DEC 2010
W9-CAZ-709

The Owl Hunt

BY RICHARD S. WHEELER
FROM TOM DOHERTY ASSOCIATES

SKYE'S WEST

Sun River
Bannack
The Far Tribes
Yellowstone
Bitterroot
Sundance
Wind River
Santa Fe
Rendezvous
Dark Passage
Going Home
Downriver
The Deliverance
The Fire Arrow
The Canyon of Bones
Virgin River
North Star
The Owl Hunt

Aftershocks
Badlands
The Buffalo Commons
Cashbox
Eclipse
The Fields of Eden
Fool's Coach
Goldfield
Masterson
Montana Hitch
An Obituary for Major Reno
Second Lives
Sierra
Snowbound
Sun Mountain: A Comstock Novel
Where the River Runs

SAM FLINT

Flint's Gift
Flint's Truth
Flint's Honor

The Owl Hunt

A Barnaby Skye Novel

RICHARD S. WHEELER

A TOM DOHERTY ASSOCIATES BOOK
NEW YORK

This is a work of fiction. All of the characters, organizations, and events portrayed in this novel are either products of the author's imagination or are used fictitiously.

THE OWL HUNT

A Forge Book
Published by Tom Doherty Associates, LLC
175 Fifth Avenue
New York, NY 10010

www.tor-forge.com

Library of Congress Cataloging-in-Publication Data

Wheeler, Richard S.
The owl hunt : a Barnaby Skye novel / Richard S. Wheeler.—1st ed.
p. cm.
"A Tom Doherty Associates book."
ISBN 978-0-7653-2201-2
1. Skye, Barnaby (Fictitious character)—Fiction. 2. Indians of North America—Fiction. 3. Fathers and sons—Fiction. 4. Shoshoni Indians—Fiction. 5. Wind River Indian Reservation (Wyo.)—Fiction. I. Title.

PS3573.H4345O95 2010
813'.54—dc22

2010035888

First Edition: December 2010

Printed in the United States of America

0 9 8 7 6 5 4 3 2 1

The Owl Hunt

one

That afternoon of July 29, 1878, was exactly like a thousand others that Dirk Skye had experienced, except that the light was dying. He glanced out the schoolhouse window and saw nothing amiss. There were no clouds.

He returned to his lessons. This day he had seven students in his Wind River Reservation school. Some days he had two or three. Other days he had a dozen. They sat at their desks staring at him in the deepening dusk. There must be a towering storm off somewhere, throttling the light, he thought.

He never knew who would attend. This was a good day, actually. In the winters he often built up the fire in the potbellied stove, but not one Shoshone child would burst into the warmth of the one-room school.

Uneasily, he continued teaching them English words in the deepening gloom. Maybe he would soon hear a crack of thunder. That would be a relief. He saw his students glance at one another fearfully. The creeping darkness had caught their attention.

They ranged from Pan-Zook, who was an adult but slow, down to So-pa-gant and Mat-ta-vish, seven-year-old twins who were from the Old Man family. Few girls came to his tribal school; they were needed at home, but boys weren't needed so much, now that they could not be warriors and hunters.

The light was turning orange.

"It is just a cloud on the sun," he said in Shoshone. "We're going to talk about the white men's words for the land. Mountains, plains, forest, grass, hills, valleys, canyons . . ."

But they were staring at the jaundiced light bathing the valley, the foothills, and the vaulting Wind River Mountains, making the whole world look feverish.

It seemed too quiet. The open windows usually brought summer breezes, the cawing of crows, the trill of red-winged blackbirds, but now the world outside seemed almost striken.

His students stirred restlessly. They would not be concentrating. He was briefly annoyed at them, but the frightening dark could no longer be ignored. The twins stared, saucer-eyed.

The faint sound of shouting drifted into the room. Not far away were the whitewashed agency buildings, the place where his father had served for years as the Indian agent for the Shoshones.

"It's a passing cloud," Dirk said.

But no one believed him. Then, swiftly, the orange faded into brown, and then into the most awful midday gloom Dirk had ever known in his young life.

"All right," he said, and headed for the door. The students did not rush out. Instead, they clung fearfully to their seats.

He opened the schoolhouse door and beheld daytime darkness, and a dying sun being eaten by the moon. A deep fear clutched him. It was the end of everything.

The Jesuits in St. Louis who had schooled him had not talked of this.

The sun had vanished behind a black ball in the heavens. A faint corona of light radiated outward, but the sun had died.

"And so we die," said Waiting Wolf. "The Owl has eaten Father Sun."

The owl was the most feared of all creatures, and possessed the most powers.

The land lay dead, as if a boot heel had pressed down upon it. Without the sun there would be no warmth, no wind, no trees or grass, no rain, and soon all who survived this hour would freeze and starve.

Dirk stared unbelieving. He could not even imagine this thing. Some of the boys were squinting at the dead sun.

"Don't look," he said. "Don't look!"

"If we look we will die," said Big Boy. He really was big, a foot higher than Dirk, and that gave his words gravity.

Now the whole world lay helpless in the gloom. The distant Wind River Mountains had all but vanished. The snowfields up high had dissolved into darkness. A bird pierced the quiet with its evensong. It would sing, and then tuck its head under its wing for the night.

"The Owl promised this," said Waiting Wolf. "It is the end of the People. We have angered him."

Off in the distance Dirk Skye saw a half-dozen people outside the agency building, staring into the dark.

What did it mean?

"Tell me the story of the Owl," he said to Waiting Wolf.

"I do not know the story. But it came to me, and it is true."

Dirk Skye pondered the dying world, the blackened sun,

the residual light that absorbed form and shape into ghostly shapes. He had no answer. He would die with the rest.

Then Mother Victoria stormed out of the teacherage. She was all that was left of Dirk's family now. Thin, impossibly old, always irritable if not angry, mostly at the pain rising from every muscle of her body.

She leaned on a staff, her legs so untrustworthy that she resorted to a stout stick. She was his Crow mother, much older than his Shoshone mother. She limped from the porch of the teacherage, where he cared for her, toward the knot of terrified youths.

"Go back to school," she said.

"But Grandmother . . ." he protested. Grandmother was the most reverent way to address an elder.

"I have lived a long time," she said. "I have seen these twice. It is nothing. It will all be over in a little time."

Over? How could such a thing be over? Father Sun lay mortally wounded, his light eaten by Mother Moon. How could it be over?

"Mister Skye called it an eclipse," she said. "Mother Moon passing in front of Father Sun. Sometimes it is very bad, like this. Sometimes not so bad, when she doesn't stop all of his light. Goddamn it, go back to school."

"It is the Owl, Grandmother," Waiting Wolf said, digging in. He had prevailed until the old woman showed up.

"You will see," she said.

The boy, on the brink of manhood, stood rigidly. "It is the Owl, and this was spoken of long ago. The Owl can change its shape and be anything. The Owl can be a black moon. The Owl will darken the sun, and the time of the People will end. This is the death of the People." Then he remembered he was in the presence of an elder. "Grandmother, you are one of the Absaroka people so you do not know this story."

Dirk saw the youth was filled with terror and defiance and something else that might have been hatred.

"Waiting Wolf, you are wise beyond your years," Dirk said to him quietly. "So we will wait a little while and see if the world ends."

Victoria said nothing, and simply waited for something known only to her to happen.

Dirk discovered his other charges rubbing tears from their cheeks. What could be more frightening than the sun being darkened by the Owl?

"Don't look," he said, remembering stories of people going blind from the sun. The children didn't heed him, so he turned them aside, and just in time. A bead of brilliant light flared on the edge of the black circle in the heavens, and the world swiftly turned from its murkiness to dull brown again.

The boys peered through their fingers, terrified at what was descending on the People.

"Mat-ta-vish, don't look at the sky," he said.

But Mat-ta-vish was mesmerized, and would look no matter what Dirk said.

Then bit by bit a rim of blinding light built up along the edge of the moon.

The world glowed eerily under light that looked almost smoky. No one said anything. Waiting Wolf turned his face away, and would not acknowledge the others, or the reappearance of the sun.

"Ah, the good sun returns," said little Noseep. "The good sun lives. Grandmother was right."

Waiting Wolf snarled.

Little by little the light crept back, the murk fled, and one could see the sunlight strike distant trees. The mountains rose once again and their peaks reached toward the blue. Shadows grew. Soon the schoolhouse cast its shadow on the turf.

A bird trilled. Life had paused, withered, and now was springing back. Dirk Skye said nothing. Nature itself, in all its mystery, was restoring order.

"Do not look at Father Sun," he told his students.

But now the sun was so bright that his warning seemed superfluous. In a while, the whole wide world was restored to what it had been, and a summer's day pulsed with life and peace.

"There, you see, Waiting Wolf?" Big Boy said.

"It was the Owl. It came. It showed us," the slim young man snapped. "I saw the Owl with my own eyes."

Old Victoria eyed them all, and retreated to the teacherage. She had done what she could to subdue the terror, and that's as much as she felt like doing.

Dirk watched her go. They were not connected by blood, but by something deeper than blood. His father, Mister Skye, made them a family.

Dirk turned to his students. "It is late in the day. We will meet tomorrow morning."

They stared at him uneasily.

"I will not," said Waiting Wolf. "I am done with white men's school."

Dirk had wrestled with this many times in the past, but still didn't know what to say to a departing student.

"I will be here to teach you," he said.

"This is a bad place. That is why the Owl came."

"I have a book about the stars and the sky. Tomorrow we will see what it says."

"The time of the white man is over. This has been sung to

me. The seers have seen it. The dark moon came and went away. Father Sun returned. It is the sign. Now we will gather our strength and see the white men go away. Now the People will be free to go where they will. We will hunt the buffalo, we will move our lodges to wherever our hearts sing. We will drive away those who are not the People." He paused. "I have seen the dark moon come and go with my own eyes."

"The dark moon?"

"I will not name them, for they are doomed."

Waiting Wolf glared at Dirk, and then stalked away. He walked proudly, his back arched, and he never looked back.

The boy's family was one of those least reconciled to reservation life. The boy's father had been a shaman of the Shoshones, stuffing Waiting Wolf with all the old stories. Dirk knew most of them, learned at the knee of his mother, Blue Dawn, who was called Mary by his father. There were many Shoshone stories, each ending in a mystery. These people didn't so much explain life as puzzle it. Their world was mysterious, startling, and sometimes tricky. The boy had seen the black moon intercepting the sun, but this was all the machination of the dreaded Owl, the ghost-bird sailing wherever there was death to be done.

There was more: Waiting Wolf's kin were simmering, waiting for a chance to visit ruin on the reservation. The youth had been sent to learn what he could at the schoolhouse, so his family might know what darkness lay within it. Still, Waiting Wolf had been the brightest light, the fiercest learner. He had learned some English, learned American history and geography, learned to spell, and was mastering writing. He was quick with numbers, too.

Now Dirk watched the boy walk down the trail that would lead to the bottoms of the Wind River. His family roamed, refusing to surrender their lodge. But now they occupied a good woodlot perhaps three miles distant, a place of abundant firewood and some small game in the brush.

There was something stiff and unyielding in the boy's gait, a defiance so profound that it radiated from his shoulders, his back, as the youth grew smaller and smaller and finally vanished far below.

Two boys headed for Chief Washakie's frame house half a mile away. He was boarding them. Some headed for the rude cabins that had sprung up around the agency. Others trudged to an old buffalo-hide lodge which had housed them all summer. It was as close as they could get to a boardinghouse. One day it might house half a dozen boys; the next day, all of them might disappear. And when the frosts came and the lodge required firewood, the boys slipped away and Dirk never saw them again.

He wondered whether he had taught them anything. He divided his days into various courses: English, writing, math, history, geography, civics, as well as various pursuits that might turn the young people into artisans, farmers, cattlemen, carpenters, mechanics, and clerks. But some days, few of them came.

He had never gotten used to it, and had never stopped trying.

The government had built a schoolhouse, as its treaty with the Snake People required it do to, and paid Dirk to teach there, as it was required to do. But Congress had balked at building a dormitory where students could board. The reservation stretched a hundred miles and the People were scattered across it, much too far from the clapboard school for their sons to attend. There was an occasional winter day when Dirk had only one student, Waiting Wolf, who came faithfully and devoured everything that Dirk could teach him—until this hour.

two

A little before the hour, Dirk tolled the schoolhouse bell and then waited for his charges to appear. None did. The minutes ticked by. He knew they had fled, just as others had fled for whatever reason over the years. He stared at the empty desks, the blank slates they used to form letters into words. He stared at the windows that let July breezes eddy through the room, vanquishing the lingering smells of wood smoke, sweat, varnish, and the bodies of boys.

He stared out the window into the sunlit pastures that descended to the Wind River, far away. He stared out the other windows, toward the whitewashed Wind River Indian Agency buildings, toward the military post that started as Camp Brown and would soon be renamed. And just below stood the shiplap house of the legendary Shoshone chief, Washakie, who had sealed a peace with the white men years before and kept that peace with a firm hand.

The schoolhouse was very quiet, and whatever was to be learned within it remained unlearned.

Dirk abandoned the silent structure and hiked toward the agency buildings, which included the Indian agent's house, reservation headquarters, staff housing, and a carriage barn and pens. He saw no one about. The greensward, brown now, was as empty as the world around the complex. He would have it out with Sirius Van Horne, the current agent. He rather liked Sirius, named after the brightest star in the night sky, while Dirk's Shoshone mother had given him the name of the unmoving North Star. So they shared something. But not much, he thought.

Indian agents rarely got rich, even those who robbed the tribes and government, and the real appeal of the position was that there was little to do. It was the perfect position for a lazy man, and Dirk knew that Sirius filled the bill.

He clambered up wooden steps, plunged into a cool antechamber, and then into Van Horne's sanctum, where his arrival highjacked the agent's morning siesta.

"You could knock," Van Horne said, lowering his boots to the floor.

"No students again. That eclipse scared them off. How am I supposed to teach an empty classroom?" Dirk said.

Van Horne eyed him lazily, from hooded eyes. "Angry again, are you? There's no purpose in it."

"Of course I'm angry. Am I supposed to not be angry?"

Van Horne sighed, rubbed a freckled paw across his red muttonchops, and sat upright. "No point in it," he said. "It's all useless. The Indians can't be educated. And don't want to."

"I don't believe that."

Van Horne smiled. "Then don't work for the Indian Bureau."

That only made Dirk madder. "Every year the bureau

wants a report. How many students attending. How many have completed courses. How many have mastered English. How many can read. How many can do sums. How many have learned a trade. And my answer is the same year after year. None. And then they tell me I'm on probation."

"It's a nice summer day, Dirk. Go for a walk."

"That eclipse set them off."

Van Horne eyed him from under bushy red brows. "Anything sets them off. An eclipse would do it, all right."

"The only bright student I have is Waiting Wolf, and he's the one who's stirring things up."

"Stirring up?" The agent pulled himself upright.

"What do you know of Shoshone mysteries? Creation stories?"

"The less the better."

The agent had meant to be humorous, but the answer annoyed Dirk. "A darkened sun means the end of their people. The return of the sun means that the People will triumph; it is the end of time for white men."

"Well, they have lots of stories, Dirk. Lots of owl stories, moon stories, all sorts of stories. That's how they explain mysteries."

"The boy went home to his people. They're a family of shamans and agitators. The rest of my class took Waiting Wolf's words very seriously. I haven't a student left."

"My oh my," said Van Horne, and he smiled.

"I thought you should know."

"Thank you, Mister Skye. I think you should go fishing."

"These people have been waiting for a sign."

"Sign? Good lord, Dirk, my boy, all of the world waits for a sign."

"The boy said the darkened sun signified the death of his people—and the returning sun signified the triumph of his people. Over others."

Van Horne sighed. "It'll pass. Superstition, my boy."

"Belief, Major," he said. Major was the honorary rank of Indian agents.

"And tomorrow it will just be another legend, the day the sun hid and then whipped the moon."

"Dreaming, Major. They dream. I dream."

"Ah, yes, your mixed blood." He smiled cheerfully. "Which are you?"

"The eclipse was the passage of the moon in front of the sun," Dirk said.

"There you go. Teach 'em that and there'll be no more dreaming."

Outside, in the quietness of a summer's morning, Dirk wondered if the agent had fathomed anything Dirk had offered him, including the warning. The Wind River Reservation seethed with dreaming, and visions, and the glistening hope that the People would soon be free forever.

This day there was no one to teach. But maybe he had nothing to teach the Shoshone boys. Maybe those boys should be teaching him.

His father, Barnaby Skye, lay nearby in the Wind River Agency cemetery, his mother Mary, or Blue Dawn, beside him. Only Victoria lived on, and he was glad to have her with him. Dirk had been schooled by the Jesuits, who ignored nothing that would help him master their European world and view and faith. That was the world he brought to the Shoshone boys at the Wind River Agency. He was schooled in St. Louis until age fifteen, but after that he schooled himself, with books brought horrendous distances. And then he had tried to school the reservation boys and girls and any adult who wished to learn, too, but little had come of it. And worse, he could not see that it had done any of his young people any good.

He stood in the sun, absorbing his aloneness. He had few friends, mostly because he didn't fit. He was too white for the Shoshones, too Indian for the whites. His mother and father lay in their graves. His anger hung about him, and wouldn't leave, and soured his life. He had no woman. Once he had eyes for Chief Washakie's daughter Mona, but his sourness drove her off, and now she was married to a full-blood Lemhi, Tissidimit.

The sun burned its peace upon the day, but that peace didn't quiet Dirk's heart. He hiked the half-mile to Chief Washakie's frame house. The old chief of the Shoshones had led his people into reservation life, saying they had little choice but to accept the new world and the ways of the white man. Dirk wondered whether the chief regretted that now the reservation starved and its people lived in despair. He had seen his people sink into misery and slow death within the prison of the reservation.

Dirk paused for a moment on the veranda of the chief's house, enjoying the shade, and then knocked softly.

The chief materialized, and motioned toward the porch chairs.

"I've been expecting you," he said.

"The boys left you?"

"They are filled with dreams, Dirk. And so are all of your students. I have heard all about Waiting Wolf."

"There was no one to teach today."

"It was the message from the sky," Washakie said. "It was a big message. I was very frightened, and then when Sun returned, very heartened."

"The seers are making something of it," Dirk said.

"Yes, and you should take heed."

"But there is nothing there. No magic. No sign. The moon passed between the earth and the sun. There's no more to it."

"You don't know your mother's people, Dirk." Washakie eyed him gravely. "And you don't know what is happening in hidden valleys, in moonlit fields. You don't know how many Dreamers there are and what they are saying. You hear the voice of the agent—a good man but blind, and eager to pass through his life without boldness—but not the voices, a hundred voices, singing ancient stories, winning new hearts every night. And now this. The great sign, signifying that all the songs are heard. Heed me, young man. The Dreamers are like a flood that washes away all things."

"But it's only dreams," Dirk said.

"Ah, the white man talks. No, Dirk, dreams are true. Believe a dream, and the rest is false or blind." He had a way of staring, unblinking. "Do you see? Have you vision?"

Dirk felt the old loneliness flood him. Why was he so different from others?

The chief eyed the young man and subsided. "You are made from red clay and white clay," he said. "It goes hard for you."

The chief's gentleness had its effect on Dirk. "Grandfather," he said. "If the People weren't so hungry, they wouldn't be dreaming. The Dreamers meeting in the shadows want the old life to return, want buffalo to eat, want to roam wherever they want, with no invisible lines around them, want hides for their clothing and lodges. But those things are gone."

"There are no fat Shoshones," the chief said. "No buffalo. The deer and elk and bear are shot away. And when we go hunting away from our land, the Territory of Wyoming tells us we must not. The white men tell us to plow the fields and plant grains, but we are so hungry we eat the horses and mules. They white men tell us to keep a herd of their cattle, but we are so hungry we have eaten the herd. And when we have a few cows, the white herders from other places slip in and take them from us. The white men tell us to build cabins and farm the land, so our bellies will be full. But that is death for boys and men who live to hunt, whose dream is to be a great warrior, just as our men and boys have always dreamed. Now there is nothing to eat, and nothing to dream. What can a Shoshone man dream now? Will he spend his days scraping the earth with a hoe? Chopping wood for the stove? Digging potatoes? It is not a life for a Shoshone man. There is no dream in it. When the man of our people kills his horse to eat it, he dreams of hunting buffalo."

"So they dream of other times," Dirk said.

"I have chosen the way of peace," Washakie said. "We have clasped hands with the white men, and now we live with the bluecoats beside us, keeping us from going where we will. Sometimes they protect us. Sometimes they drive away white people who want our land or our grass or our water. I do not regret that decision, mostly because we had no choice, and what was coming to the People was going to fall upon us, no matter what."

"And now the Dreamers dream," Dirk added.

"And the People are hungry. They eat turtles and fish and badgers and eggs and lizards and snakes and weasels and gophers. They eat anything that crawls."

Some of it was Indian Bureau policy. The rations doled out to enrolled Shoshones fed them only two days a week, and much of the meat or flour was bad. There was intent in this: force the Indians to start farming and ranching. Make them take up agriculture and become less and less dependent on white men for their survival. But the idea ran into walls and barriers, for there was no honor in stoop labor. That was for women. A man fought wars and hunted, and took care of his people, and won honor with his skills. Now the white men were turning Shoshone men into drunks and bums, and sometimes Shoshone women sold themselves to the soldiers to get enough food for their lodges.

Both Dirk and the chief knew all that.

"You have lost Waiting Wolf," the chief said in a voice so quiet that Dirk strained to hear. "And his kin, too. They own the dreams. My voice is no longer heard. There was a time when I could say no and they would honor me. Now they will not hear me. They will not hear the words of our Indian agent. Once they listened to your father and honored him. The People listen only to dreams. There is no way you or Major Van Horne or the bluecoats can stop what is coming, or keep the sacred ground beneath our feet from soaking up our tears."

three

The dream came to Waiting Wolf in the middle of the darkness, when the moon had eaten the sun. He stared into the heavens, and it came to him just then, so ice-clear that he knew he had been changed for all time. Owl stared at the boy with big eyes and spread his wings across the entire heaven. Then Owl glided away. Waiting Wolf was transfixed, for in that moment he was burdened with the salvation of his people. Now he would wear that which had been given to him. Even as a bead of light burst on the other side of the dark moon, Owl glided away into the stars.

Waiting Wolf only dimly fathomed what his mission would be, how he would do this thing, and how the People might receive him. An Owl vision? The most dreaded of all the creatures, the harbinger of evil, the omen of doom had come to a fifteen-year-old youth. Waiting Wolf knew that there would be some who would respond sharply; this could not be. But it would be. And no one of the People could ever disdain a vision.

Now, on a night filled with misty darkness, Dreamers gathered far from the eyes of white men. No moon offered a lantern to this place, and everyone had found it almost by instinct, there being only the faintest of starlight. There were twelve present, all older men save for himself. Many had war honors from times past. Younger ones dreamed of them. All of them had become Dreamers, ritually bathing in sweet grass smoke, crying for a vision. All had received a dream. All were quietly recruiting others who were open to the dream.

Now they bathed their bodies in the smoke of the sweet grass, which took away corruption of heart and body and made them clean. The smouldering fire lay in the bottom of a gully that emptied into the Wind River, unseen even by someone nearby.

Waiting Wolf let the fragrant smoke drift over his flesh until he was purified, and then he climbed to the top of the bluff, a signal to the rest that he would give them his words.

The rest collected below, attentive to the youth, and silent.

"I dreamed my dream," he said. "It came upon me at the moment when Moon ate the Sun and the People were crushed by darkness. Hear me now. For this is a mighty dream. And it truly came upon me. In that moment, when all seemed lost, Owl spread his wings across the entire sky, from horizon to horizon. Owl was a terrible presence, and my heart quaked in me. Owl stared at me until I felt small and then I knew all things. Owl told me to take heart; in a moment Sun would return and with Sun, a new-made People. Hear me, and believe me. Owl told me what I must do, and then glided away, even as Sun burned a bead of light on the edge of Moon."

Waiting Wolf stared calmly at the rapt faces below. None of the Dreamers had missed one word.

"I am taking a new name, as was given me. My name is Owl."

That brought sharp gasps. No Shoshone could imagine such a thing. Owl was the harbinger of evil, dreaded more than any creature. Still, no one objected.

"I am Owl. And Owl will spread his wings over the soldiers and they will be taken sick and fall down. Owl will float over the agency, and the agent and his staff will tumble down and go away. Owl will float over the white man's school, and all who are in it will fall to the ground. Owl will float over the lines that imprison the People, and the lines will go away and the People can go anyplace. Owl will glide over the mountains and plains, and drive the buffalo to us, and the elk and deer to us, and the People will have meat and be well fed."

Some of the Dreamers were frowning, but Owl knew they would come around.

"I have been chosen to be this one; I have dreamed it," he said.

His oration met with silence. How could any Shoshone be named Owl? It was a sort of sacrilege. It turned the world upside down. Yet no one among them challenged him. A dream was sacrosanct.

The fire flared a moment. He saw warriors with long scars upon their arms and backs, the victims of lance and arrow and clubs and knives and axes and bullets.

It was Owl's own father, Buffalo Horn, who finally asked the only question: "Will Owl glide over Chief Washakie?"

"The Owl will do whatever the Owl will do," the youth replied.

That evoked a stir. This was something unthinkable.

He sensed anger among those who listened. But none

dared protest. A dream carried its own weight, and that weight could not be questioned.

"The time of the white man is over," he said. "You will see with your own eyes."

"I am with the Owl, then," said a voice from the darkness.

The young man newly named Owl felt a chill but set it aside. Men twice and thrice his age listened raptly and he marveled at it. He was yet a youth. He had never counted coup or gone to war. He had barely killed anything in a hunt because there had been no game. But there he was, a prophet and Dreamer.

"There will be more signs," he said. "The Owl, my spirit helper, will glide through the nights, and the hearts of the white men will grow cold. The Owl will visit their hearts and make them sick. The Owl will fill their minds with regrets. The Owl will turn their faces east and they will yearn to return to the lands they came from."

"Who are you to say these things?" an old headman asked.

"I had a dream."

"So have we. But we know nothing of this."

"I can only tell you what was given to me, Grandfather."

That one didn't like it. Owl, as he now called himself, knew who it was. This one, old Runner, was a petty chief, a friend of Washakie, and a brother of Blue Dawn, the woman who had mated with Barnaby Skye. And therefore, a man to be wary of.

"Young people can be hotheaded."

Owl contained his irritation, but nodded. He would not let an old fool bleed this moment. What good was caution when the People were hungry?

"I will tell you what I know," Owl said. "Watch for the buffalo. They will drift here, and feed us. Watch for the elk. They will run through the mountains. Watch for the soldiers to leave. They will load their wagons and march out. Watch for the missionaries to go away. These missionaries with their books and rules, they will go away with the soldiers. Watch for other peoples, like ours, to rise up. Watch for the Bannocks to rise up. Watch for the Paiutes to rise up. These are all signs we can all watch for, and when you see these good things, you will know that the sun is rising on our People."

The youth sensed a grudging respect. Could the fate of the Shoshones really rest in the hands of one so young?

He turned to his father. "See me, Buffalo Horn. The dream you wanted has come to your son. See me, and be proud."

But his father stood motionless in the night, barely visible, and Owl could not tell what was passing through his father's heart. Owl waited for an acknowledgment that didn't come. Ah, so his father was envious. Too bad for him. He wasn't given the dream.

"I am Owl, and I have a dream," he said, directing the remark at his father, and his brothers, too.

He felt light-headed. His voice was more powerful than all other voices. More powerful than Chief Washakie, who quaked before white men and served white men and surrendered to white men. Owl's word would soon be the only word, and the old chief would fade away. Old Washakie, traitor to the People! Owl would take back everything that the old chief had surrendered, and then erase even the memory of Washakie.

"Now is the time to spread the word. Go to every corner of our land and tell them that Owl, born of another name, will spread his wings against the white men, and soon they will fall sick and dead, and leave the land, and all will be healed."

"Grandfather," came a voice out of the night. "Grandfather, when will this be?"

Owl savored the moment. They were calling him grandfather, a term of utmost respect. "It will be when it will be," he replied. In truth, he didn't know and wouldn't say. "Soon," he added. "Soon."

The Dreamers drifted into the night, and no sign of their meeting would exist save what lay in their memories. But soon the Dreamers would be gathering throughout the Shoshone lands, cloaked in darkness. For here was the salvation, voiced by a chosen one of the People, to lead the Shoshones to the sweetness of the life they knew.

Soon this cruel and pointless existence would pass away. The starvation would pass. Eating bugs and snakes would pass. There would be buffalo meat to fill their bellies, buffalo hides for their lodges and winter coats, elk hide for moccasins and shirts. And the liberty of all of nature would return to them. Ah, quaking hearts, take courage from the Dreamers.

He hiked the long trail upriver with his father and brothers, pitying them because their dreams were not the smallest part of his own dream. This was a good thing, for he was the eldest of three sons, and it was right that he would be honored. He did not scorn his brothers; they were simply boys, and without gifts.

His parents kept a traditional lodge, scorning white men's cabins. The Shoshone way was good; nothing else was good except for guns gotten from traders. He slipped inside, along with the rest, and lay restless in the blackness, his mind seething with plans. He would take his dream to the People. Let them see Owl, let them hear Owl. Let them heed Owl.

But first there was one thing to do.

In the morning he bathed at the creek, paid homage to the sky and earth spirits, and set out for the Wind River Agency and the schoolhouse. It would do no good at all to talk to the Indian agent, whose ears were full of wax. But it would be a joy to tell Skye, that two-blood traitor to his mother's people, what he had dreamed, and what his name was now.

He walked a long while before the white agency buildings hove into view. He hated them, these structures inhabited by the invaders. The military buildings at Camp Brown he didn't mind so much as the agency itself, where a white man ruled over the whole tribe. That was almost more than he could bear. Buffalo Horn's family had even despised Barnaby Skye, the second agent, who struggled to keep the tribe fed. But that old man was merely the agent of the Yankee masters. And even worse was his son Dirk, who chose that side. It was a pity he had not chosen his true name, North Star, and made himself one of the People.

Owl knew he was not the youth he had been hours before. His walking was different, his way of standing was different, his way of addressing others was different. He was no longer Waiting Wolf. When Owl spread his wings and glided through the darkness, the world quaked.

Owl found Dirk Skye in the schoolhouse, where he was obliged to be by those who paid him. Owl saw that he was reading at his desk, and approached boldly. The teacher swiftly sensed this was not an ordinary meeting, and set his book down.

"I am pleased to see you, Waiting Wolf," Dirk said.

Owl smiled. "You do not look closely. Why do you think I am still what I was?"

Dirk smiled. "I see a confident young man ready to resume his lessons."

"Why do you think I need your white-man lessons?"

Dirk paused, weighing that. "You have come to tell me something, and I am ready to listen," he said.

"I have come to tell you that I am a Dreamer, and I have a new name."

"Good. It is fine for you to take the name given you."

"My name is Owl."

The teacher visibly startled.

"Owl, Owl, Owl," the Dreamer said. "Owl was the name I dreamed, and Owl is now my name."

Dirk paused, obviously weighing his words. "And what do your family and clan and the People think of this?"

"They have made me the chief of them all," Owl said. "I carry the Shoshone nation on my wings."

four

No doubt of it, the young man had changed. Owl was no longer Waiting Wolf, the bright youth who would tackle the three Rs one week and drift the next. Now he was Owl, the most dreaded spirit animal known to the Snake People, as the Shoshones were also called.

Dirk digested all that. Owl was only a few years younger than himself, but somehow seemed a man now. Owl slowly smiled, but it wasn't a friendly smile, it was the gloat of triumph, and then Owl swept out of the schoolroom.

Dirk wasn't puzzled. These people dreamed. These youths went off on vision quests. This one had found a dream waiting in the middle of an eclipse. Their universe was not governed by impersonal forces, but by powerful spirits. By an owl. An oppressed and dispirited people had suddenly found a messiah. Owl could be Owl only when his beak faced white men; if his beak faced the Shoshones, they would somehow drive him away.

The boy would stir them, and there might be painful

confrontations with soldiers and the agent, but those would pass. Owl would remind them of their misery, maybe even win some concessions from the government, and then he would fade from memory.

Dirk empathized with the youth. There were times when the Shoshones needed an Owl to deal with obtuse Indian Bureau officials or boneheaded military officers. Dirk felt his two bloods warring with each other, for Owl had stirred up in him the bitter mingling of white and red.

He had never harmonized his two bloods, and finally had stopped trying. His mother's blood stirred at the sight of Owl; his father's blood had congealed in his veins. His two bloods hung over him as a curse; he wished he might be one or the other. Either! It didn't matter which. He would have been a proud Shoshone, his mother's son. He would have been a proud Englishman, his father's lad. His father's blood ached to see the Shoshones settle into farming and ranching, educate themselves in the manner of his people, and enjoy the settled world. His mother's blood resisted; it rose in the middle of lessons, when sometimes he wished some student or other wouldn't learn English, but become a medicine man of his people.

It was unending, this strife in his bosom, and maybe that was why after years on the reservation he was no further along than when he started. Where was he? His teaching was a failure; he had no wife, and had managed to drive away the one girl he cared about, Washakie's daughter Mona. He had drifted, doing his duty in the schoolhouse, sliding into apathy because nothing was better than before.

Heat hung over the agency. Nothing stirred. A cloudless sky was merciless. The schoolhouse offered shade, but even with windows open it was miserable.

Dirk stared at the empty desks, the unused slates, the pegs where no coat hung, the dried-up inkwells.

"You're excused," he said, and watched the ghosts drift away.

He left the one-room building, drifted past the two-hole outhouse, and walked toward the somnolent cemetery, a rough and ill-kempt patch of bone-dry soil. He saw the old woman there, as she often was these days. Victoria's heart was yearning to be with Skye. Dirk sometimes thought his own heart yearned to be with his father and mother, who lay beneath clay mounds in the somber sunlight.

The headboards were gray wood, the names burned into them with a branding iron. BARNABY SKYE, B. 1805, LONDON. D. 1876. MARY SKYE, B. ? D. 1876, BLUE DAWN.

Victoria sat on the clay between the graves.

"The boy gave you trouble," she said.

"Were you there?"

"No. But he walks a new way. Like trouble in his footsteps. I saw him walk. I know that goddamn walk. Plenty sonsofbitches walk like that."

"He has changed his name to Owl."

She stared sharply at him.

"And the People have gathered to him. At least that's what he says."

"More tears. Is there no end to tears? Is that all of life on the earth?"

Dirk smiled. "You visit with my father and mother?"

"He was never so big as his last years, North Star, sitting there where Sirius Van Horne sleeps in his swivel chair. His heart was never bigger. One day he would be roaring at ranchers for stealing cows from the People. The next day he would be roaring at the army for letting stockmen graze on reservation land. Oh, his heart was so big."

There was more, Dirk knew. Once he was appointed as Indian agent for the Shoshones, his father had been a whirlwind. He had tapped some source of energy that was astonishing in an old man. Half of his task had been to educate the boneheads at the Indian agency itself, a task harder than bringing new ways of life to the Shoshones. The bureau had expected the Shoshones to settle down and farm. But it didn't happen. Planting and hoeing and weeding and harvesting were women's work, and the men wouldn't do it. They were hunters and warriors. The officials in Washington City couldn't grasp it, and faulted Skye for the lack of progress. But Skye knew the change would take generations. He struggled to create an agency cattle herd, knowing the reservation men were far more open to caring for cattle than for plowing and planting. But the agency herd he fought so hard to build was stolen by white cowboys, eaten by hungry Shoshones, or starved by a lack of winter feed. Still, Barnaby Skye had never faltered, never abandoned his wife's people, and when age finally overtook him, his Shoshones were better off than before his tenure.

Now, though, the Shoshone starved, drank, gossiped, gambled, and panhandled.

"You have a decision to make," Victoria said.

"I've made it."

She eyed him closely. "Goddamn, you're Skye's boy."

How she knew his choices, he couldn't say, but she did.

"Let him sleep," he said, glancing at the agency building. "That's all he does anyway."

Victoria's eyes lit. A little rebellion, a little mischief, lit her as much as ever.

He didn't really know what he would do. The Dreamers

could inflict disaster on their own people. But the Shoshones were already immersed in disaster, hungry, rootless, dispirited, and feeling more and more as if they had been sentenced to a lifetime in prison.

"Grandmother, come," he said.

She rose stiffly, but once she stretched, she was as lithe as ever.

He led her toward Chief Washakie's house, and sensed she approved.

He helped her up the veranda stairs, and then knocked. This time the chief himself answered, eyed them, and suggested that the shade of the porch would be a good place to visit.

They waited for him on comfortable wicker chairs, and when he returned Dirk saw at once that he was wearing a white-man's suit coat.

"I am pleased to see you, Mister Skye, and madam. If this is a social call, you will surprise me."

"There's trouble, Grandfather."

"Ah, yes, Owl. He came here after visiting you. The Dreamer is collecting a storm cloud around him, and soon will rain lightning upon us."

"Then you know."

"As much as he's told me. He's an honorable young man who does not skulk around behind my back. He told me of his dream, and the meetings of Dreamers in the dark, and how the world will change. He turned my blood cold. I told him that dreaming would make things worse."

Dirk expected as much. "Grandfather, I will tell you that I have not spoken to the agent about the Dreamers, or to the soldiers. This is something for the People to deal with."

Washakie eyed Dirk sharply, a faint smile building in his seamed face. "Then it will stay that way unless Owl himself announces his intentions to Major Van Horne. But I doubt that he will."

"Grandfather, what do you make of it?"

Washakie turned somber. "Nothing yet. Young Mister Skye, suppose you were to obtain the agency trap and drive me to our people. And of course with you, madam, if you are inclined."

"I have the use of it. I'll be back directly," Dirk said.

He trotted to the agency, told a yawning clerk he was taking the chief for a ride, and swiftly harnessed the dray in the pen. A half-hour later he settled Washakie on a quilted seat, his Crow mother beside the chief, and they were off. It was midmorning. They could talk with many people this long summer's day.

They rolled down a golden road that angled toward Crowheart Butte, a favorite summering place of the People. On Sage Creek was the ruin of a model farm. It had been Barnaby Skye's prized project, intended to teach these people how to grow their own food and care for themselves. Now it was deserted, some graying clapboard buildings, weed-choked fields that had once been virgin prairie, and an aura of desolation over it all.

"Stop here," Washakie said, as the buildings rose before them.

He stepped nimbly to the dusty clay, toured the sorry place, and then clambered aboard.

Dirk ached to know what the chief was thinking, but Washakie didn't offer a clue.

Farther along Sage Creek were the ruins of a few log cabins, simple structures with dirt floors, shake roofs, and gaping glassless windows. Some of the fields around them had been scraped into furrows and planted once, but only weeds grew there now. This had been the Indian Bureau's dream: families on farms, raising crops. But simple realities had demolished the good intentions, not least of which was the lack of firewood for heat and cooking. So the People returned to their lodges which they raised wherever there was wood and water and game.

Another hour of riding, with the dust sifting over the carriage wheels and eddying behind them, brought them to the first of the encampments, seven lodges in a spring-fed gulch with jack pine and brush to meet the needs of those people. There was no shade to speak of. But the creek was cool and clear. It wasn't the best of places to summer, but it was close to the agency, and thus close to the dole of flour and salt and sugar.

Chief Washakie waited quietly in the trap, eyeing the camp. His gaze caught the shabby lodges, patched over many times, some of them a mixture of canvas and hide. His gaze caught the children, dressed in rags, the boys sometimes naked. He surveyed the horses, three in the village, the rest probably eaten. He sniffed, not missing the rank smell of a camp that had been in a place too long.

The Shoshones were quick to discover their chief in the carriage, quick to note his black coat, white collarless shirt, and black hat. Only his two braids of jet hair were familiar to them. The women shied away, but slowly the men collected around the buggy, their expressions ranging from pride to suspicion to defeat.

The chief was in no hurry, and let these miserable people congregate as they would.

Dirk felt their gaze upon him, and his old Crow mother, both of them strangers, in a way; sojourners among the People.

Washakie seemed to know the moment to begin, and he greeted them warmly, calling them his own people.

But then he addressed the younger men, who seemed to collect in a knot, a little apart from the rest.

"I will speak now to the Dreamers," Washakie said. "Come gather around, you who dream."

No one moved. Some of the younger ones eyed one another furtively.

"Ah, my young friend Wolverine, are you a Dreamer?" the chief asked.

The young man, with brooding eyes and heavy bones, considered the request.

"Yes, Grandfather," he said.

"And what did you dream? Tell me what you saw. We shall all listen to your story."

"I saw . . . Grandfather, I am waiting for my dream."

"But you are a Dreamer."

"We follow the Dreamer."

"Owl?" the chief asked softly.

The young man remained silent, a deepening defiance in his face.

The chief waited patiently. "Do others among us dream?"

The knot of young men gradually hardened into stony silence.

"I see," said Washakie. "The Owl is the most dreaded of all creatures. The Owl can visit death upon the People. The Owl can trick the People."

"The Owl can do that to others, Grandfather," said Wolverine. "The Owl came when the moon was eating the sun."

"Wolverine, wait for a true dream, your own dream," Washakie said. "And I will say the same to the rest of you. Look for your own dream."

The stony gaze had returned to their faces.

five

Dirk Skye drove patiently toward Crowheart country, where most of the People had congregated because there was wood and shade and a little game drifting out of the mountains. Chief Washakie sat quietly, undisturbed by the turmoil on the reservation. His clothing contrasted sharply with what he, or any other plains chief, might have worn a few years earlier. He meant it to be so.

If Dirk had seen rebellion in the faces of those Dreamers, so had Chief Washakie. But he paid it little heed. Dirk steered the trap over two-rut trails that sufficed for roads on the reservation. The iron wheels coiled the dust up and around, so it was always tumbling back to earth behind the carriage. They would not return to the agency this evening. Washakie plainly intended to confer with most of his people.

The next stop was where a few lodges had collected in the Wind River bottoms. The river formed a silver streak through the sun-browned plains there, with bands of green on either side. A life of sorts might be gotten from the area if there were roots and berries and rodents enough. Dirk steered the wagon into the center of the encampment, where the lodges stood in a semicircle. Stately cottonwoods and willows sheltered the place from the burning heat of midsummer. The camp seemed deserted as they drove in, but it was an illusion. The women were quietly working in the shade, and the men were dozing in the dried grasses. There was nothing of a manly nature for them to do; no war to be fought, and nothing much to hunt, though a few were usually prowling for anything they could kill and eat.

The white man's regime had rendered Shoshone males all but useless. They could not be warriors; the army protected the People from their enemies. They could not be providers; the agency dole of flour and sugar and coffee and occasional blankets sufficed to sustain life. And that was what burned in the bosoms of the Dreamers, who wanted nothing but to restore the Ways of the People.

Dirk drove the trap to the edge of the encampment and waited. It was a courtesy to wait to be invited in, and even the chief of the People needed an invitation. It was granted by an old headman Dirk knew as Last Dog. Slowly, he steered the trap toward a shady place where these people would congregate. Washakie studied the camp with knowing eyes, and the tableau was not heartening. Still, the males bestirred themselves and gathered around the carriage. They wore rags, their hair was not groomed—the usual insignias of honor, a feather in the hair, a painted emblem on their brown flesh, were absent. They were a sorry lot, and their demoralization hurt Dirk.

Washakie waited leisurely. Haste simply was not part of Shoshone life, except in dire circumstances. But in good time, the encampment drew around the trap, making the dray horse restless.

Washakie stood, eyed them calmly.

"I greet you, my People," the chief said. "I see my friend Walks at Night here. I see Rabbit, a man of great courage. I see Nighthawk, and Mare. All good People. I see my beloved ones. I see my brave women. I see my beloved children. I see the People, and I have come to listen."

"What brings you and the old Crow woman and the half-blood to us?" asked Walks at Night.

Dirk knew that was not a friendly greeting, and it placed the chief among those who were not full-bloods.

"You know our son Dirk Skye, and his honored Absaroka mother, Many Quill Woman, who live in peace among us. They were kind enough to hitch the wagon and come with me, and I honor them now with the best wishes of all the People."

Dirk saw no change in the faces gathered around him. Always before, Chief Washakie had warmed his people, won smiles and assent and loyalty. But now he was facing a crowd whose thoughts were hidden deep.

"We are not receiving from the white man what was promised to us," Washakie said, suddenly shifting ground. "We have been protected from our enemies, and that is good. But we have not received what was promised. Our young friend here, Dirk Skye, was hired to teach us the new ways, so that we might possess the skills of the Americans, but the promised school is unfinished. And we have not been taught what we need to learn about planting crops and keeping cattle and learning to read and write and do numbers. This is a great sorrow to me. I am saddened to see you here, digging roots to live, catching snakes for meat, when we were promised so much more. So I have come to listen; tell me what troubles you and what you are doing. I will take these things to the agent and make life better for us."

Dirk saw disbelief in the faces around the trap, and knew the chief was making no progress. No one, not Washakie, not Dirk's father, not any Indian agent or government official, had succeeded in any of it.

Washakie saw how it was, even without hearing from any of the crowd.

"There are things to learn. We need to grow foods. We need to raise beef. That requires work and patience. We could do these things without help, if we try. We are a wise people, and we can do these things."

The male Shoshones looked pained. Women's work. They would die first.

Washakie gauged the mood of his listeners very well. These people were not receptive to any arguments, nor did they believe the chief could accomplish anything.

Washakie stood quietly, and then addressed them in a new tone.

"Some of you are Dreamers. Come, tell me who you are. Are you a Dreamer, Walks at Night?"

The old headman stood straighter and met Washakie's powerful gaze with his own. "I am a Dreamer," he said.

"And what did you dream? What did the spirits bring to you, old friend?"

"I am a follower of Owl. His dream is true."

"Have you dreamed?"

"I listened to Owl, and his dream is good. It is what will be."

"Ah, but you call yourself a Dreamer."

"I hear the Dreamer, Grandfather."

Washakie nodded, and turned to another, Mare. "My friend Mare, are you a Dreamer?"

Mare's gaze was hard. "Owl came to me. I dream. The Owl will glide over the white men and they will vanish."

"How will they vanish?"

"The Owl will drive them away for all time."

"And how will Owl do that?"

Mare slid into silence.

"Will the white man decide to go away, and turn his ponies east?"

More silence.

"Will Owl summon warriors to drive the white soldiers away with bullets and arrows?"

None in the crowd responded.

"Who among you are Dreamers?" Washakie asked.

The silence only deepened. Dirk could see that the tenuous peace between the chief and this crowd had vanished, and a certain defiance had risen in its place.

The chief waited. Time stretched thin.

Dirk wondered who would speak first, but the chief, easy in his authority, chose to talk.

"Very well. I have learned from your silence. You are not true Dreamers who have been visited by a spirit. You follow a young man whose vision you do not doubt. That is a courtesy among us: we never question the vision received by any of the People.

"I will tell you what will happen if you rise up against the white men. They will send more soldiers, and more and more. The Lakota and the Cheyenne defeated Custer at the Little Big Horn, and defeated our Shoshones and the Absaroka. But look at the result. Where are they now? They are being rounded up and put on reservations. If the mighty Lakota could not drive away the white men, why do you think you can?"

"We are Dreamers," said Mare.

Washakie's reasoning wasn't getting anywhere with these angry men.

"If we die, then we will die bravely. If the People die, then the People die," Mare continued. "For what life have the People now?"

Dirk knew enough to keep silent, though he wanted to respond. The People could have a good life if they changed their ways. They could have a good life even if the Yankee government never did another thing for them. But only if the People let go of their past.

"The People will have as good a life as they choose for themselves," Washakie said.

Dirk thought it was a superb response.

"We will not turn ourselves into girls," Walks at Night said.

That stirred a sharp response.

"Owl, Owl, Owl," one chanted.

They took up the chorus. "Owl, Owl . . ."

Washakie raised a hand, an ancient gesture used by men given authority, but no one paid him heed. It dismayed Dirk. In all his time on the Wind River Reservation, he had never seen any Shoshone treat the chief with no respect. And that struck Dirk as somehow menacing.

Washakie knew it. He stood tall and quiet, letting his hawkish gaze survey each of these men, one by one by one. Something critical had passed here. Dirk could only sense its outlines, because he had been too far removed from his mother's people to grasp what was happening. But clearly, these men were throwing out the chief who had paved the way into reservation life.

They would not be girls.

They would not do women's work, and everything except warfare and hunting was the office of women. Everything that the Americans wanted them to become was a threat to their manhood.

And the odd thing was, Dirk thought, he empathized with them. It would take generations, not a few months or years, to transform them—if ever. People forced to let go of their deepest beliefs, passions, visions, habits, and comforts might choose to die because nothing would be left to them.

Victoria struggled to her feet. "Goddamn Snakes," she said. "Owl will eat your heart out."

She sat down painfully, her rheumatism tormenting her.

That stopped the guttural chanting, slowly.

"Go away from us, Absaroka woman. You are not welcome here," Mare said.

"Go to hell, Snake," she replied.

Dirk stared sharply at her.

"You mess with Owl, and Owl will eat your heart out, and then your brains and then your liver and then there ain't nothing left to eat." She addressed Mare. "Where is the boy, the one who calls himself Owl now? He's a half-grown fool. I want to talk with him before he does any more foolishness."

"The Dreamer? You will never know, Absaroka woman. And you, half-blood, will never know. And you—who is called chief by a few women—you will never know."

That shocked Dirk. It was a calculated insult to the chief. It also shocked the rest. He saw men grimace.

"Send the young man to me," Washakie replied, once again shrugging off the offenses against his person and office. "I wish to learn about his dream."

In the ensuing silence Dirk saw no softening.

Washakie motioned, and Dirk hawed the dray horse forward, and along the river trail, but Washakie urged him to turn toward the agency. The chief sat in stony silence as the day waned. They would not reach the agency until long after the summer sun had fled.

"This is a good land," Washakie said. "See how the peaks still are white even as summer dies. See how the forests rise up their slopes. See how clear and sweet is the water that tumbles down to the valley. See how the sun blesses the home of the People. I won't waver. Our friends the white men have given us a good place. It is up to the People to make it comfort us.

"If they follow the boy, they will lose this place, and maybe their lives."

six

Sirius Van Horne yawned, his mouth a tunnel between orange muttonchops.

"Dirk, my boy, these are Shoshones, not Sioux. A few bad apples, so what? Who cares? Old Washakie's got the lid on 'em and that's that."

"They are dreaming, sir. Their sense of reality is altered."

"Eh? You don't say. Bloody thundermugs, the whole lot."

"Sir, they're on the brink of . . . madness. That's not the word. Purging their land. Purging their world. Purging their life, by any means."

Van Horne smiled. "Very good, my boy. You did the right thing, letting me know. Now you get back to your books and chalkboard, and I'll deal with it."

"Sir—I think you should take this seriously."

"Why, boy, I am."

Van Horne smiled toothily, waved a languid hand, and dismissed Dirk.

"Your safety is in your hands, sir."

Van Horne chuckled. "It's never been in anyone else's hands, my boy."

Dirk abandoned that, and headed into the bright morning, glad to get away from the stink. What was it about Van Horne? Did his flesh exude sour fumes?

The impersonal sun scoured the whole world and Dirk felt its heat upon him. Back in that agency office, Major Van Horne would be digging into his desk drawer for the first nip to smooth over the long day. It had been a comfortable office when Dirk's father occupied it, redolent of leather. But Van Horne's body exuded a sourness that permeated even the wallpaper.

Camp Brown stood nearby. In a few weeks it would be renamed Fort Washakie, the only military reservation to be named for an Indian. Dirk wondered whether to talk to the commanding officer, Captain Prescott Cinnabar. It was hard to say. Dirk had already done what might be required, which was to alert the Indian agent of trouble. But Major Van Horne had been so disinterested he had scarcely wanted an accounting, and was not even interested in the names of those who were dreaming. He didn't even express much interest in what was stirring this sudden turbulence on the Wind River Reservation.

Dirk decided he probably should take his news to the captain. The thought tore at him. He shared the distrust of the blue-bellies, just as his mother's people did. On the other hand, what the Dreamers were goading themselves into doing would be well classified as suicide. He decided to hike over there and see the commander.

It wasn't much of a fort and was staffed by two undermanned companies of mounted infantry, which devoted their time to patrolling the region, sleepy reconnoiters of sleepy trails more populated by game than by human passage. The post's principal occupation was subsisting itself. There were firewood details, hay details, garden details, kitchen details, slaughter details, carpentry and building details, and only occasionally did the infantry train for battle, usually by firing five rounds or doing drills. The monthly target practice was so rare that the crack of rifles startled the whole agency and set the crows to cawing.

A flag hung limply, and beneath it the regimental colors, on a staff before the whitewashed headquarters. Dirk thought that the limp flag reflected a limp life, served by enlistees and officers doing duty-time. No one thought of the place as home, least of all the six officers who whiled away their lives at an obscure army outpost.

Dirk barely knew Captain Cinnabar, even though the man had been posted to this remote camp for over a year. The camp boasted little social life, what with only six officers and two or three of those usually on leave. Only a few women endured life with their officers. Cinnabar's wife and daughter were sometimes among them, sometimes not. They lived in Galena, Illinois.

It was approaching noon, so the commander would be about, probably preparing for his afternoon siesta, which was a favorite occupation at this post in the summertime, shared by enlisted men and officers alike. Dirk climbed the three wooden steps to the veranda, and then clattered through a screen door and into the antechamber, occupied by a buck sergeant who was sweating in his buttoned-up blue blouse.

"He ain't in, Mr. Skye."

"Where might I find him?"

"He's inspecting the outhouses and laundry. You need something?"

"No, but I want to talk to him."

"If it can't wait, try him at his billet at noon."

Dirk nodded, wandered the parade, watched a detail bucket water out to the potato patch, and then tried the commanding officer's quarters, knocking lightly.

Much to Dirk's astonishment, a young woman responded.

"Ah, do I have the right place? Is Captain Cinnabar here?"

"You probably have the right place. My father is half here and half somewhere else much of the time. You are—?"

"Dirk Skye, madam. I teach school."

"Miss, not madam."

She had the mournful face of a bloodhound, with soft eyes peering from heavy cheeks. A pear-shaped figure had been carefully swathed in a blousy dress. She noticed Dirk's glance and withstood it with dignity.

"Ah, you must be the captain's sister."

"Daughter." She eyed him. "I am Aphrodite Olive Cinnabar, but I prefer to be called Olive for obvious reasons. My parents thought they were doing me a favor."

Dirk smiled. "I think they were doing you a great favor."

Olive reddened but otherwise didn't yield to good humor.

"You wish to see my father? Is it about something urgent, that can't possibly wait until after lunch, or would you prefer to come back at a more civil hour?"

"Ah . . ." This was a new species of female for Dirk, and she would take some getting used to. "I'll come back at, say, two?"

"Who's that?" bawled a male voice from the parlor.

"It's the teacher," Miss Cinnabar said.

"Oh, bloody hell, show him in and get up a sandwich for the fellow."

"I've put the beef back into the springhouse."

"Well fetch the fellow in, and fix him up."

"Oh, Captain, I'll come back."

Miss Cinnabar intervened. "Go in there and have your man-to-man. I'll do my duty in the kitchen."

"Your duty, miss?"

"When among men, be a scullery maid."

"Ah . . ."

Captain Cinnabar loomed suddenly at the door. As always, Dirk was first aware of the captain's vast soup-strainer mustache, which curled ornately around his mouth like shark's teeth.

Miss Cinnabar vanished, with a rush of limp gingham.

"Bloody woman. I brought her out here for a while. I get bloody tired of living in a house without a petticoat in it."

"She's an asset to you, sir."

"Asset is she? Asset? You have quaint notions."

The captain led Dirk to a settee.

"Sit there and spill it, and don't mind if I gnaw on the sandwich while you jabber. I don't want the bread to dry out."

Sitting there, Dirk wondered why he'd bothered to come. This was alien turf. Maybe he should go. But oddly, he wanted to experience more of Olive. There was little about her that he liked, neither her bloodhound face nor her strange demeanor, but at least she was interesting, and only a few years younger than he was.

"There's been some trouble among the People, sir."

"Ever since the eclipse, yes. It set them to howling like timber wolves in January."

"Then you know about it."

"My staff tells me. Is there something else I should know? Battalions marching in the night?"

"Yes, sir, that's a good way to put it."

"With howitzers and Gatlings and repeating carbines?"

"No, sir, with dreams that they believe lead them into what is to come."

"Ah, bloody superstition."

"No, sir. Fate."

Captain Cinnabar munched steadily, but he was listening.

"My student, Waiting Wolf, comes from a clan of seers and medicine men. He's bright but not focused, and tends to vanish now and then. At the moment of the eclipse, he claims to have received a vision, the Owl spreading its wings over the dead sun, followed by the return of the sun, which he took to mean the end of the subjection of the Shoshones by white men. He took the name of Owl, and made his vision known, and now he commands most of the Shoshone males, though he is only in his mid-teens. They are Dreamers, Captain. And they dream they will see white men leave here. And maybe Chief Washakie, too."

Cinnabar stopped munching long enough to absorb that. "I've heard some of it. What does Major Van Horne think of it?"

"You'd have to ask him, sir."

Cinnabar grunted and nipped off a huge chunk of sliced beef encased in bread.

"Bloody nonsense, but it might be best to stamp it out fast," he said. "Where's that boy?"

"Owl? He's vanished and you won't find him easily," Dirk said. "It's a large reservation, with a thousand secrets."

"Well, we'll round up a few of these Dreamers and make them dance."

"When a vision grips the soul of an Indian, sir, you won't make him dance."

"Hmm. Bloody saints. You ever wonder about saints, what's in 'em, Skye?"

"All the time, sir."

"You're an emperor in Rome, running a bloody model of an empire, and off in the hinterlands somewhere a bloody visionary gets himself born in a stable, and the next thing you know, he's conquering the world, not with swords but with belief, vision, whatever it is. It's unstoppable, and pretty soon the visionary's conquered the empire. Get the drift, boy?"

"I do, sir."

"What would you do, eh? You can't behead soothsayers, even if it'd improve the world."

"Go to the things that trouble them, sir. The government's welshing. It's not feeding them as promised, or giving the annuities as promised. The government's not letting them off the reservation to hunt up enough food to keep from starving."

"Well, they don't have to starve, you know. Find me one bloody Snake who'd plow up a garden patch or raise some beef."

Olive swept in, carrying a black-enameled tray which she set down in Dirk's lap. She stepped back to admire her handiwork, and Dirk caught the glint of her glossy brown hair, which framed her face.

The service was exquisite. There before Dirk was a finely wrought sandwich of sliced beef, on Tiffany china, a snowy napkin in a silver ring, a cut-glass decanter of water, a salad of greens with walnuts and diced apples, nestled beside the sandwich.

"This is a handsome lunch, Miss Cinnabar," he said.

"If you're going to be in service, you may as well do it up proud," she said.

"Tasty, my dear, tasty," the captain said.

"I do what I'm required, and then some," she said. "I will serve the world."

Dirk watched her retreat from this man-to-man, as she had put it. He saw force and grace in her movement, as if she viewed all of life as something to be assaulted. He wondered what her station was, her true object in life; certainly it wasn't spending her years in her father's service. She assaulted everything before her, and she did it to please herself.

Dirk bit into an elegant sandwich, the beef sliced so fine it melted in his mouth, but his thoughts weren't upon the food, remarkable as it was, but upon the sad and probably lonely woman who transformed herself into sheer elegance by force of will.

"I don't know what to do with her," Captain Cinnabar said. "She's never had the slightest interest in domestic life. She's never had a swain. In all the years I've introduced her to society, she's not snared anything resembling a suitable husband, and in fact scares the hell out of 'em. Sometimes she scares the hell out of me. Good sandwich, eh?"

"She reminds me of my Crow mother," Dirk said. "In her own way, she was the strongest in our family. And still is."

Captain Cinnabar demolished his sandwich, ate the last scrap of salad, wiped his shark-tooth facial hair with a napkin, and eyed his guest.

"The Shoshones are simply in a funk," he said. "The Arapaho are being settled downriver, and the Shoshones don't like it. It's their land, but Uncle Sam doesn't seem to care. The two tribes are enemies, but that never bothered the Indian Bureau. It certainly makes life difficult for the army. Frankly, Skye, I'm surprised there hasn't been more trouble. Washakie's kept the lid on or there'd likely be some bloody battles just outside of our parlor windows. That's all this is. And things will settle down soon enough."

Dirk wanted to believe it, but he couldn't. And he couldn't very well explain why he didn't. It was Indian knowledge.

"It's not that, sir. It's the vision. It's what Waiting Wolf saw in a single moment, saw things that lie beyond this world. Once he saw Owl—the feared totem of these people—across the face of the dying sun, everything changed, and now he's picking up followers day by day. Believers, sir, believers, like the apostles."

Captain Cinnabar merely smiled wryly. "Heard a lot of that sort of thing, but it doesn't beat a Springfield trapdoor carbine."

At the exact moment that Dirk finished his sandwich, Aphrodite materialized and collected the Tiffany plate.

"A saint in rags will defeat an army with swords every time," she said.

"Well, the Shoshones aren't saints, my dear, and what I have in mind will bloody well keep the peace. I'm going to march my whole command across the entire reservation, two companies of mounted infantry, each with a carbine and a revolver, riding on fat horses, with a Gatling gun behind. I think that'll quiet the Dreamers. Just watch!"

seven

Captain Cinnabar was sure putting on a show. He assembled his column on the parade while most everyone for miles around watched. A hundred men would march this morning, with a handful left to man the post.

These mounted infantry were carrying carbines and revolvers, with spare ammunition in their saddle packs. They wore blue blouses, yellow scarves, visored campaign hats. Their horses had been groomed until they glowed. A pack train would carry three days' worth of rations, and a pair of big mules would drag the Gatling gun and its caisson. This was more than a patrol. Cinnabar meant to show the flag, and that meant a color guard in the van, with Old Glory and the regimentals curling softly in the morning zephyrs.

The juniormost lieutenant, Gregorovich, would command the post and its skeleton crew, mostly stablemen and clerks, but the rest of the officers who weren't on leave—two or so were usually away—were shaping up their companies. The enlisted men were mostly immigrants from Ireland and Germany. Some had barely fired a weapon, but that didn't matter. The show was the thing, and show was what Captain Cinnabar wanted. Show that blue column to every Shoshone on the reservation, and to the Arapahos being settled over on its eastern reaches.

Dirk watched intently. This was the same army that had gotten licked at the Little Big Horn, along with Washakie's scouts who had gone along for the fun of licking their enemies the Sioux. The same army, but if anything even weaker, with few experienced enlisted men in its ranks. Most of these men had never been in a fight.

The chief stood silently, with space around him even though he had twenty or thirty Shoshones for company. He wore his white-man clothing this morning. Dirk wondered whether he had been consulted and what he thought of it. The rest of the Eastern Shoshones watched impassively, their gazes taking in everything, their stance straight, their bodies lean. Deep silence pervaded the clot of natives.

It seemed half the morning was consumed by all the prepping, but at last the captain took his position at the van, lifted an arm, and shouted an order. There was no band here, no bugler, either, but no doubt Cinnabar was wishing he might have a musical send-off. One could almost hear the bugles and snare drums.

The agent, Major Van Horne, watched intently, flanked by clerks. The two officers' wives, Jane Wigglesworth and Glory Merchant, stood to one side, waving their parasols. They were jointed by Amy Partridge, wife of the Episcopal vicar, the Reverend Thaddeus Partridge, and their little boy Robert, who they called Bobolink.

The Indian reservations had been divided up among the denominations, and the Episcopalians had gotten Wind River. Off a way was their mission, St. Michael's, and a vicarage. A gaggle of soldiers watched from the edge of the parade. And not least, Aphrodite Olive Cinnabar was studying the sea of blue-bloused soldiers with obvious amusement.

"Miss Cinnabar, something has tickled your fancy," Dirk said.

"Men are such idiots," she replied.

"I take it you're not impressed."

"The Shoshones won't be."

"What would impress them?"

"A government that keeps its promises to them."

Her logic could not be faulted. He smiled at her.

The column circled the parade and then clattered down the creek toward the Wind River, flag flapping, guidons snapping. In a while it diminished to a blue worm, and then disappeared. The agency and post were suddenly quiet. Oddly, no one drifted away. Van Horne stood there, as if contemplating the meaning of life. The vicar and his wife simply gazed blandly. The Shoshones stood in deepest silence, no doubt pondering this show of friendly force by the friendly whites.

Aphrodite was grinning.

"Gunboat diplomacy. You want to guess what's going on inside the heads of those gentlefolk?" she said, gesturing toward Washakie's people.

Dirk glanced uncomfortably toward them. Even Washakie, faithful to his Yank friends to the last, seemed pensive. The rest stood like rocks. Then, suddenly, Washakie wheeled away and the rest of the Shoshones broke into knots of two or three, and drifted toward their lodges and cabins, their lives entirely in the hands of the Great Father in the city of Washington far away.

"You appear to be at odds with your father, Aphrodite."

"Olive. Never call me that other name, which I will not

speak. Of course I'm at odds. I was born at odds with him. I'm an army brat. Army brats and ministers' children are born to rebel."

"Olive, then."

"Olive isn't much of a name, either, but we're stuck with what we get. The captain interprets his orders, namely to keep the peace, very liberally. I'm looser. I reject all orders, especially his."

Dirk scarcely knew what to say to that, but was rescued by his Crow mother, Victoria.

"Goddamn," Victoria said.

"Ah, Olive, this is my Crow mother Victoria, one of my father's wives."

"This is an entertaining day," Olive said. "Was your father a Mormon?"

"No, he was in the fur trade and then a guide. He met my Crow mother at a trappers' rendezvous, and later met my mother, Blue Dawn, at a summertime visit of the Shoshones and Crows."

"I have no intention of adhering to any faith," Olive said. "I'm leaning toward free love and feminism."

"Well, dammit, that's me," said Victoria.

Olive looked a little flustered, but was rescued by the Partridges, she petite and demure, he with a noble Roman profile, with an especially fine nose, which caused him to stand slightly sideways of his auditors so it might be admired.

"Why it's Madam Skye, and I do believe you're the captain's daughter Aphrodite," Amy Partridge said.

"Olive. Aphrodite's the name of a lewd goddess."

"I see," Amy said. "Virtue is its own reward."

Thaddeus rescued the moment. "What a sight! Oh, when I beheld that blue column, the flags flying, the horses and men marching toward their destiny, words failed me and my heart fairly burst with pride," he said. "Never was I so proud to be an American."

"Goddamn," Victoria said.

The Partridges were familiar with Victoria, and simply treated her as if she didn't exist, which she didn't in their minds. She was a relic.

"We all put our pants on one leg at a time," Olive said.

No one had anything to add.

"Has your attendance dropped off?" Dirk asked the missionary.

"Now that's a funny thing. They've all run off. Ever since the eclipse. It's as if they all reverted to their old ways. I was catechizing a class of six, and now there's no one. I fear we'll have to start all over again. I hear the school's empty, too."

"I have no way to board them," Dirk said. "There's not much I can do until there's a way to board all the children. I rarely have ten."

"Oh, it's coming, Mr. Skye, but far more slowly than we might wish. It's so hard to get the attention of anyone Back East."

"I'm on the side of the Shoshones," Olive said.

"Why, miss, aren't we all?" the vicar asked.

"No, I mean I think they should just be themselves."

"Surely you don't mean that. Why, with some enlightenment they could accept our faith, cease polygamous marriages, support themselves by farming, start up businesses, have Fourth of July celebrations."

"They may prefer to celebrate their own Independence Day, July twenty-ninth, to be specific," Olive said.

"The day of the eclipse? Independence?"

"That's how it's shaping up. They have their minutemen,

and one of these hours they'll collect at some local Concord Bridge and fire the shot heard 'round the world."

Thaddeus Partridge stared.

"Sonofabitch," said Victoria.

"What does your father think of that?" Amy Partridge said.

"I'm too busy serving him hand and foot to utter subversions," Olive replied.

Dirk laughed, but no one else did.

The conversation ended on that note. Dirk intuited that he would enjoy a lot more of Miss Cinnabar's company.

Olive headed forcefully for her quarters, her gait willful, while the Partridges gathered up their tow-haired Bobolink, who was prowling the stables, and they drifted toward the distant white Episcopalian compound: a small clapboard church, a Montgomery Ward prefabricated vicarage, and a prefabricated sexton's cottage, occupied by God, or at least an imitation—an old man with a flowing beard, sandals, and a gray monk's habit. His name was Alfred, but Dirk didn't know anything else about him. He either lived in his own island of the mind, or else was mentally slow. He swept, dusted the plain pews, tended a garden, served as handyman, and squinted at the Shoshones from watery blue eyes. Some of the Shoshones were sure he was Jesus come to earth and the Partridges either didn't know that, or didn't discourage the idea.

If anything, that afternoon was sleepier than usual, and Dirk scarcely knew how to occupy his time. He was obliged to keep the school doors open, which meant being there, which meant that he occasionally spent hours reading whatever came to hand, which wasn't much, considering the remoteness of the agency. On some days he was reduced to reading tea leaves.

"Tonight Owl visits," Victoria said at the supper hour.

"What do you mean?"

"Owl will come. You'll see."

"How do you know that?"

"I'm a goddamn medicine woman."

"What will happen?"

"Scare the hell out of white men."

"Should I alert the post?"

She started cackling. She'd lost a couple of teeth, and now her wheezing whistled through the gaps. "Hell, boy, I like Owl," she said.

The drumming began sometime around midnight, when the whole world was fast asleep. Dirk awakened with a start, something within him responding to the muffled thump of drums. He found himself fully awake instantly. Outside his window, the sky was dotted with stars, and a gibbous moon glowed—and yet it didn't. A curious cloud obscured it, darkening this place but not blocking its bold light on nearby fields and slopes. That was an odd cloud, and then Dirk was chilled by it. He swore it was an owl cloud, an owl with spread wings, glowing eyes, curved beak, its claws tucked under. And it hid the moon.

Dirk dressed swiftly, plunged into the parlor only to discover Victoria grinning, and then hastened into the night. The drumming rose to the east, beyond the military compound, somewhere near the Episcopal mission. He hurried that way alone. The drumming hadn't disturbed the post, or awakened the agent or his minions. The drumming hadn't even stirred Chief Washakie's house. But it was drumming nonetheless, and every little while the drums climaxed into a brief violence and then returned to the soft heartbeat that somehow choked the night.

The Dreamers.

Dirk hurried there, wherever they were, but could not see them, and began to question his senses. Surely the Dreamers were somewhere, collected together to drum, their urgent chanting soft and knife-edged in the peaceful night.

The Dreamers had collected here after the soldiers had marched. The Dreamers would disturb, maybe even terrify, this small collection of houses and buildings. The Dreamers would sing their dark message until they awakened this whole scattered community known as the Wind River Agency.

A part of Dirk responded to this night-song, which followed the rhythms of his heart and set his own Shoshone blood to singing. He felt an odd empathy toward Waiting Wolf, whose prophesies and visions had inspired this. This was a song of defiance, a song that cried out to all listeners. You are not welcome here. Leave our homeland. Give us our lives and ways and visions. Go away, white man, go away, with all your armies and churches and condescension.

He reached the mission and found the Partridges in their nightclothes on the porch, staring into the moonlit night. He didn't see the sexton. The drumming was clearer here but lay somewhere beyond this place, perhaps in a copse of cottonwoods down the slopes. The Partridges stared at Dirk but said nothing, and Dirk acknowledged them with a wave. He saw that Thaddeus had a fowling piece in hand. Dirk had nothing, wanted nothing, for he would not need to defend himself.

He pushed toward the cottonwoods, passed the first trees, which rose like sentries, and then into a small park where the brown grasses had been trampled. There was no one, no swift shadows. And the owl cloud had passed away.

eight

The moon cast a sickly light over the slumbering slopes, a lantern for Dirk Skye. He made his way back to the vicarage, where the Partridges huddled on the porch, she wrapped in a vast angora shawl, he in a greatcoat over his nightshirt, and Bobolink barefoot in a nightshirt.

"They're gone," Dirk said.

"How do you know they won't come back?" Partridge asked.

"I don't. But they made their point."

"It was awful, just awful," Amy said.

"It rose up from the bottom layers of hell. It was savagery, the howling of demons. This was the devil's own work," Partridge said.

Dirk scarcely knew how to respond. "The Shoshone people have their own traditions, sir."

"I tell you, Skye, this was something out of the bowels of the earth. That fiendish drumming, rising to some sort of crest and then fading away, only to rise again, sulphurous and sinister, unloosing all the demons of the netherworld."

"They would not see it that way, sir."

"Well, you're one of them, Skye. It was an assault, that's what. They'll come closer next time, and closer, until they do this under our windows. Deliberately terrorizing us. If we become martyrs, like the Whitmans in Oregon, then that's our fate. We're Americans, sir. We're bringing truth and goodness to these savages. We're offering them the hand of reason, and the keys to everlasting life. I'll tell you what I'll do. I'll talk to Van Horne in the morning. These ghouls must be punished."

"I'll want the army here every night," Amy Partridge said. "I'll insist on it."

These people were plainly distraught.

"They're probably the Dreamers," Dirk said. "They've received a vision of life as it was for them, life without the presence of white men. Life following the buffalo herds. Life honoring their traditions and mysteries."

"Exactly, and it must be stamped out! Exterminated!"

Dirk tried another tack. "Have you heard of the Jesuit Father De Smet? For years, he wandered the West, befriending the tribes most hostile to white men, teaching them his faith, inviting them to masses. He helped them deal with settlers. He was their friend and they trusted him, and he was never harmed, and was much loved. He walked freely among the Blackfeet and the Sioux."

"Yes, and all he did was delay the inevitable. We all saw the result at the Little Big Horn two years ago."

Dirk found no opening in that closed mind. "Well, you're safe now. You can go back to bed."

"I won't sleep a wink," said Amy Partridge.

But they drifted into the rectory, and Dirk heard the door shut behind them.

Dirk drifted through the pale light. He saw a single lamp burning at the army post, and no light at all at the agency. No light burned at Chief Washakie's residence but Dirk was pretty sure the chief hadn't missed a thing. The Dreamers had announced their presence, choosing a moment when the army was miles away. This was probably the work of Owl, Waiting Wolf, and Dirk didn't doubt that the youth could run circles around the blue-shirts. The army probably would never catch the boy, not on a reserve with so many hidden refuges and mysteries tucked into its vast size.

As he passed the chief's residence, a quiet voice caught him.

"North Star, come sit with me."

Dirk discovered the chief sitting in deep shade, staring out upon the moon-washed night. He was wrapped in a red-and-white Hudson's Bay blanket, the red barely discernible.

Dirk settled himself in the next wicker chair.

"It is a good night, brother," Washakie said.

"The Dreamers came."

"And went away."

"They frightened the vicar and his family."

"What did you tell them?"

"I told them about how Father De Smet had made friends of the very tribes most feared by white men, and how the father looked after their needs and helped those people deal with the tide of white men."

"And what did this man Partridge say?"

"He said Father De Smet only delayed what was to come, and the result was the Little Big Horn."

"Then he is not a friend."

"No, sir. He burns with the need to civilize the savages and bring them to the True Faith and make the savages just like white men."

Washakie exhaled his exasperation. "And the Dreamers are devils, yes?"

"Yes, sir. He thought they rose out of the pits of hell, out of the very earth."

"They left something for me."

Washakie handed Dirk a furry feather. It had to be from a Great Gray Owl.

Washakie eyed Dirk. "I don't plan to die anytime soon, but the Dreamers seem to have other ideas."

"It is a threat?"

"Will they seek my life? No. But Owl, the great bird, will pursue me. As the whites might say, it is written. It has been seen."

"My mother didn't explain all these things to me."

"Shoshones have no religion in the sense that white men have one," Washakie said. "We are led to our own universe in our own way. Your mother had nothing to teach you because each Shoshone pursues his private path, often in secret. There is no white men's Bible, no tracts, no catechism for the People. These mysteries are discovered by boys when their time comes to listen and wait. It is something for you to find, not for her to teach."

"I was taken away at age eight, put in a Jesuit school in St. Louis. That's what separates me from you, Grandfather."

"Yes, and it was good you went to St. Louis. You are a brother, North Star. You are one of the People, and you will help us learn how to live the new way."

"Brother? Not by blood."

"By all the mysteries that bring life to the womb of a

Shoshone woman. We live in a world we barely know, and some of what we know is not what we see, but what rises inside of us. It rises in me to call you brother of all my People."

"What will you do with this owl feather, Grandfather?"

"Tomorrow I will ride in my wagon to the encampment on the river, and give the feather to Walks at Night."

"And?"

"He will not accept it, but let it drop to the clay."

"And it will lie there."

"The winds of time will take it away. They will lift it a few feet, and blow it into the reeds. And the Americans will still be here. I have made them my friends. They call me a friend and are naming that army post for me in a little while. In a way, they are what they say. But their focus is not upon us, not upon their Shoshone friends. Their hearts are upon their lands and settlers and ranchers and farmers and the towns and mines they will start, and they will forget their Shoshone friends. And they will forget the Dreamers, and an owl's feather will not change them in the slightest."

"And the People?"

Washakie stared into the mysterious night. "The bodies of the People will live on, make babies, survive. But the People, the Snake People, they may be lost. The Dreamers believe it will not happen that way. Everything will return to what it was. But white men come with guns made of iron, with wagons and horses and steam engines, with plows and looms that make cloth, with steamboats, and the time of the owls and the buffalo fades into the past and will not be seen again. Only the bodies will live on, and those will be poor, small, sickly, and ill-made."

There was something prophetic in Washakie's vision.

"I have made my choices, for myself and for the People,"

he added. "The Dreamers might put me on the spirit road, but the fate of the People would be no different. Go now. There will be an owl feather at the teacher house."

That chilled Dirk. He hurried across the empty fields to the shadowy schoolhouse and to his teacherage, only to find old Victoria waiting for him, sitting on the front stoop, wrapped in a striped blanket. She handed him the same furry feather that had been given to Chief Washakie, and maybe others this fateful night.

He took it wordlessly.

"Stuck in the door. Big goddamn medicine," she said.

"No, no medicine in it. It has no magic. A Gray Owl did not fly here and drop this feather for me to heed. It's a warning, though. A Dreamer brought it. Maybe Waiting Wolf himself. The Dreamers are telling me something."

"I don't know what. In the old days, when I had the inner eye, I could tell you."

"You still have medicine, Grandmother."

"I don't see the magpie no more," she said.

He puzzled it, and remembered that the magpie had been her spirit helper all her long life, and in some strange way, she and magpies had bonded. For her, Magpie was one bird, even if she had seen thousands in her life. It was as if all magpies had become her spirit counselor. But what did her magpie have to do with this?

"Grandmother, when did Magpie become your spirit guide?"

"I was still a girl, and I asked for a spirit blessing, and went by myself into the mountains above our village, and there I waited, and then Magpie came. She walked right up to me, where I lay on a robe, and she looked at me with one eye, and turned her head and looked at me with the other, and then I saw her above me, big as the whole sky, and I came down from the mountain and told our chief, Rotten Belly, that I had received the gift, and he told me I had received great powers. This was before I ever met your father, Mister Skye. Such powers didn't come often to a girl, but they came to me. But now I don't see Magpie, and I tell myself that we will meet on the star trail soon."

Dirk settled on the stoop beside her. The moonlight seemed eerie, and sometimes Dirk swore he saw shapes gliding across the meadows. But these were nothing, figments of his imagination, ghost warriors, ghost dancers, ghost spirits playing hob with the peace. Odd how jittery he was, even though the Dreamers had vanished.

The feather seemed cold to his touch, not just lifeless but radiating the coldness of death. It sent chills through him. He ascribed this to his imagination, but no matter how much of a white man he tried to be in that moment, his other blood froze in his veins.

"The feather is telling you something," she said. She had a way of seeing through with eyes that fathomed the unknown. "Magpie was always with me. I saw Magpie where she could not be. Magpie beckoned to me, or warned me, or chattered greetings, or let me know of a bear or a moose or a wolf. Magpie saved our lives, you know. Without Magpie, or your father's grizzly bear medicine, you would not exist. Mister Skye didn't know anything about living in this place and only his medicine and my medicine kept death away. He might have died a dozen times before he met your mother, but for Magpie, and the great bear claws that rested on his chest. They are medicine, even as that owl feather freezing your fingers is medicine."

Dirk didn't want to believe it. Everything stormed inside of him.

The arrow whacked into the porch post two feet from his head. He jerked back, and tumbled into the shadow of the veranda. Victoria didn't move. His heart raced. He slipped to the floor of the porch to make himself smaller.

But there was nothing to be seen. Only eerie white light from the impersonal moon, and those strange spectres that somehow shifted the light here and there. Someone had almost killed him. And still could. He debated what to do, how to hustle old Victoria into the safety of the house. He studied the deeps, the shadows stretching from the school building and the distant agency, and the slumbering fields.

"You get inside, Grandmother," he whispered tautly.

She ignored him, and stood in the light of the moon, a small wraith waiting there.

He could barely discern the bushes from where the arrow had flown. He had nothing else to go on, so he sprang up and raced straight toward the brush, expecting more arrows to fly. He leapt into the brush, thrashing toward whatever was there, but found nothing. No one was fleeing, either. He roamed the area, but found nothing, and finally stood still, hearing only the hammering of his heart.

He slowly made his way back to the porch, alert to any movement anywhere.

She stood there, and sang softly. He knew it was not her death song, but an Absaroka song of courage. They stood while she sang her song, and then she turned toward the house.

"Your father's spirit is in you," she said.

He got his first close look at the arrow buried in the post. It had a steel head, was dyed totally black, and it was fletched with the soft feathers of the Great Owl.

nine

Owl knew the fate of the People was intertwined with his vision. He found himself almost alone now, a mystic, a visionary who was sought out for counsel that rose not from his own youthful wisdom, but from a larger and more terrible source.

Like the great Lakota visionary and warrior Crazy Horse, who had defeated the blue-bellies led by Colonel Custer two years earlier, Owl chose not to adorn himself. He was only a vessel, one whom the spirits had appointed in one galvanizing moment to carry their message to the People. He was scarcely into his manhood, and only days earlier he had been a youth named Waiting Wolf learning white-man things in the schoolhouse.

Now he wore only a breechclout and moccasins, his body at home with nature. Whenever he spoke of his vision, the Great Gray Owl stamped on the face of the dead sun, and the return of the brightness that lit the world of the People, he was heard with respect. Who had ever imagined such a thing? Who could dispute this sign from the all-knowing spirits?

Who could bear to receive a prophecy from the Owl, harbinger of death, terror of the night, the aerial stalker floating murderously on the currents of chill air?

And so the Dreamers had sprung up. Other men were seeking a vision, and dreaming, and receiving the Owl courage. The Owl Dance had begun, sung in the depths of the night to the soft melancholy of flutes, punctuated by a single drum, flute and drum, a death knell drifting over the lonely reaches of the Wind River Reservation, the prison fashioned by the white men to contain the People.

Now there were Dreamers in every hamlet, and almost nightly they gathered in hidden valleys far from the ears of the Yankees, to dance the Owl Dance, to hear the flute send owl chills through them until they fell exhausted upon the dewy grass, still dreaming of the time to come whenever Owl should declare the moment was at hand.

For Owl himself, it was all very strange. He was scarcely fifteen winters, but old men, seasoned warriors, battle-hardened scouts who had returned chastened from the Custer debacle, where a contingent of Shoshones had supported the bluecoats, all these now paid heed to this quiet, uneasy, sometimes arrogant boy. They called him Grandfather, the ultimate respect, yet he was barely into his manhood. They hung onto his every word.

"I do not speak for myself," he told them. "I speak only what comes to me, for I am no more than a bowl carrying the blood of life. I have taken the name of He who Speaks to the People."

He retained his humility, seeking nothing for himself, avoiding any declaration of his own authority, and because of that he fevered his followers all the more. For he was the vessel of great tidings for the People.

He drifted into the hidden chasms of the Wind River Mountains, faded into distant camps, lived on high meadows, prayed incessantly to receive the word of the Owl, most dreaded of all the spirits. No white man saw him; no blue-belly army would ever find him. And yet the People somehow always knew where he was, many misty layers of foothills from the eyes of the whites. The Owl Dance spread, and now Dreamers danced it in every hamlet from one end of the reservation to the other, the flutes whispering the song of liberation, which somehow all the Dreamers learned and repeated and made into a ritual that swelled across the whole reservation.

Owl himself was the principal Dreamer, and often took a blanket out to a breezy hilltop to listen, and always received new visions from the Great Owl. Sometimes those visions were slow to form in his mind, and then he supplicated the fearsome bird for direction. But sometimes he was transfixed, taken out of himself, floating through the night skies, so he could see his own resting body below. And then he received word. This he carefully conveyed to several trusted lieutenants, chief of which was Walks at Night, who spread the new understanding to the Dreamers, who now were located in every cranny of the reservation.

The only unfathomable thing was the attitude of his own father, Buffalo Horn, himself a shaman, who glared angrily at the young man, as if he were committing sacrilege. But Owl simply stared back. Let the dead bury the dead; his was the true vision, the future brought to the present. And now many Dreamers had been given the vision.

"How do these visions come to you?" Buffalo Horn had asked him.

"It is not for you to know. It is my own medicine," Owl replied.

"Have you taken your visions to Chief Washakie?"

"I have not. I will not."

"Have you called all the People together and told them of your vision?"

"I do not share my visions. They are for the Dreamers, who also hear and dream."

"The Owl is the most feared of all creatures. Because he is death, he brings death to the People," his father said. "All the People fear the Owl."

His father's gaze was unblinking, so the youth met it with his own unblinking gaze, and then the older man turned away.

That was the only trouble to befall the young man.

They were all waiting for the moment when they would drive the white men away from their home, and the buffalo would return, and they would be free to go wherever they would go.

Then came word that the blue-bellies had formed into an armed column and were marching. Could this be war? Murder? The column marched out in the morning, its flags flapping, its ponies groomed. It looked like a parade, just what the Yankee army did when a visiting general arrived to inspect them. Within half a morning, Owl knew all about this new thing. There were a handful of soldiers remaining at the post. The agency settlement was undefended but for those. The column slowly heading upriver was intended for show, not war. The white men's message to the Dreamers was plain: stop it. Go back to your quiet ways.

Now his lieutenants crowded around Owl, waiting for word. The young man slid easily into the authority granted to him. "Let them march. Let our camps vanish before the blue column. Let them seek the People and find no one except the older ones. Let them go where they will and return to their fort puzzled. Let those remaining at the agency, the mission, the school, learn that they are not safe. But do not harm them, not until the vision comes. Let them know that Owl has spoken." He eyed his lieutenants. "And if the People go hunting away from the reservation, there will be no blue-bellies to stop them."

The lieutenants liked that. They liked taking direction from this stripling boy who could peer into the spirit world. They liked his authority. So Owl's word was carried to every corner of the reservation except where the Arapahos were settling, and soon all the People knew what to do. They kept an eye on the blue column, led by Captain Cinnabar, and well before the column arrived in some camp, the lodges were dismantled and spirited away, and the place vanished. And some among them were well beyond the reservation, hunting game on white men's ranches.

Wherever the column rode, the soldiers were observed by many eyes watching from the surrounding hills. Plainly the captain was puzzled, and sometimes sent patrols out to follow the lodge trails, the furrows of the dragged lodge-poles, and sometimes they found a lodge filled with elders living peacefully beside a creek. But when the villages dispersed, they took their lodges in all directions, so there were dozens of trails, and Captain Cinnabar had little understanding. If his was a show of force, it was proving futile because there was no one who saw it.

Mare and Walks at Night were reporting each day's events.

"We drummed near the mission, not the Dreamer songs, but the drumming from old times, and soon the mission man and woman were frightened," said Mare. "Skye's boy appeared, and we slipped into the night. Later we put an owl arrow near him, always heeding Owl's word not to kill, not now. But how I itched to plant that arrow in his chest. He was born of a Shoshone woman, and now he spends his days destroying the old ways. How I itched!"

"What did he do?"

"He rolled into the moon shadow of the porch, frightened, but then he sprang at me, and I reached the shadows just in time."

"He had no courage and sought the shadow," Owl said. "His time is coming. He is a mixed-blood, born of the People only to betray the People."

Of all those whom Owl despised, Dirk Skye was chief among them. Dirk Skye had Shoshone blood but taught white men's wisdom.

"Let him think about the owl arrow," Walks at Night said.

"When the moon comes up, put an owl arrow close to Buffalo Horn," Owl said. "Let him see the power of the Dreamers."

"Your father, Owl?" asked Walks at Night.

"He does not see with true eyes and does not honor the vision of his own son," Owl said.

"But your father?"

Owl stared at the older man until the man seemed to wilt into his moccasins.

Someday all the People would rejoice in what Owl had done. The People would be free, and the land would be scourged of evil, and the Dreamers would be honored at all the lodge fires of all the old men. And Owl would be remembered even as Sweet Medicine was remembered among the Cheyenne, the lawgiver and the savior of the People.

But that was not for now. That was for the time when Owl received the vision that would change everything.

The Dreamers brought him food, this time rabbit, and he nibbled at it. Ever since the time of the darkened sun, he had not eaten much and had felt little hunger. Yet he was no thinner. It was one of the mysteries that he could live on almost nothing, and it had not escaped the Dreamers. What sort of being was this son of Buffalo Horn who had swiftly become the prophet of the Shoshones?

Sun by sun, runners kept Owl informed of the progress of the blue column wending its way up the river for the purpose of showing the power of the white men. Now it was a joke. Wherever the soldiers went, there were no Shoshones to see it. Only once in a while did the soldiers even encounter a lodge of old people, who watched impassively. All the rest of the People were long gone, so that Captain Cinnabar found only cold ashes, tepee rings, some of the refuse of living in a camp, but scarcely a soul who might set eyes upon his mighty column.

In time, the captain reached the western edge of the reservation, and continued a few miles farther upriver for good measure, perhaps hoping to uncover nests of Shoshones, but he still found few of the People, and finally turned his column home, this time on the north side of the river, where he had as little luck impressing anyone as he had on the other side. If he had actually seen the People, he would have found them in rags, their bones poking from their flesh, or in skins that were falling apart, for the agency had given them almost nothing by way of cloth or leather to replace what they had gotten from the buffalo herds.

Owl mused about that. What if the blue column had been seen by all the People? What difference would it have made to see the fat horses and well-clad soldiers? The People had no meat. What they needed was buffalo meat, a tongue or hump ribs. The People needed good buffalo hides to scrape and tan and sew into their lodges. The People needed robes to sleep under because the agency had not given them all the blankets that had been promised to them. The People needed to live beside a bison herd, where there would be food and clothing and comfort, and all of it more reliable than the promises of the white men.

Soon, oh so soon. Soon there would not be a white man anywhere near.

ten

A woman and two children were sitting patiently at the door of the schoolhouse when Dirk arrived the next morning. They rose at once as he approached, and he discovered a young Shoshone mother and her two daughters.

She seemed overwhelmed with shyness, but finally managed to speak, in her own tongue.

"Grandfather, I am Dawa, the woman of Pan-mook, of the People, and these are my daughters, Kills Bird and Lizard. I give them to you now."

"Ah, teach them?"

Dawa nodded sternly. "Give them magic."

"I would be glad to have some students. I have very few, so I can give all my time to them."

"Nine winters has Kills Bird, eleven winters has Lizard."

"And have they a place to stay? Have you brought your lodge here?"

"The grandfather, Washakie, he said bring my girls to him for a while."

"The girls will stay with him?"

She nodded. "For a moon."

"Is there anything I should know about them?"

"Pan-mook is not a Dreamer!"

So, Dirk thought, this passion overspreading the reservation was not universal, and might be generating some resistance.

"I will keep that before me, madam."

"Our lodge is a long way." She pointed upriver. "I must go now."

"But tell me about these girls . . ."

She was a pretty woman, with golden flesh and bright eyes, but now she seemed distraught. "I go," she said, and retreated.

The girls stared at him solemnly. Then at their retreating mother. They revealed nothing of themselves.

"Well, my new friends, come inside and we'll start somewhere."

They girls eyed him fearfully, this schoolteacher they knew so little about. Lizard seemed more confident than Kills Bird, but the empty schoolhouse subdued them both.

"This is where you'll go to school," he said. "Every morning, you'll come here as early as you can, and I'll usually be here, or in the house over there." The girls studied the empty place, making no sense of it.

"I'll be talking to you in the tongue of the People, except when we learn to talk English. I'll teach you that language because it will help you in the future. We will learn words and phrases and how to write and spell. Then I'll teach you numbers, which you already know. How to multiply, divide, subtract, and add."

They were plainly bewildered.

"You'll learn many good things. How to use money. How to preserve food. How to grow cattle, how to cook meals on a woodstove. You'll learn about how the United States is governed and what your rights and duties are. I'll show you a map of your home, the Wind River Reservation, and we'll learn the names of places."

They listened silently, and he knew they understood little. But they would pick up things quickly; the ones who cared to learn usually did learn quickly.

He was so glad to be teaching. For several days he had opened his classroom only to stare at empty desks and hear only a sad silence. The Dreamers had stolen his students. The girls listened, and even if they were shy, they were absorbing whatever he talked about.

He taught them a few words of English. He showed them arabic numerals and what they meant. He showed them the slate boards, and showed them how to draw letters. Soon they had a sense of much of the alphabet.

Two shy, eager students. Dirk felt rich.

Then Harvey Patella popped through the open doorway. "Skye, the major's called a meeting. He's ready to see you."

"I'll come later. I've some new students."

"Now. He's got every interested party over there except you."

The agent's commands were law on the reservation. Dirk nodded. "I'll get my Crow mother in here."

Patella vanished, and Dirk scraped Victoria out of her bed, where she was having her morning doze.

"The major wants me, and I've two new girls."

Victoria wordlessly followed him into the schoolhouse, where the girls craned to see an old Absaroka woman wearing a blanket even on this hot day.

"This is our Crow grandmother and she will teach for a while. She understands your tongue, and she'll teach you some English."

"You gonna learn a bunch of goddamn good words," Victoria said.

Dirk fled, and soon found himself in Sirius Van Horne's lair, along with the Partridges, their sexton Alfred, Aphrodite Olive Cinnabar, a sergeant with two enlisted men, and a few clerks. Apart from some soldiers, the only white people missing were the two officers' wives, Jane Wigglesworth and Glory Merchant.

"Ah, at last, Skye. Always bringing up the rear."

Dirk didn't reply. Notably absent from this gathering was Washakie, the other real authority living at the agency. This was to be a white man's party. Van Horne seemed more ruddy than usual, which translated to hundred-proof ruddiness.

"I'll be swift and to the point. We're under siege. There's a rebellion on this reservation. Lives are in peril. This strange cult, called Dreamers, have set the Shoshones aflame. The Partridges were threatened with an owl arrow, a sure sign of death. I've dispatched a trooper to find Captain Cinnabar's column and bring it here on the double for our protection. And I've sent a trusted man south to Laramie to wire for help. This insurrection must be stopped, and these rebels caught and hanged."

"What insurrection?" Dirk interrupted.

"Of course you would think that way," the agent replied. "It's out there, and it could strike any time. I'm ordering the remaining troops to guard the agency and associated settlement. And I've ordered the post to prepare to receive civilians in the event of a siege."

"And what of Chief Washakie?"

"We can't trust him. He's not included here."

"Have you talked to him?" Dirk asked.

"No, and I don't intend to."

"Then you're not aware that he received an owl feather."

"So what? He's a Shoshone."

"He still has a large following, Major. He probably could quiet the reservation just by commanding it."

"Bah! Bah! This is for me to handle."

"Everyone's off in a tizzy," Aphrodite said. "Some Dreamers drum, and a few owl feathers decorate a few porches."

She was amused.

"Not a bit funny, miss. I suggest you hold your tongue," Major Van Horne said.

"Before I get the vapors," she added, her smile widening.

"This is a clash of worlds, miss. Their superstitions have driven them over the cliff."

"So they want to deprive us of our superstitions, I take it."

"Sergeant, please escort Miss Cinnabar safely home."

"I'll do so," Dirk said, "if Miss Cinnabar agrees."

The agent studied Dirk levelly, as if escorting her was an act of insurrection. "Well, what do I know about teaching aborigines?" the agent said.

That struck Dirk as piquant.

"There is no wisdom to be gotten here," she said. "So I'll retire."

He reminded himself to call her Olive, even though he preferred Aphrodite, mostly because she inspired Aphrodite-like sensations in all quarters of his person. He discovered that every eye was upon himself and Miss Cinnabar, and the general look on all those faces was Good Riddance.

"Thank you for your gallantry, but I didn't need rescuing."

"I took it as a chance to escape the collective madness, and snatch you for my own pleasure for as long as you will have me."

She simply smiled at him, a smile so warm and pleasured that he smiled back at her with even more pleasure.

"So they've sent a courier to fetch my father," she said.

"And another to bring up a brigade or two from Laramie."

"Is it that grave?"

Dirk was tempted to play the expert, but something in him bridled at that. "I wish I knew," he said.

"At last! A male who isn't sure. You're a card, Dirk. I've waited a lifetime for this moment."

Aphrodite would take some getting used to.

"The Dreamers are fevered with a vision of a homeland purged of all whites, a return to their old ways. But so far, their leader, Owl, hasn't given the word."

"But the drumming last night, and the owl feathers."

"They make themselves known, and stir up some dread. It seems a good tactic."

"Should my father return?"

"I'm not a mind-reader, Aphrodite."

"Olive."

He smiled wilfully. "Aphrodite. It fits you."

She stared at him too long.

"Olive, then," he said.

"I think I should like the comfort of two companies of troops."

"Green troops."

"We're very vulnerable here."

"Your father should be back soon. He's not far away."

They reached the teacherage.

"I could escort you back to the fort, or I could invite you to help me teach two Shoshone girls. Lizard and Kills Bird. This is their first day in school."

"I think Aphrodite's a better name than Lizard. But Kills Bird's a better name than Olive."

"I think the presence of a woman would help the instruction."

"I don't speak—"

"I'll translate."

She acquiesced, so he steered her to the schoolhouse, where they discovered Victoria sitting in a student desk, a girl on either side of her.

Dirk made the introductions, and spoke to the girls in Shoshone. "This woman lives at the soldier post and her name is Olive. She will help teach."

Victoria was enjoying herself. "Goddamn, I think I'll go to school," she said.

So now there were three students.

The day passed quietly. Dirk and Olive taught words and numbers, and the Shoshone girls ended up filled with delight, for it was almost a game, and the very presence of old Victoria and young Miss Cinnabar made the schooling an adventure.

But outside the window, something had changed. Dirk noted pairs of armed guards steadily patrolling the agency and surrounding buildings. Not that a few armed guards and a handful of soldiers could make a difference.

Dirk thought it unwise to push the schooling too long.

"All right now, Lizard and Kills Bird, you come early tomorrow, and if I'm not here, I'll be over there." He pointed toward the teacherage. "Look for me."

Victoria retreated, but Dirk and Olive escorted the girls to the chief's home, and left them there. Washakie's women collected the girls and hustled them into the chief's house. Dirk hoped to see Washakie and discuss matters with him, but the chief remained within, which was unusual for the hospitable Shoshone.

Dirk and Miss Cinnabar drifted along the weedy pathways that had become the lanes binding this settlement. It all seemed peaceful enough.

"I would like to teach again tomorrow if you would let me, Mister Skye."

"I was going to ask if you would."

She hesitated. "Do you think anything will happen tonight? The Dreamers?"

"No. They had a chance to kill us all last night, and didn't take it. They aren't ready for that. Drumming, owl feathers, an owl arrow—all warnings."

"Arrow?"

"A black arrow with owl-feather fletching. Sunk into a post near me while Victoria and I were sitting on the stoop, absorbing the night. It was intended to warn me. The Dreamers believe I'm betraying my Shoshone blood by teaching in a white man's school. Whoever fired that arrow could easily have put it into me—but didn't. That's very important. The Dreamers are not murderous—at least for now."

"You didn't say anything about it to the agent."

"There was more than enough hysteria in that room."

"I can't tell you I have no fear, Dirk."

"I'm just as fearful as you, but we have to go on. Fear is what the Dreamers are dreaming of; fear in us so large that we flee for our lives—even when no one follows. In the shadow of the Owl."

"Your figures of speech mystify me," she said.

"I have Indian blood."

They reached the point where she would turn off to the post, and she turned to him.

"Thank you. This has been a lovely day."

"Miss Cinnabar—"

"You can call me Aphrodite if you want, Dirk," she said.

"Only if you want me to."

She smiled and nodded. "I'll be Aphrodite for you alone."

eleven

A great commotion late that afternoon proved to be Captain Cinnabar's column, which trotted into the agency on the double, flags and guidons flapping. Dirk hurried from the schoolhouse to see what this was all about, and discovered weary soldiers, still on horseback, awaiting word from their captain and Major Van Horne.

Little by little, a crowd collected outside the agency. Dirk lent a hand to Victoria, who hobbled, squint-eyed, toward the bored troops. Clerks and officials, storekeepers and Shoshone servants, gathered near the soldiers.

Eventually the captain and the agent emerged. Van Horne chose the moment to address the quiet throng.

"We're in a state of siege here and the army's going to protect us. We've sent for additional troops from Laramie. Soon we'll have the means to stop this rebellion and punish the hostiles."

Dirk listened, amazed. What rebellion?

"I'm requiring that everyone in the agency, as well as our

missionary friends, report in the evening to the post for their own safety. By day we'll resume our duties, protected by patrols sent out by Captain Cinnabar. It'll take a week for an additional column to arrive, so we'll have to resort to these measures until help is at hand."

"Is there an uprising, Major?" Dirk asked.

"You, above all, know of it," Van Horne replied.

"Has anyone been attacked, Major?"

"Death threats, young fellow. Owl feathers. We all know what that means."

Cinnabar interrupted. "For your own safety, we're offering quarters at the fort at night. And be prepared to retreat to the fort by day if we sound the bugle."

"How many hostiles are there, sir?" Dirk asked.

"Several hundred, if the Bannocks are included."

Dirk chose not to get into an argument. He doubted there were more than a few dozen Dreamers, and he doubted that the half-starved and poorly armed Shoshones could collect even a hundred warriors ready to fight. But these were white men, and they were afraid, and prone to exaggerate, and itching to manufacture trouble.

"Oh, God bless you, Captain. You've reached us in our moment of need," said Amy Partridge. "Now we're safe."

"We'll see," Cinnabar said. "This will require the utmost caution. I have two companies of green troops, both undermanned. Colonel Custer had twelve companies and look what happened to him. Be prepared. Stay armed. Know exactly what you'll do if trouble comes. Bury your valuables. The savages might burn your mission to the ground."

"You make it sound so dreadful," she said.

"These are times to test men's souls," Cinnabar said. "Be strong as steel."

"And don't let the redskins fool you," Major Van Horne added. "They're tricky devils."

"Goddamn right," Victoria muttered just loud enough for Dirk to hear.

"All right then, at seven in the evening, report to the post. I'll prepare quarters."

"We'll all be there, Captain," Van Horne said.

Cinnabar returned to his sweat-stained mount, clambered up, and led the column toward the military grounds. The captain had returned before a mob of howling savages scalped and shot and burned the Wind River Agency and its environs to the ground.

"Kill all them Indian bastards," Victoria said.

"You going to the post at night, Absaroka Mother?"

"Hell no."

"Neither am I."

"You been threatened by them Dreamers."

"They made a point of not killing me."

They watched the weary blue column ride over to the post and then vanish among the whitewashed buildings.

"If you don't go, North Star, they'll think you're a Dreamer."

"They know better."

She squinted up at him. "Wanna bet?"

He didn't want to bet. Imagined redskin threats were as real to white men as the genuine ones. And anyone with a drop of Indian blood might be suspect.

"I don't know what I'll do," he said. "Maybe join the Dreamers."

He surprised himself by saying it. Now, suddenly, his two bloods were warring again. There was something shouting in him that he didn't want to admit. He was tired of the Yanks and their broken promises, their policy of slow starvation, their shrug-of-the-shoulders belief that Indians should either settle into European life and belief, or become extinct.

"Maybe a few arrows through agency windows might improve things around here," he muttered.

But he knew they wouldn't. A serious rebellion would mean more death and starvation for the Eastern Shoshones even though Chief Washakie was considered a tame Indian.

Dirk watched the crowd dissipate. The Shoshone servants seemed to vanish into the ground, plainly fearful. Clerks whispered and went back to work. The Partridges headed back to their mission.

Peace had returned to the agency—or had it? Sirius Van Horne vanished into his agency offices. No commotion rose from the post. The flag barely fluttered. The summer sun hovered in the west. Dirk's schoolhouse remained empty. But peace was not in the air, and not in the advancing shadows. There were no thunderheads piling up in the sky.

"You want to walk with me to the chief's house, Crow Mother?"

She shook her head. Often, at this hour, she trudged out to the cemetery to visit with Barnaby Skye and Blue Dawn. There was now a yearning in each of her visits. She talked to them daily, and for all he knew, their spirits talked to her. When the weather permitted it, she settled in the rough grasses beside them, and was content to be with them for a while. Sometimes Dirk went with her and felt some presence that made him uneasy.

"I'll see you later," he said.

She reached out to him and touched his arm, and then slowly retreated on her daily mission. The touch of her old hand, dry as parchment, felt like a good-bye kiss.

He found Washakie himself sitting on his porch, and a motion from the chief steered Dirk to another chair.

"I did not want to hear them," Washakie said.

"Then you knew what they would say."

Washakie smiled grimly. "Yes, and that is how they live and think. They speak with honeyed words, but I know them well enough."

"Then you know we're in the middle of a rebellion, or so they say. They've sent to Laramie for more soldiers."

Washakie laughed softly. "I watched Captain Cinnabar return with his soldiers. I watched the crowd gather at the agency. I watched the captain and Major Van Horne. I thought maybe to walk over there to hear what they were saying and then I thought maybe I shouldn't. Let them come to me if they have anything to say to me. Which they don't. Major Van Horne, he says nothing to me. Does he tell me there is trouble? Does he ask me to call a council of the elders? To gather the headmen and talk this over? Does he ask me about the Dreamers? Does he propose going out to the People to talk, eh? No, I am chief of the Eastern Shoshones but I'm an Indian, and so he does not come here."

"Could you stop the Dreamers?"

"I think you know the answer."

"Could a council of elders stop the Dreamers?"

"A few of the elders are Dreamers. No, North Star. It is not in my power. The Dreamers have taken their own road. Come with me. We will have a talk with the Indian agent. I have been thinking about this."

Dirk and the chief walked quietly across the weedy fields to the agency, and found Van Horne stuffing papers into a small black safe painted with cherubs. A revolver lay on his desk.

"You, is it?" he said, annoyed. "You're lucky I didn't shoot. We're under siege and you walk in without knocking. What do you want?"

"Ah, my esteemed friend Major Van Horne, agent to the Eastern Shoshones for the government of the United States of America. I, Chief Washakie, friend of the Great Fathers in Washington, have come to tell you that the Dreamers will not assault you this night."

Van Horne straightened up and stared. "You have some sort of moccasin telegraph telling you this?"

"I know my people."

"Maybe that's what they want you to say."

"I plan to sleep soundly in my own bed, Major."

"Well, of course, they wouldn't touch you."

"And you could sleep just as soundly in your bed, Major. And so can the missionaries. And so can Mister Skye, here."

"You've been in touch with the Dreamers. Tonight's not the night, eh?"

"No, the Dreamers have said nothing to me. No Shoshone whispers in my ear. No elder visits me in the night. I hear nothing of their plans but I know something of their purposes. If you know the wisdom of the Owl, you know the Dreamers. The Owl is their night-bird."

"Hoodoo," Van Horne said. "If you sleep well tonight, you can thank the patrols that the army's putting out in the field."

"My good friend, Major Van Horne, that's what I wish to see you about. When armed men make mistakes, innocent people die."

"Innocent people die? You call Dreamers innocent?"

"It is very difficult for a blue-shirt patrol to shoot only at Dreamers, and not at hunters or root-gathering women, or boys cutting firewood, or women washing in the river, or old men sitting in front of their lodges."

"My old friend, Chief of all the Indians, are you suggesting that the army's not competent?"

"My fine and treasured friend Major Van Horne, who tells his red children all good things from the Great Fathers and is a friend of all the Shoshones, I say only that no one who lies in his bed in his own house this night is in peril, but many of my people are in great peril, because our friend and good father of the Shoshone people, Captain Cinnabar, has many in his command who would not know a Dreamer from a girl washing her hair beside a creek."

Van Horne laughed shortly, baring yellow teeth in the middle of orange whiskers. "My friend, Chief of all the Shoshones, you let us worry about that."

"My dear friend, Indian Agent Van Horne, that is exactly the problem. I remember that peaceful Cheyenne were butchered at Sand Creek, and a peaceful village of Blackfeet, suffering from smallpox, were slaughtered in their lodges on the Marias River not long ago."

"Chief Washakie, friend of the Great Fathers in Washington, I will take your concern to Captain Cinnabar, and ask him to make sure his soldiers shoot only at Dreamers."

"My friend, Major Van Horne, why shoot at Dreamers who have done you no harm? Have they killed? Have they stolen? Have they violated your women?"

"Chief Washakie, my friend, who wisely leads his esteemed People, the Dreamers have threatened us all. A boy called Owl has made himself into an outlaw, and with each day he gathers an army together to drive white men away. It's well known."

"Major Van Horne, who kindly protects his red children

from white men seeking land and animals, let no red woman or man or child die this night, or any night."

Van Horne straightened up to his full height, until he was a formidable force standing behind his oaken desk.

"If any person, red or white, perishes, it won't be the fault of my army, Chief."

Washakie nodded tightly. The exchange could go no further.

A certain fire built in the major's ruddy complexion. "I take it you gentlemen and your families will enjoy the protection of the fort this night?"

"My women and I will stay in my house, Major," Washakie said.

The Indian agent turned to Dirk. "And you?"

"There is little peril, sir."

Van Horne studied him. "Even though I have directed all salaried people to stay in the fort this night?"

"We will stay at the teacherage, sir."

"I see," said Sirius Van Horne. "I take it you don't need the protection of the United States mounted rifles."

"No, sir," Dirk said.

twelve

Victoria filled Dirk's coffee cup as he settled at the kitchen table.

"Goddamn Indians scalped us last night," she said.

"While I was asleep," he added.

"You get oatmeal today because you got white blood in you."

"What if I was all Indian, Grandmother?"

"Buffalo balls," she said.

Dirk ate the gruel, not minding even if Victoria made a dry paste of it. She was grinning wickedly at him downing his white man food.

"Beats buffalo hump, don't it?" she asked.

Nothing beat buffalo hump.

He faced another boring day at the schoolhouse. It was anyone's guess whether any Shoshone children would appear at the door. Even the girls staying with Chief Washakie weren't showing up in the midst of this tension affecting the Wind River Reservation.

But his intention to wander over to his empty schoolroom was trumped by the arrival of a messenger, Pontius, one of the clerks at the Indian agency.

"Himself wants to see you, real quick," Pontius said.

"No students in sight anyway," Dirk replied.

Dirk left the dishes to his Crow mother and hiked across the grassy fields to the agency, on a peaceful August morning. Maybe not so peaceful. He saw armed sentries patrolling the outskirts of the whole Wind River Agency complex. Still, but for that, it was just another sleepy day in a remote Indian agency in western Wyoming Territory.

He found Sirius Van Horne awaiting him, red in his eye, like the red of his hair.

"Ah, there you are, Dirk. Sleep a heap?"

"I did, sir."

"You're still wearing your topknot. You can thank Cinnabar for that. He put two-man sentry patrols out all night."

"I'm sure they held off the hordes of savages, sir."

Van Horne cackled. He was plainly in a jolly mood. "Serves me right," he said. "You know the hoodoo better than I do. I'd have sworn there'd be a few hundred howling savages swarming through here last night."

"You could listen to my Crow mother, sir. She has medicine powers."

"Hoodoo is all there is out here, Dirk. Now I've got a mission for you. I'm calling a council of the headmen."

"Then you'll have the chief summon them?"

"No, boy, you will. You're going to lasso all the bastards and drag them bodily to the agency, where they will receive 'the lecture.' "

" 'The lecture', sir?"

"Damn right. They're going to live peaceable or have their rations cut in half."

"Their rations are already half of what they need, Major."

"Damn right."

"Starving people could turn desperate."

"That's right, my boy."

"Why send me?"

"You speak their tongue. You're the best Shoshone speaker around. And you're paid by Uncle Sam—at least for now."

Dirk didn't miss the nuance.

"I'm sending a patrol with you to protect your ass."

"I'd prefer to go alone, sir. And a patrol wouldn't protect me for a minute if it came to that."

"No, not alone. I'll send Sergeant Muggins with you."

"I can't imagine why, sir."

Van Horne smiled so widely all his yellow teeth came into view. "He speaka da tongue, right?"

"I think I'll take my Crow mother if she's up to it."

"I like the old crone," the Indian agent said. "If I get scalped, I hope she does it." He laughed. "But no, I'm sending you on a double-time trip."

"Ah, when is this meeting? When do you want the headmen and elders?"

"Just tell them to bust their asses. We'll wait. We're going to have us a little lay-down-the-law session about those Dreamers."

"You're not having the chief invite them?"

The major smiled. "This is my party. I'm running this little powwow. If Washakie calls them in, it's his show."

"It would be a courtesy to include him."

"Schoolteacher, are you lecturing me?"

"Yes, sir."

Van Horne pulled a cigar from the humidor and scratched a lucifer and puffed until the tobacco glowed. "He's sulking in his house. That's where I want him. I'm bypassing him. We're going to have us a meeting with all the headmen, and he's not invited."

"When?"

Van Horne sucked hard, expelled a cloud of blue smoke, wheezed, and smiled. "Fort Laramie's sending two companies. We can expect them in a week. You tell all those headmen to show up in a week. We're going to have us a conference, you translating, with all the Shoshone subchiefs, and two hundred blue-bloused United States Mounted Infantry and Cavalry making a nice little circle."

"I will tell them what to expect."

"No, my boy, you'll just tell them that their kind father, Indian Agent Van Horne, requires them to show up on the seventh sun. They've got fingers; they can count to ten." He paused. "Sergeant Muggins, he's the army's interpreter, and he'll stick to you like glue."

"And what will you tell them, Major?"

"Bring in the Dreamers before anyone gets hurt. Bring in the Dreamers, the whole lot, and we'll reward them."

"Reward them?"

"We won't cut their rations." He pulled a turnip watch from its nest and studied it. "Muggins will be here in an hour. You'll be ready then. You'll have army mounts."

"I would suggest, Major, that you invite them yourself. I'll go along as interpreter."

"Sonny boy, I've more important things to do."

The agent knocked some gray ash to the floor.

"What will you do with the Dreamers, sir?"

"That depends entirely on the Dreamers, Skye. But they can save their asses by taking a loyalty pledge and surrendering their arms."

"And if they won't?"

"The government has its ways, my young friend. Say, Skye, you do know who the headmen are, don't you?"

"Most of them."

"I want all of them. I'll give you a list. You bring every last one of them in."

"If I can find them, Major."

"You'll find them, my boy. That's what schoolteachers are for."

"I'm a teacher. I'm not paid to run your errands. I'm supposed to open the schoolhouse every day and teach. That's my job, sir."

"You'll go because I'm telling you to go, and if you don't go, you won't end up teaching. You're becoming a problem. You have no students. What would the bureau think of that?"

The autocrat behind the desk was making himself very clear.

Dirk left the agent's office lost in melancholy. Everything was wrong. And he was to be the errand boy. His mother's people were friends, not hostiles. If there was trouble now, it was largely because the government had reneged on most everything it promised. And he was being stuck with the job of bringing the headmen into the agency. He thought wildly about quitting on the spot. He was being used. He wasn't teaching, and he was being paid to teach, not to be the emissary of the Viceroy Van Horne. Or the jailer for Prison Warden Van Horne. The command he would deliver to the headmen would insult them. The presence of two hundred soldiers surrounding the meeting would insult them all the more. Which was what the agent intended.

The veneer was wearing thin. The Wind River Reservation was papered over with a lie—that the Shoshones were a sovereign tribe, in permanent friendship with the Yanks, and that the tribe could live its own way on land guaranteed them by treaty. And not be punished by cutting rations. It all was official malarkey.

Dourly, Dirk repaired to the teacherage, told Victoria he'd be gone a few days, put a kit together, and waited for Sergeant Muggins.

Victoria hobbled up to him. "Make it work for the good of the People," she said. "It is a chance for them to come in and tell the Indian agent a few things. He has eyes and ears but doesn't see or hear."

He wondered about that. Van Horne seemed to know everything as fast as it happened, and it was rumored that he had a small army of paid snitches reporting everything, all for an extra pound of flour or an occasional sack of beans.

"A column is coming over from Fort Laramie," he said. "They'll be here just in time for this little powwow."

Victoria laughed malevolently.

Sergeant Muggins showed up with two saddle mounts and a loaded pack mule, and Dirk added his gear to the mule pack and climbed aboard.

"You steer me," Muggins said. "You know where all them outlaws is hid."

"No, Sergeant, I don't. They're scattered across a hundred fifty miles, and probably won't be in sight when we ride in."

The sergeant was in uniform, with a nonmilitary lever-action repeating rifle in his saddle scabbard. He could spray a lot of bullets fast with that. He rode side by side with Dirk, tugging his pack mule behind.

"You know where them headmen are?" the sergeant asked.

"No, and at best we'll find four or five. Right now, the Shoshones are scattered in small camps from the west end eastward to the Arapaho settlements. I've met most of the headmen, but there's a dozen I don't know and wouldn't recognize."

"Why'd he send you, then?"

"I'm half Shoshone. My father was an Englishman."

"You favor one side over the other?"

"Well, Sergeant, whose side are you on?"

The sergeant laughed. "Funny thing is, I'm favoring the Shoshones. They've been licking spit around here."

"You're a speaker?"

"Comanche, boy. I was stationed in Texas. I know Comanche real good, so I can understand some Shoshone if I try some. It ain't that different."

"They're sending you along to check up on me."

"That's what they're up to, my boy."

"I'm a two-blood, so I'm not trusted?"

"You got her."

"And you're telling me this?"

"Know somethin', Skye? I got me three stripes because I make sure everyone I'm with knows I'm on the level. I ain't keeping no secrets from you. You know what? I stay square, and that's saved my life a few times."

"They think I'd betray them?"

"Who knows, buddy boy? But I don't think so. They just think you ain't predictable. Like not going to shelter at the fort. It says to them, it says, maybe this Dirk Skye, he's plugged in with them Dreamers."

"I'm not, but I think the People have some grievances.

And I know something of their thinking. They're waiting for their spirit helper, the Owl, to steer them, and when they have a vision, it'll be shared with everyone. It'll be the most public news on the reservation."

"Hoodoo," Muggins said.

There was no arguing with the sergeant. Dirk thought of all the ways his people had interacted with their spirit guides. Even his father, Barnaby Skye, had bear medicine and a sort of bear knowing, and that had steered him out of danger, or helped him in times of need. And his old Crow mother Victoria always drew some mysterious wisdom from the magpie. It wasn't just the magpie in sight throughout the countryside, but Magpie, the spirit of all the magpies. He remembered that the Jesuits in St. Louis had tried hard to dismiss such things as superstition, but it wasn't. It was another way of knowing. Let the whites dismiss it as hoodoo. Maybe it was good that they were so blind.

"Glad you think so," Dirk said.

Muggins was watching him intently. The sergeant's stare was almost a physical force.

They rode through a day that was quiet in the valley and stormy in the mountains, mostly quietly but not without a certain silent camaraderie between them.

"Them Snakes sure are scarce," the sergeant said.

"This time of year they'll be as high as they can get," Dirk said.

They rode past garden patches, mostly abandoned or seriously lacking attention. There wasn't anyone in sight.

"Looks to me like the whole tribe jumped the reservation."

The brown grasses of midsummer stretched silently toward the river bottoms, where a green bottomland stretched endlessly east and west.

"How often do they come in for their allotment?"

"Their flour and beans? Once a month."

"They gotta come a long way."

"It's a long way to flour and beans, and a long way to whatever game they can find in the foothills and slopes. So they move two hundred miles a month, or more, to stay fed."

They rounded a shoulder of land, and beheld a green valley, and a dozen lodges drawn into a semicircle there. It would have a headman, maybe several.

thirteen

The runner clambered the last steep grade to the hanging valley, and headed for the nest. Owl knew what he would say; Owl knew all things. Owl had received another runner, Weeping Woman, at dawn. Now Father Sun had climbed over the lip of the ridges illumining the valley where the Dreamers gathered.

Owl rose to meet the runner. With each passing night, Owl looked more and more like the spirit bird who had entered into his heart and now transformed him. Above all, Owl didn't walk anymore; he glided over the land so softly no creature heard the flap of wings until too late. And now he had owl eyes. Every Shoshone knew it. Owl's eyes were huge and unblinking and could see through everything to the innermost spirit. That was because the Owl had entered the youth, Waiting Wolf, and occupied his human body.

But Owl also wore an owl cape, fashioned by his sister, who had stitched the soft owl feathers into wings falling away from his elk-leather sleeves. This was a good cape, which blessed him with his owl nature, and identified him as the keeper of the Owl secrets. When any Dreamer approached, Owl stood very still, never even a facial muscle twitching, a ghost of a birdman, awaiting the moment of triumph. For Owl, there was no present; only the future, when his spirit bird inside of him would peck at his heart and a long night would begin.

Thus did Owl wait immobile while the runner, panting slightly, trotted across the mounting slopes. Owl knew this runner, too, a brother of Ah-Chee, who worked as a woodcutter for the agency. Owl knew the things that happened at the agency almost before other white men in the white men's camp knew of them.

At last the runner, a certain boy, stood panting before him.

"You have come to tell Owl that the teacher and a soldier are even now seeking our elders and headmen," he said.

The youth stood, amazed.

"Owl knows what there is to know," Owl said.

"Owl, Grandfather, you have spoken truth. The teacher will tell the headmen they must attend a meeting at the agency after seven suns."

"There will be many soldiers at the meeting," Owl said. "They will be there to show the muscle of the white men."

"Truly, Grandfather, you have spoken what I came to tell you. Your eyes are large and see all things."

Owl was scarcely older than this runner, but he enjoyed being addressed as Grandfather, the term of greatest respect.

"Is there anything else, boy?"

"The headmen seek your wisdom, Grandfather."

"Tell them to go to the white men's meeting, as requested. I see outrage. I see insult. This must pass before Owl begins the new world, when the People can go where they will, and the buffalo are thick on the prairies."

"Truly you have spoken, Grandfather. I will tell those who sent me of your wisdom. That they must attend the meeting at the agency, and be prepared for insult. Have I your message well remembered?"

"You have it. Rest and eat, and then go."

The youth backed away, for it was not good to turn one's back on Owl, and soon settled at a campfire where some Dreamers had a pot of elk stew bubbling.

"You have great eyes, Grandfather," said one of the Dreamer subchiefs, Walks at Night.

"It is the Owl who has taken hold of Waiting Wolf. It is Owl residing in me, my friend. I am only a clay bowl holding what is sacred."

Owl glided through the camps of the Dreamers, a hush surrounding him wherever he went. The Dreamers knew Owl to be surrounded by silence, and some said that even the wind stopped whispering where Owl walked. That is what made the People so respectful. Owl brought with him a world of stillness which wrought fear and obedience in all who approached him. What was greater than the power to quiet the wind?

This hanging valley was a good place. It was guarded by vaulting slopes on three sides, leading upward to perpetual snow. And it could be approached only by a steep and treacherous path from forested slopes below. A rill offered snowmelt, and game was still available to the patient hunter. Most of the People knew exactly where the Dreamers had gathered, but none would tell the agent or the teacher or the missionaries or the soldiers. Not if one expected to live.

He approached one knot of Dreamers and won their instant attention. "The agent is requiring the presence of the elders and headmen. This is not Chief Washakie's doing. The headmen will discover more soldiers than they have ever seen before. The agent Van Horne will tell the headmen to bring the Dreamers to the agency, and there bad things will happen to the Dreamers. Owl has seen these things, and they must come to pass before the Time of Change we have dreamed will begin. Let it happen, for it is all a part of Owl's design."

"The headmen will betray us, Grandfather?"

"No, the white men will betray the headmen. These friends of the People have put us in a prison. Now they want to talk. But they don't want to listen. They want to threaten."

"Truly, Owl has peered into the thing that will come."

Owl nodded, and glided to other knots of Dreamers, who had organized themselves into a war camp, making lances and arrows because they had so few firearms. Owl didn't encourage that; he knew that when the moment came, the white men would flee this land in terror, their hearts frozen by fear. Then the People would possess all that had been given them from the time of the grandfathers long ago.

Still, some blood would be shed, so he did not discourage any Dreamer preparing himself to do battle with the soldiers. He wished he had a weapon of his own, but none had come to him. He glided from group to group, and was always greeted as the salvation of the People, and that is how he saw himself.

The Dreamers had received a new dance, and now they danced it each night, often in utter darkness when it was far more engrossing than by the light of a fire. The Dreamers danced the Owl Dance, in which they glided silently, arms outstretched, not in a circle but each Dreamer on his own path, gliding without noise but for the thump of a single drum. It was the quietest dance anyone had ever known, so quiet that a pounding heart seemed noisier. The Dreamers glided through the evenings, immersing themselves in owl medicine, sometimes led by Owl himself, sometimes not. For it was night vision that the youth sought, this Waiting Wolf who now was a spiritual force among the People. Often at night he glided upward to the snow fields and made his vision bed upon a shelf of rotting ice, there to listen to the spirits. The Dreamers said that Owl returned to camp transformed, some mysterious force radiating from him after he had opened himself to the Other Ones who ran the highest ridges.

Owl knew where the teacher, Dirk Skye, and the sergeant would camp. He did not know how he knew; it was simply one of the mysterious powers he had acquired when the most dreaded of all creatures inhabited Waiting Wolf. The teacher and the soldier would invite eight or ten headmen to the meeting this day, and tomorrow would invite the rest, and return to the agency. But this night they would camp about two hours away by horseback.

He would greet them.

He found the swiftest horse among those herded by the Dreamers, slipped a hackamore on it, glided to its back, and steered it away from camp. A few Dreamers stared, but Owl's lonely and mysterious trips were familiar to them all. Owl was forever communing with his spirit guides, and often left camp on his spiritual voyages. But this time Owl did not ride toward the great ridges and snow-choked chasms, but down from the hanging valley and then along a tumbling creek, and finally into the broad valley of the Wind River. He saw no one. His fine horse glided, even as Owl glided, and they covered much ground. He came to the place his inner eye had told him to come to, and found no one there. Unfazed, he picketed his pony and sat quietly. It was a good place to camp, and many before him had sojourned there, where grass for the ponies lay thick, and no mosquitos buzzed, and a fire could be hidden in a shallow drainage, and the wind didn't whip.

So he waited patiently as twilight stretched toward darkness, and then his guests arrived just as he had foreseen. He stood quietly, letting them spot him and his pony. The blueshirt was instantly alarmed, but Dirk Skye simply stared, saw a young Shoshone wearing only a loincloth and moccasins, unarmed, standing quietly in the blue last-light of the day.

"Who greets us here?" Skye asked in the Shoshone tongue.

Owl did not reply. Let Skye name him.

The sergeant trailed along behind Skye, his hand ready to draw a sidearm, but even the sergeant could see Owl had no weapon and was not dangerous in the slightest.

"You," Skye said, finally recognizing the youth. "Waiting Wolf, is it?"

"The name you have spoken you must not speak, for he is no longer alive," Owl said.

"Owl, then. I am pleased to see you. This is Sergeant Muggins, and we're on an errand for Major Van Horne."

"Yes, you are asking all the headmen to meet, so that something will be done about Owl and the Dreamers."

"You are well informed. Would you join us while we make camp and cook a meal?"

"Owl will join you. And how shall I call you? North Star, the name given you by your mother?"

"My mothers called me North Star; my father called me Dirk. I have taken that as my way. I am pleased when my mother's people call me North Star," Dirk said, staying with the Shoshone tongue.

The sergeant set himself to picketing the horses and making camp once it became plain there was little to worry about.

"I will call you Dirk," said Owl.

The teacher glanced sharply at him. "You've come here to tell me something. Or to give me a message to take to the Indian agent."

"Owl sees many things. He sees a column of soldiers coming from Fort Laramie. He sees many soldiers at this meeting of the headmen and the agent. He sees that the white men are afraid of Owl and the dreaming, so afraid they would stop at nothing. Many Shoshone would die from their bullets. This is what Owl sees."

Skye stared pensively at the small blaze that Muggins had kindled. "It's not fear," he said. "For them, an owl is not something to fear. It is a night-bird, nothing more. Some white men think the owl is very wise. But no one dreads it."

Owl smiled. "An owl feather is left with missionaries. An owl feather is left with others. And the white men summon the army."

"An owl arrow struck wood near me," Skye said. "It was not meant to kill me."

"Owl is a thief. Owl will steal what is in the heart of white men."

"What are you saying?"

"Owl will steal the souls of white men. That is why they are so afraid. That is why a hundred more soldiers are marching. That is why Major Van Horne and Captain Cinnabar would like to catch me and put me in a prison and keep me from the People, and stamp out the Dreamers."

"I'm not following you at all, Owl."

Owl felt annoyed. There was too much white blood in this fool. "Owl glides quietly and pounces on its prey. The white men take the land and open the earth and plant grain and run cattle over the land and drive other people off the land and pen us up in reservations. That is their way. And then Owl comes and steals their spirit from them. They send an army and Owl steals their courage. They send missionaries and Owl steals their spirits and eats them. Owl steals the hearts from ranchers so they don't know why they run cattle. Owl steals the heart from farmers so they don't know why they plant. Owl glides through the times, in plain sight, and everything white men build and believe crumbles, because Owl has taken their souls from them."

Dirk Skye was frowning. The soldier was trying to understand, and was having difficulty. Owl watched them closely. They did not know Owl, and did not know what the Dreamers saw, and now they sat beside the wavering flame not knowing anything that Owl was talking about.

"Why are the white men so afraid of Owl?" the young Shoshone asked. "They are strong and have many guns. But they are afraid of Owl because the Owl glides in the night and pounces on their spirits—ah, the word comes to me. Their souls. Those missionaries, they would know it best. Owl comes to steal their god, and soon they will see their god fail them, and when their god fails them, they will go away, and the army will go away, and the Indian agency will turn to dust, and the People will be a nation once again."

That stupid Dirk Skye stared, without understanding.

"You are blinded, so Owl will show you how it will be," he said.

Owl rose, walked to his pony, climbed onto it, and rode into the soft night.

fourteen

And then he was gone.

Muggins stared into the night. "I'll be damned," he said.

Dirk intuitively backed away from the flickering firelight, fearing an arrow out of the dark. But none came.

There was something about that boy that tugged at him. But even more that bewildered him. What were the Dreamers dreaming? And what did they want?

"Tell me what you think, Sergeant," he said.

"You was talking too fast for me to follow. Owl talk, and I don't know a beak from a tail feather."

"It was about things of the heart."

"He probably wanted to cut out my heart and eat it," Muggins said. "We shoulda nabbed him, took him in."

"For what?"

"Just for being himself, starting up a rebellion."

"Has he killed or injured anyone?"

"You defending him?" Muggins asked.

"What has he killed, threatened, wounded, or destroyed?"

Muggins sighed. "He's gonna do it. We could've nabbed him and stopped it. If we took him with us, this whole Dreamer business would've gone the way of the passenger pigeon."

"I'm a schoolteacher on an errand," Dirk said.

"You'll have to explain it to Van Horne and Cinnabar," Muggins said. "How you could've ended this whole uprising but didn't."

"What has Owl done?" Dirk asked.

"He's—who cares? Catch him and we stop it."

"Sergeant, do you really want to know what Owl wants? He's a missionary. He wants to enter us, pierce our hearts, toss out white man religion, and foster his own."

"Missionary!"

"Do you think it's only white men, Christians, who collect souls?"

"Jaysas, Mary, and Joseph," Muggins said.

Something in this tickled Dirk's humor, and he chuckled.

"We shoulda shot the little bastid," Muggins said. "Now he's loose."

"Owl is collecting souls. That's how I read the boy."

"The boy's a witch, that's what. We should be drivin' a stake through his heart and burying him in a swamp, sez I."

"Muggins, why?"

Muggins glared at Dirk. "Because I say so, is why."

"No, I want a reason."

"You're a half-blood, so you'd not know even if I told ye."

Dirk marveled that the young Shoshone could evoke such malaise in white men. It was as if Owl had triggered every nightmare that could affect a white child in its crib.

The night passed peacefully, except for the time Dirk awoke to the hoot of an owl, bolted upright in his bedroll, and then settled into a fitful sleep. The next morning they forded the Wind River at a gravel bar and started east, planning to contact whatever Shoshone encampments lay on the north bank of the stream.

The reservation slumbered peacefully in the early sun, unchanged from time immemorial, as Skye and his military escort threaded their way toward the encampments. These were usually families or clans living as close to small game or berries or roots as they could, scratching food from a reluctant land to supplement the monthly flour allotments they received from the agency. In the decade of reservation life, little had changed. They still lived in lodges, but now that buffalo were no longer available, the ragged buffalo-hide lodges were being replaced by duck-cloth ones, which offered much less shelter against heat and cold, but did turn rain. Here and there were ragged garden patches, begun at the insistence of the white agents, who wanted the People to become farmers. But most had gone to weed for the want of cultivation and weeding, and yielded little to these hungry people.

The sight of them depressed Dirk. Shoshone men would not tend the fields, and it seemed that little would change until a new generation would replace those who clung to the old ways. The thought left him restless. The things that had made the People hunters and gatherers of roots and berries might never diminish, and then where would these people be? If they survived at all?

He and Muggins steered up a tributary creek tumbling from the Owl Creek Mountains, and found a desolate collection of patched leather lodges beside the creek, and people listlessly sunning themselves. These encampments exuded a sort of hopelessness, which was evident in the disorder, the middens of garbage, the stink of offal. The reservation life was tearing the soul out of the Shoshones, and the sight of these shabby camps pierced Dirk's heart.

Dirk and Muggins rode quietly into the place. No dogs greeted them. Every mutt had vanished into cookpots. These people looked gaunt. Dirk knew many of them. This was the Brother Otter Clan, and its headman would be Swimmer.

They found Swimmer readily enough. He lay on an ancient blanket, staring into space, in some sort of trance, ignored by his women. This autumnal day was chill, but he wore only his loincloth, and not even moccasins. No one in the encampment cared who came in or out; in times past visitors would have gathered a crowd of boys and girls, barking dogs, men and women collecting to greet the newcomers. It chilled Dirk to see the stupor and squalor.

Swimmer had been smoking. A pipe lay beside him, cold now, and Dirk wondered what weed the graying headman had burnt. There were some, he knew, that induced voyages of the soul, weeds that took a smoker to a distant place. The old healers of the People knew of them, or sometimes traded for them when tribes exchanged visits.

Swimmer, like most Shoshones, lacked facial hair, save for a small tuft between his lip and chin, and that was gray. One of the tribe's labels for white men was "hairy men," because most white men had hair sprouting from their cheeks and chins. But hair was rare indeed on the faces of the People, and when it did occur it might grow from the face of either sex.

The headman stared upward for some while before he wrestled himself up.

"Greetings, Swimmer; it is a good day when we can see you," Dirk said in the Shoshone tongue. We greet you, Father," he said, adding the traditional words of respect for a tribal leader.

"Ah, you, eh? Well, you caught me listening to the spirits."

"May we sit with you a while?" Dirk asked.

It would be impolite to get on with business, as white men did. It would take a while, one could almost call it a courtesy period, to get around to delivering the word from Indian Agent Van Horne.

One of Swimmer's women, as emaciated as he, brought gourds of water and set them before the guests. The old courtesies had not vanished among these people. She wore brown gingham, gotten from the agency as part of the allotments. Dirk knew that the People had almost nothing to fend off winter now. There was no leather for coats and skirts and shirts and moccasins because there was no game, and the People had no access to buffalo. So many of them wore layers of rags, there being nothing else.

"This is Sergeant Muggins, Father," Dirk said. "He comes with me as we go to all the camps in the Shoshone home. He knows the tongue of the Comanches."

Swimmer smiled. "It is a bad tongue. They took our tongue and made it different. Tell him that the People speak the true tongue, and the Comanche words are no good."

Muggins nodded, and removed his forage cap.

Swimmer eyed the sergeant. "He got my words."

"I got your words, Father," he said.

"The blue-shirts got killed by the Sioux, eh?" Swimmer said. "Washakie sent many of our young men to help Custer, and we got whipped, too, eh? No one's any good anymore, eh?"

The Little Big Horn was fresh in the minds of the Shoshones, Dirk thought. Maybe fresh in the mind of Owl, too.

"You are looking well, Father," Dirk said.

"Ah! There is nothing left."

"I bring you a message from the agent, Major Van Horne, Father. He wants you to come to a big meeting at the agency five suns from now. There will be big talk, and he has things to give to the headmen of the People."

"Big talk, eh? Go catch Owl, and stop the Dreamers." He laughed. "Big talk. Maybe we get a plug of tobacco, eh? Hey, Teacher, does the chief want this meeting?"

"No, the Indian agent does."

"Chief Washakie, he's coming?"

"I don't know, Father."

Swimmer stared into the bright sky. "It's a long walk."

"Not far to ride, Father."

"Walk, that's what I would do."

Dirk studied the camp and the fields beyond it, seeing no horses at all. He knew, suddenly, that this camp had none. They had been eaten when there was nothing else to eat.

"It would be a long walk, Father. Maybe I can send a wagon for you."

"Ah, I don't feel like going. Why go to this meeting? To hear the agent tell us what the fathers want? I think I won't go."

That was familiar. Several of the headmen in the camps across the reservation had simply shrugged off the invitation. But there was more. Van Horne was showing disrespect for Chief Washakie, calling the meeting himself instead of asking the head of the Eastern Shoshone tribe to do it.

"I will tell the agent that you will not come," Dirk said.

"Maybe I will, if I feel like it. Why should I go all that way to listen? He will talk and I will listen. I am tired of listening."

"Maybe you should go and tell him what the People need, Father."

Swimmer laughed softly. There were gaps in his incisors. "It is a good joke, Teacher."

One of Swimmer's women appeared with a small kettle that issued steam.

"Eat, eat," Swimmer said.

The woman smiled and handed gourd bowls to Dirk and Muggins.

Dirk glanced at the stew, and needed some excuse to decline. There were boiled prairie dogs floating in it. Or maybe gophers, their bodies white and limber.

And there was no escape from this hospitality.

"We thank Swimmer and his family," Dirk said.

"Eat! Eat!"

"Jaysas," said Muggins.

"We must," Dirk replied.

He dipped his half-gourd into the stew and extracted some juices, leaving the rodents behind. Muggins sat rigidly while Dirk glared, and finally dipped his gourd into the stew, until he had barely a tablespoon.

Dirk sipped. Muggins sipped.

Swimmer dug his gourd into the stew and filled it, including a pale gopher floating on it.

He was laughing.

A few sips later, enough to show some courtesy, Dirk and Muggins stood, wiped their mouths, and thanked Swimmer and his women.

"We have a long way to go, Father," he said.

Swimmer smiled. He had downed two gophers. "Tell the white father that the Dreamers see a better world for the People, who will live in peace and friendship," Swimmer said.

Dirk nodded. It wasn't a message that Major Van Horne would gladly hear.

Dirk mounted his horse, and the sergeant collected his pack mule and mounted, while a small crowd of Swimmer's clan watched.

They rode along the north bank of the river, returning now to the agency as fast as they could.

"Jaysas, they'd eat anything, them filthy people," the sergeant said.

"It's all they have to eat, Sergeant."

"Naw, it ain't. Look at all them pumpkin patches they didn't weed, and the gardens they didn't plant and hoe. They ain't even herding a few cows and hogs and sheep. Too much work for them folks, I guess."

There was no arguing with that. The People preferred to eat whatever they could scrounge from nature to the toil of raising food.

"We sure ain't getting much from the headmen," Muggins said. "I think Van Horne's little parley's gonna be a bust."

It was true. Scarcely any of the headmen in the encampments across the reservation made a firm commitment to attend. It was almost as if Owl and his quiet army of Dreamers somehow reached out to them all, and told them to stay away.

fifteen

An overcast sky, a harbinger of autumn, dulled the flat in front of the agency buildings, and the air had an edge to it. On this, the appointed day, a table stood in the grass, while in front of it were fifteen chairs spread in a semicircle. Behind the table sat Indian Agent Van Horne, flanked by two agency clerks, along with an American flag that wavered half-dead on its pole. The other party behind the table was Chief Washakie, wearing a black suit and a dour expression. This was not his meeting.

Dirk sensed that the chief would much rather have occupied one of those fifteen chairs facing the table. His face was stony. On a nearby auxiliary table were the ritual gifts for the headmen: twists of tobacco, trade blankets, small sacks of sugar.

Dirk was to translate, an office he would just as soon not fill, but the agency had few two-speakers, so he had been dragooned. Some of the civilians had collected to watch the proceedings. Dirk spotted several officers' wives, along with Aphrodite Cinnabar, plus some teamsters.

The post loafers, a dozen or so Shoshones who cadged a living around the place running errands or doing chores, had collected, along with full- and half-blood clerks, woodcutters, kitchen workers, and laundresses. All of these stayed far apart from the military wives and children.

Over at the newly named Fort Washakie, Dirk could see blue-bloused soldiers hurrying about, but none were present at this conference—not yet, anyway.

Major Van Horne fidgeted and examined his turnip watch and studied the three headmen sitting uneasily in the chairs facing him. There were a dozen empty ones. The three headmen had sat far from one another, as far as they could get, intuitively wanting to be isolated rather than to form a small clot of Shoshone leaders. Dirk knew them slightly. By coincidence, they were Big Foot, Big Nose, and Big Belly. All had come with their women, who sat demurely in the brown grasses off a way. All three were old men, chieftains long past their time of commanding a Shoshone band. He didn't see Swimmer, Natoosh, Bad Ear, or any of the others, and wasn't surprised. The younger chieftains were mostly Dreamers; others were starved, sick, or simply uninterested in these proceedings.

This whole business had a sour quality to it that dismayed Dirk. He saw his Crow mother, Victoria, standing quietly, wrapped in a red blanket against the chill, looking like an axe.

Van Horne gestured to Dirk, who approached the polished table.

"Why are there only three headmen?"

"I invited all I could find, Major."

"Invited! I asked you to compel their attendance."

"There is no word in the language to compel them, Major. Nor would I do so."

"You failed me! Three headmen! Big Nose! He's ancient history. So's Big Belly. I wanted every leader and elder present because they are going to get an earful."

"I suppose the others didn't want to attend, sir."

"I should have rounded them up with bayonets."

"Yes, sir, that might have done it. Captain Cinnabar's troops would have managed it."

Van Horne eyed Dirk. "I've put a lot of work into this. If it fails, I'll know who to blame. We have an entire cavalry column up from Laramie, and I intend for every Shoshone headman to feast his eyes on it. They are going to get my message, one way or other. If this conference is a bust, then I'll march the cavalry across the whole agency and into every camp until the whole tribe gets the message."

There wasn't anything worth saying, so Dirk kept the peace.

Van Horne fidgeted another half-hour, but no more headmen showed. The three who did come were all ancient, and an affable lot, mostly engaged these days in telling jokes to their clan members. But now they sat and waited. And a lot of other people were waiting also.

The Indian agent, trapped by events, opened the proceedings with a rap of a gavel on the polished table. A clerk opened his ledger and dipped his pen into his inkwell.

Dirk eyed the chieftains, who sat eagerly, their gazes straying to the table stacked with gifts.

Oozing annoyance, the Indian agent eyed his audience.

"This is an important meeting, and it is most unfortunate that the leaders of your people didn't bother to come. I have important things to say."

Dirk translated, using hand gestures and applying a little diplomacy. "Major Van Horne welcomes you who are chieftains of your people, and wishes more headmen were on hand. This is an important meeting, he says."

The three Bigs nodded cheerfully.

"I'll get directly to the matters before us," the agent said. "We have a crisis at hand, a crisis that could tear apart the peace of the Wind River Reservation. A crisis that could end up in blood and horror and starvation and tragedy. I have gathered you here at this hour to do something about it, and am seeking your utmost cooperation in the tasks and programs that I will lay before you."

Dirk was able to reduce that to a few words. Washakie was listening closely. He knew both tongues. But so far, at least, the chief had not frowned or corrected Dirk.

"I speak, of course, of the Dreamers, whose announced goal is the expulsion of white men from this entire area, and the restoration of life as it was lived in ancient times. I speak especially of the young Waiting Wolf, who took a new name and now leads an insurrection against the United States of America.

"I am here to tell you that the great fathers in Washington City won't allow this to happen, and that the full force and might of the United States and its military will be brought to bear against this insurrection, and that the fathers in Washington will not permit this rebellion to take place on the soil of the American republic."

Dirk wasn't sure whether the three Bigs were getting it, but he translated it into something the chieftains would understand, while Washakie listened closely, his face granite, his eyes impassive.

"The government of the United States is a friend of the Shoshone people, and its Indian agents are leading the People toward a peaceable employment of the lands guaranteed them, toward a time of abundance, ample meat and grain, secure homes, and good educations, self-governance, and democracy. The fathers want their Shoshone children to live in peace and contentment. I am always available to listen to grievances and to act upon them to the extent that my office and wherewithal permit. That is the way of peace and prosperity, and the way I and the agents before me, and those who will follow me, wish things to be here in this fine land of the Shoshones."

Dirk wrestled his way through that. The three Bigs got most of it. Washakie listened as well, not intervening or correcting any mistranslation. Dirk saw the crowds listening intently; the white men restless, the Shoshones intent. A chill wind flapped the Stars and Stripes.

"Now hear me well, my friends," the major said. "Hear me well. Hear every blessed word I have to say."

He paused, staring with an unblinking gaze into the seamed copper faces of the three Bigs.

"The Dreamers are engaged in an uprising against the sovereignty and authority of the government of the United States. They will be stopped one way or another; by peaceful surrender, or by bloodshed. One way or the other. If they wish blood, we will give them blood. If they choose the way of peace, we will give them peace. We will give them ten days to surrender. To come out of the mountain fastnesses where they are hiding, show up here, take an oath of allegiance, and be paroled on their honor. That is their choice.

"If, after ten days, they have not surrendered, abandoned their dreaming, returned to the pastoral life they were enjoying, then they will be declared hostiles and subject to military discipline, with whatever results they choose. The Army of the Republic of the United States is fully prepared to invade the most distant fastness, pierce the most remote alpine refuge, and gather up these devotees of an outlawed and criminal sect.

"We leave it to you, the chieftains of the Snake People, to convey this choice to the Dreamers, near and far, in every village, every camp, every valley where the nighttime dancing transpires. It will be entirely up to you, who govern the Snake People, to take the word to the outlaw sect and require that they disband at once and report to the agency."

The three Bigs sat stoically and Dirk wondered whether they really cared. The Shoshones were caught on a reservation, and did not govern themselves, and finding their next meal was all that mattered.

Major Van Horne drew himself up and waited dramatically for Dirk to translate and for it all to sink in. "Now, one last matter. The youth, Waiting Wolf, is in a state of insurrection against the government of the United States, and is therefore a wanted man. We all know how this started; we all know that he professed to see the hallucinations that now fill his brain. We all know he is preaching a new religion of liberation, that is false and abominable. We all know that it can lead only to tragedy and the spilling of blood. We all know that until he is brought to heel, my children, you all will suffer." The major stared straight at the headmen. "Therefore, if he does not surrender, does not sign the parole we offer him, he will become a wanted man, and we will offer a large reward—two fat cows—for information leading to his capture."

That did create a stir, mostly among the post's loafers and native workers.

"Of course we hope it will not come to that. Waiting Wolf is just a youth, and as a youth he is entitled to clemency, so long as he surrenders and disavows his scandalous religion.

And if he fails . . . he will face a military court of justice as an enemy combatant, and will suffer whatever punishment the officers of that tribunal should choose to impose on him."

Dirk somehow had trouble translating all that, and when he did, the three old chieftains weren't smiling.

"Are there any questions?" the agent asked abruptly.

Of course not. He wasn't there to take questions; he was there to make demands.

The gray overcast seemed even lower by the time all this had passed.

"Now then, we have a special treat for you gentlemen," Van Horne said. "We have at Fort Washakie two troops of the Third Cavalry from Fort Laramie as well as our own mounted rifles, and these fine men will be patrolling the entire reservation and the country nearby during the next weeks. On this fine day we will witness a dress parade, and then something very special, which not even I have seen before: a demonstration of the army's powerful Gatling gun, which can fire three hundred and fifty rounds a minute."

Somehow, Dirk didn't need to translate that.

At a signal, the columns waiting at Fort Washakie formed up and began their march toward the agency and the commons before it. Bugles sounded, snare drums rolled, shining horses settled into a fast walk, and arms clattered. By fours, the infantry column, rifles shouldered, plunged toward the waiting spectators, while just behind, the cavalry clattered toward the meeting ground, its own flags and guidons flapping. The clatter of all those shod hooves made a fine racket as the column smartly rounded the rim of the agency field, and negotiated the perimeter of the entire agency. Everything shone, even on that dullest of days, and Dirk found himself transfixed, even as disgust seeped through his every pore.

Bringing up the rear was a team of draft mules dragging a caisson and a Gatling gun on its limbers, its six shining barrels describing a cylinder. It rolled easily over the turf, accompanied by a crew of four gunners.

That was what caught the eyes and transfixed the multitudes. For here was something new and terrible. The weapon had been around since the Civil War, but only recently had it been perfected and deployed by the army. And now it rolled behind the column, a black instrument of doom, and Captain Cinnabar on a white steed led the two hundred men twice around the agency grounds and then stopped.

The gunners unhooked the Gatling gun and swung its snout around so that the six shining barrels pointed toward the uplands above the agency, mostly grazing ground and empty of life. The red men stared at it, and stared at the pasture above, and a terrible silence settled over the agency.

One of the gunners led the draft mules away and held their harness, while the others aimed the piece, choosing a lonely jack pine halfway up the slope. They attached a magazine to the piece. Its genius was that fresh rounds dropped automatically into each barrel as it revolved by, thus enabling rapid fire.

Captain Cinnabar stood next to the gunners and when all was ready, he lifted his saber and let it fall. At once the burly gunner yanked the crank around and the Gatling chattered to life, spilling bullets at a pace never before seen by anyone at the agency, a stream of bullets faster than anyone could count, a white streak of bullets that caught the lone pine and severed it from its roots until the hapless tree tumbled to the ground. Powder smoke drifted away. Dirk's ears rang. The heated barrels sometimes crackled and protested. The sight mesmerized everyone present, and the silence that followed was very like a sob.

sixteen

Aphrodite Cinnabar watched pensively as the elderly chieftains departed on bony horses, with wives beside them. They had lingered on the commons a while after Major Van Horne's tirade, conferring with Chief Washakie. But then they ambled away, returning to their camps, while the chief walked back to his house.

It was an odd moment. Only a while before, a column of foot soldiers and mounted cavalry had ridden the perimeter of the agency, making a great show of blue and gold, trumpet and snare drum, the rattle of shod hooves and the clatter of arms. But now the two troops of cavalry and two companies of infantry had vanished. The Gatling had been wheeled away by its mule team, and the acrid smoke of its firing had dissipated in the chill wind blowing over the grounds.

Her father had staged his show, all right, and his message was now burned into the brains of the Shoshones. Don't mess with the United States government. There seemed to be a vast amount of energy expended in all this, she thought. Even if all the headmen had been on hand, it would still have seemed . . . she hunted for a word. Excessive. Too much. What had gotten into her father? What had gotten into that shifty Indian agent, Van Horne?

Maybe they were right. Maybe there was a crisis here, a threat to the sovereign authority of the United States. Maybe they would all live in dread of a shower of arrows sailing out of the night. Maybe they would all be tomahawked in their beds. Maybe she should defer to her father, who, after all, was a career officer and a good one by all accounts. Maybe she shouldn't meddle in men's business.

Only something deep within her resisted everything she had heard and seen this afternoon.

She wanted the viewpoint of Dirk Skye, and thought to get it before he and his ancient mother Victoria vanished into the teacherage. She was curious about what he made of all this. That was as good a reason as any to drift his way, across the dusty commons where only a while before armies had marched.

He looked worn, but smiled as she approached, carrying a parasol she never had opened that gloomy day.

"Miss Cinnabar," he said. "You remember my mother, Victoria?"

"Goddamn good army show," the old woman said. "Your father, he looked like a real boy."

"He loves the command," she said.

"It impressed our Shoshone guests," Dirk Skye said.

"I'm afraid so."

"You don't sound enthused, Miss Cinnabar."

"It just leaves me, I don't know, uneasy."

"It was all for nothing. The Dreamers are dreaming a religion, not a war."

That intrigued her. "Why do you say that?"

"Heard it from Owl, himself."

"A religion?"

Dirk smiled. "He's a missionary. If white people can send missionaries to red men, why can't red men send missionaries to white men?"

Victoria Skye cackled softly.

"The Dreamers dream of a world without white men. A world in which everything wrought by white men is washed away."

"I suppose that includes us, then," Aphrodite said. "We're to be sent packing."

"I don't know," Dirk said. "I don't know how it works, or what the vision is that seems to be galvanizing them now. But it seems to restore the world they knew before, a world without white men and their ideas. It's the cleansing, the washing away of white men's ideas, beliefs, religion, that seems to excite these people."

"So why did two troops of cavalry arrive here on the double?" she asked.

"Armageddon," he said. "The war of the worlds."

"I don't understand nothing, dammit," Victoria said.

"The Dreamers prefer the wisdom of Owl to the wisdom of the missionaries, Grandmother."

"Well, ain't that a toot!"

"I should like to invite you to a picnic, Mr. Skye," Aphrodite said. "I'll prepare a little basket for us. Meet me at four, and we'll hike up the slope and picnic beneath that poor old pine tree that got shot to death."

"Picnic? Pine tree? Why, yes, I'll be at your door at four."

She smiled. "I want to see that poor tree."

"Yes, a sight to see. Mr. Gatling's revenge on all pine trees," he said, a tight smile on his face.

"I want to pick up the splinters. I want to dig the bullets out of the tree," she said.

"I'm sure your father would be most interested," he said.

"Yes, but not the way I'd be interested. I would like to see how the tree was murdered."

"Murdered?"

"Yes, executed by command. My father raised his sword, whisked it downward, and the pine tree was murdered."

Dirk Skye was staring at her.

She smiled. "See you at four," she said, whirling her unopened parasol.

That's when Major Van Horne boiled out of the agency, waving something small. He started toward the encampment, his whole person in disarray, maybe even alarm.

"Trouble, Major?" Dirk asked.

"This! This!" The Indian agent was waving a feather. When his hand finally slowed down, Aphrodite discovered it was soft and gray.

"Is that the feather of a Gray Owl?" she asked.

"It is the feather of rebellion! Of war! Of disobedience! Insurrection!"

"What about it, sir?" Dirk asked.

"What about it! It was lying on my desk. I returned to my office after our little meeting, and there it was. Put there insidiously, put there to threaten me. This is war, and I'm going to direct Captain Cinnabar to take appropriate measures."

"War, sir?" Dirk asked.

"War, war, war. Can't you grasp that, Skye?"

"Has a shot been fired? Has anyone died? Has property been destroyed?"

"War, sir. Disobedience. The perpetrator will be tried and

punished. It's Owl himself. He slid in here and did this while we were on the commons. I'll put a price on his head."

"You have proof of this, I presume."

"This is my proof!" The agent waved the feather, which did indeed seem almost sinister to Aphrodite, a sinister feather exuding menace and threat and arrows and tomahawks. "Look, Skye, it doesn't matter who put it there. Maybe he sent some skinny little pup of a Snake. But it's Owl's doing. This came out of that boy's head, and I'm going to round up that boy."

"On what charges, sir?"

"Insurrection. He's stirred up the Snakes and the Bannocks and God knows what else. We're on the brink of a major uprising that could drive civilization out of the whole area. And I intend to nip it before it happens."

"How will the Dreamers drive out civilization, Major?"

The agent glared and subsided. "If you don't know, Mr. Schoolmaster, you'd better study history. Enough of this."

He stormed toward the post, where he would swiftly be in touch with Aphrodite's father, and a few more officers newly arrived from Fort Laramie.

Aphrodite smiled. "They may not let me out for a picnic."

"I'll come anyway."

"I won't tell them where we're going."

He grinned, and they parted.

When she reached the grounds of the post, she found the place seething with activity. Over at the stables, troopers were unsaddling their mounts, brushing them, or turning them over to the stable detail. The mounted rifles were stacking their weapons. And a knot of officers had collected around her father, who was listening intently to the Indian agent.

Why not? She headed that way, delighting to poke her nose into the middle of it. She knew at once that Van Horne was waving the owl feather about, and talking war.

The post brass scarcely noticed her. Maybe it was the amusement in her face.

"Now, Major," her father was saying. "It's one feather, and it looks a little bit like a joke to me. I don't suppose you want to put the whole post on a combat basis for that—do you?"

"It's no joke!" Van Horne bellowed.

But the officers were having no part of that. They stared skeptically at the incensed agent, and at the soft gray feather.

"Tell me again what an owl feather means," asked a lieutenant from Fort Laramie.

"It is the sign of the Dreamers, a cult of Shoshone warriors hiding high in the mountains, preparing to descend on us all," Van Horne said.

"I think it's a religion, Lieutenant," Aphrodite said.

They suddenly realized she was there, in the middle of men's business.

"Well, now Miss, that's nice, but we need intelligence," the lieutenant said.

She refused to give ground. "It's been explained to me. The Dreamers believe the day is coming when the ways of white men will vanish. The world will then be the one they knew."

"Well, that's conjecture, dear," her father said.

"It's so far removed from what really is happening on my reservation that I trust you gentlemen will dismiss it," Van Horne said.

Her father turned to her. "Yes, you'll want to see what needs doing in the kitchen, and help out. We're entertaining these gentlemen at dinner."

Dismissed.

"The big feather war!" she said, mocking.

Oddly, that seemed to have its effect. They stared at her, and at Van Horne.

She poked her parasol into the sky and sauntered away, with an unladylike sway.

She wished she might know what would transpire. It was the fate of army wives and children to be kept in the dark. An entire fort could prepare for war, for a sally into enemy ground, and army families would be the last to know.

She walked briskly, enjoying the admiring gazes of the enlisted men. They weren't supposed to gaze at the commander's daughter; they weren't even supposed to acknowledge her presence, but most of them hadn't seen a girl in many months, and they furtively feasted on the sight of officers' wives in crinoline and lace and taffeta and gingham. She didn't mind.

She didn't see her mother anywhere, so she simply set to work on her picnic supper. She wiped the wicker basket clean, added a small dining cloth and two napkins, and rummaged in the root cellar for a few things to nourish them beneath the shattered jack pine. Her mother had several covered bowls of things ready for dinner, so Aphrodite left those alone, found a loaf of uncut bread, several slabs of cheese, some fresh apples from somewhere far away, and some sarsaparilla. To these she added some tin messware and cups. A simple meal beside a mortally wounded pine tree that had lived its life in all innocence until the army arrived. She truly felt sorry for the tree, and wanted to apologize to it for its demise one chilly afternoon when the tree was least expecting to depart from life on earth.

That done, she examined herself in the looking glass, and

discovered a flush of color on her cheeks, and eyes that seemed to open on a secret world inside of herself. She didn't know whether Dirk Skye would think much of her company, because she was always on the edge of getting into trouble, but she thought he might. He was never far from trouble himself, so maybe they could make some trouble together.

She discovered that her mother was lying down in her room with a sick headache; that was nothing new. Her mother had a sick headache before almost every dinner party, perhaps because Captain Cinnabar sprang those parties on her, announcing only hours beforehand that he would be entertaining Lieutenants Smith and Jones, Captains Murphy and Peterson, or Lieutenant Colonel Digby and his second wife, Lettie. So her mother did what army officers' wives do, and prepared a dinner, and if the company was all male, she would retreat to the kitchen while the gentlemen ate and enjoyed brandy and good Havanas.

Aphrodite knew that was the life she could expect; indeed, her father was steadily introducing her to young gentlemen under arms, all suitable of course. But it wasn't a life she planned for herself if she could help it. She had an eye for someone else.

seventeen

Dirk discovered Aphrodite on the veranda, a wicker basket in hand, awaiting him. She hastened down the steps, smiling, and steered him away from the commander's residence. It seemed almost as if she wished to escape something, or wished not to introduce Dirk to anyone there.

He knew all about that. A man with Indian blood in him dealt with that most every day. But that didn't make it easier.

"I'll take that basket, Aphrodite," he said.

He collected it even as she smiled. "I need to get away from the post," she said. "And you're my rescuer."

He hadn't thought of himself as a rescuer. He steered her along a grassy grade and up the flank of the foothill that stretched past the post. Fort Washakie was quiet now in the late afternoon.

Unlike the agency, a deep serenity pervaded the grassy slope. Breezes toyed with the tan grass. The white agency buildings grew smaller, and so did the tensions and alarms radiating from them. The sky was cloudless and anonymous.

Ahead of them loomed the shattered jack pine, which sagged like a broken crucifix, its limbs jagged against a blue heaven.

Something about the broken tree seemed sinister. Its green boughs flailed out from the shattered trunk. Dirk and Aphrodite approached warily, not knowing why. It was nothing but a shattered tree. The trunk had splintered perhaps four feet up, the yellow wood reduced to toothpick shards. Apparently three shells, grouped close, had severed the trunk. A breeze or maybe just deadweight had toppled the top, scattering green and brown needles. None of the shells were buried in wood; all had passed through, and some disturbed earth upslope hinted at where the Gatling shells had buried themselves.

"I guess it's not a place for a picnic," Dirk said.

She eyed him somberly. "We shouldn't have come here."

"I was curious. I wanted to see why an innocent jack pine died this morning."

"I don't like this place."

"Bad medicine. That's what my mother's people would say. But there's no meaning in it. There's nothing here but some shattered wood and a dead tree. It may not even be dead. The roots may throw up new shoots."

"I agree with the Shoshones," she said. "There's something awful about this."

He disagreed. Some shells had shattered a tree. That was all. But he chose not to talk about it. "There's some trees up a little, over there. We can picnic and look down on Fort Washakie."

She nodded and plucked up her gray skirt. They would have to traverse some deadfall to get to the glade upslope. He started ahead, and then held back, wanting her ahead of him.

He simply wanted to watch her walk; wanted to absorb her. She proceeded eagerly toward the grove of aspen. She held her skirts in both hands and lifted them slightly to walk over deadfall, and the sight of her filled him with an odd yearning.

"I think Captain Cinnabar was happy that the Gatling felled the tree," she said.

"Do you prefer to call him captain?"

"No, he's usually Father. But this was a captain event. A military event. Shells demolish trees and people."

"And maybe whole ways of life."

"Yes, if a tree can be shot to death, so can everything someone believes in. So can every habit or custom, too."

They plunged into a golden-green glade, with sunlight filtering through bright leaves, and patches of blue sprinkled with lime leaves. There were windows behind them, affording a view of the peaceful post and agency, slumbering in the sunlight.

Owl was waiting for them there. They hadn't even seen him sitting on an old bare log until they closed upon him, though he had sat quietly as they approached.

Dirk was astonished. The youth wore only a breechclout and moccasins, and if he possessed a weapon it was not visible.

"Oh!" Aphrodite said, and shifted closer to Dirk.

Owl gazed solemnly at them. "There, you see? The fast gun didn't kill me."

"It wasn't aimed at you, Owl," Dirk said.

"I was at the pine tree."

"You were? No one knew that."

"No one sees Owl until it is too late."

They stared uneasily at each other.

"You have brought a lunch," Owl said. "Eat."

"We will share it," Aphrodite said. "I brought enough."

"You are the captain's daughter."

Dirk said, "This is Aphrodite Olive Cinnabar. She prefers to be called Olive. And Olive, this is Owl, who was one of my better students at the schoolhouse."

"Call me Aphrodite," she said.

"The Greek goddess," Owl said. "Even a Snake knows it."

She busied herself spreading a tablecloth and setting out cheese, a knife, and some bread. Owl watched, faintly amused at her malaise.

Dirk sawed off some cheese and handed it to Owl, who lifted it high, in the four directions, before nodding.

"Owl follows what the fathers taught us all."

Oddly, no one spoke. The cheese was too sharp for Dirk's taste, but the others seated on that tablecloth seemed to enjoy it.

"They are hunting for you," Dirk said, after a while.

"Ah! I am hunting for them!"

"That's what they all believe, and why they would like to catch you and put you in their prison."

"Owl glides through the night. Will you tell them I watched their entire parade?"

"Do you want me to?"

"Yes. It will madden them."

"Why are you here, Mr. Owl?" Aphrodite asked.

"You are a polite woman. Owl awaits the vision that will begin the new world."

"Vision?"

"The end of your time, when you will be naked."

"Naked?"

"When there is nothing in your heart."

Dirk sat, transfixed. This was so far removed from what Van Horne and all the rest thought that it was as if he were on a different planet, and not just a thousand yards or so from Fort Washakie.

"What will happen?" she asked.

Owl peered into the cloud-specked sky. "It is not for anyone to know. I am only an empty bowl. I was given the promise. I know nothing more."

"But the Dreamers dance . . ."

"The Dreamers invite the Owl to come. We dance to invite the Owl to change the world. We wait, and dance, and wait for the New Day."

In some visceral way, Dirk fathomed the boy and his vision, and yet nothing made sense to him. "Why are the white people afraid, then?" he asked. "If the Dreamers are only inviting a visitation from a creature dreaded by the Shoshones, what has that to do with white men?"

"You have eyes but do not see, Dirk Skye."

"Why don't you simply go to Van Horne and tell him about your vision?"

"He would not understand. He thinks the Dreamers are planning to massacre white people." Owl smiled for the first time. "Then there would be iron bars between me and the world. They would capture my body, but no one can capture Owl."

Dirk fought back his impatience with this boy and his mysticism.

"Owl, tell me plainly. You are pleading for a vision. When the vision comes, what will happen? What will the Dreamers do?"

Owl smiled, something glowing in his face. Dirk thought of saints and martyrs, of oil paintings of early Christians whose gaze was upon heaven even as they were being led to the flaming pyres.

"When the vision comes, I will die. The Shoshone people will be born again. The white men will be emptied of everything in their hearts and minds, and walk away because there is nothing inside of them and no reason for them to be here."

"Nothing inside of them?"

"That is what they fear most. Not an uprising, not blood and death, but to have their ways stolen from them." He stared at Dirk, and then at Aphrodite. "Just as white men have stolen all the ways of the People. We cannot be ourselves now. They have taken away our heart."

It made little sense.

Owl rose suddenly. "Here I am. Take me to the Indian agent. You have captured Owl. You can put Owl in a cage and stop the Dreamers and they will all go away to their families." He held out his arms. "Tie my hands and feet. Take me. You can stop the Dreamers. You will have your reward. The Indian agent will praise you. The blue-shirts will praise you. You will be Dirk Skye, and the name, North Star, will no longer be spoken by the People."

Aphrodite was staring at Dirk.

Owl smiled, and that smile seemed almost a mock. Some embers lit in his eyes, as if to hint of well-lit rooms behind that boyish face.

An odd numbness stole through Dirk, almost a paralysis, as if the two bloods within him had come to a fatal separation.

"Owl," Dirk said at last. "Go from here, quickly."

"Ah, North Star, I will go. When the New Day comes, maybe Owl will give you dreams."

With that, the youth stood, nodded gravely to them, and

slipped upslope through the glade until he had vanished. Dirk half-expected to glimpse the boy striding softly through the azure skies, over white clouds and joyous rainbows. But there was only the rustling aspen leaves gilded by a low sun and a strange quiet. Dirk felt energy hemorrhage from him, and sat limply.

Aphrodite sat gravely, and then reached across the cloth to him and took his hand and squeezed. "I don't know why, but I'm glad you didn't take him up on his offer," she said.

"He's a saint," Dirk said. "And you know what the world does to saints."

"More of a mystic," she said. "He has a mystical vision. It's just the fevers of his imagination. White men won't be emptied of all meaning and walk away and leave this world to the Shoshones. We're here to stay."

Dirk remembered the catechizing of the Jesuits when he was being schooled in St. Louis, long before. They believed, and they ached to instill that belief in their Indian and half-blood charges. That wouldn't change. And yet . . . there was something in Owl's vision of the world to come that was unbearable, if not frightening. Hollow white men without dreams.

"I've spent years here teaching the Shoshone children what white men have taught me, and now the Dreamers are pleading for a vision, a coming of an Indian Christ, who will sweep it all away," he said.

She smiled brightly. "He's so beautiful. I mean, he's so naked. Oh! I shouldn't put it that way. He's not hiding anything. He's just, a beautiful boy."

Her cheeks had flamed, and Dirk looked elsewhere out of pure instinct. And maybe envy. He wished Owl would vanish from her mind.

"He's just an angry boy," he said.

She smiled wryly.

They sat silently, neither of them hungry enough to finish the picnic she had so carefully packed. He wanted to say things, just to talk, to whisper in her ear, but he felt iron bars between her and himself, the bars of blood and breed—and now something else. Owl's talk had stirred something in him, some deep yearning to return to his mother's people and become one with them, share their fate, teach white men the mysteries.

A single cloud obscured the low sun, which shot golden rays from behind the cloud and cast an odd shadow over the agency and the military compound below. Chill air eddied past them, on its long journey from alpine meadows somewhere.

"Dirk, I'm glad you showed me the tree," she said.

"It was a perfectly innocent tree," he said, "sacrificed to send a message."

"Do you think it will regrow?"

"There are live limbs below where it was shattered."

"Then it will regrow. Some things are hard to destroy."

"Yes, one of those small limbs will become the new trunk, and it will reach upward once again. I will take it for a sign."

eighteen

They straggled in for distribution day, and Dirk watched them uneasily. Things would be different this time. Scores of blue-clad soldiers milled about, eyeing the Shoshones as they gathered at the agency warehouse. At least the soldiers were unarmed, but their mere presence changed everything.

Once a month Shoshone families gathered at the agency to get their allotments, the food guaranteed by treaty. They came from afar, some on horse, a few with pack animals, others with travois. A handful had a wagon drawn by a bony mule or burro. Traditionally these were happy days, the promise of flour and beans and maybe a little beef, along with some calico or gingham, brightening the moment.

Many were worn by the hard trip, older Shoshones especially, who would struggle thirty or forty of fifty miles each way to load up their groceries. Still, hard or not, the distribution days were moments of celebration on the Wind River Reservation. With each distribution, sheer hunger was held at bay a while more.

Dirk was usually on hand to translate when a two-speaker was needed, and few were coming to school anyway. He saw so many people he knew. Old Agnes Snake-eyes was waiting in line to collect flour for her and her bedridden man, White Bird. Young Turtle, heavy with child, waited patiently along with her three children. Dirk saw Deer Stalker sitting impassively on a mule. The knot of Shoshones kept growing as they waited, but there was only silence from the warehouse and the agency. Dirk wondered what had delayed Van Horne, who usually was eager to begin the handout, something the agent took pleasure in doing.

The Shoshones huddled and gossiped and watched the soldiers watch them, and whispered to one another about the blue-bellies. The soldiers were unusual, but there was no cause for alarm; no one was at war, and no friendships had shattered. And the soldiers themselves had gathered in knots to gossip, or just watch.

Then, when a goodly crowd had at last collected, Van Horne emerged from the agency, flanked by the clerks and warehousemen who would hand out the annuity goods as provided by treaty. The agent looked uncommonly important this day, in a black frock coat and bow tie. The man's sideburns seemed almost to bristle.

The Shoshones quieted, and watched as Major Van Horne mounted the warehouse platform and turned to face the goodly crowd.

"Skye, come translate," he said.

Dirk, uneasy this time, joined the agent.

"We will begin our distribution as usual," the agent said. "Each enrolled member will make his mark. My clerks will see to it."

That was simple to translate, but Dirk knew what a shock

it would be to the Shoshones. Up until now, heads of families could collect the allotments for the whole family, and the clerks would record the transaction.

"People, Mothers and Fathers, the white father will give the food to each person who makes the mark," he said in Shoshone.

That was all. In the silence that followed, Dirk sensed the despair that snaked through these people. Only about a third of the enrolled members of the tribe were on hand, and they had planned to collect the distribution for the whole people.

"We'll begin now," Van Horne said.

No one moved.

Dirk turned to the agent. "What of the old and sick? The ones who can't travel?"

"Sorry, Skye, no exceptions. That's policy from Washington."

"That's what they've told you now?"

"No, it's always been policy. Enrolled members must make their mark to receive annuities and distributions."

"Why now?"

Van Horne chuckled. "It's mighty inconvenient, isn't it?"

The clerks settled on chairs at a table and spread the ledger before them, along with a nib pen and ink bottle, and waited officiously.

The soldiers watched idly. This didn't concern them, or did it?

And still no Shoshone moved. There was an odd anticipation among them, as if they were all expecting something. Or maybe they were simply waiting.

Would two-thirds of the People starve the next thirty days?

"If the missing show up in the next few days, can they collect their food?"

"Oh, as a concession I'll permit it tomorrow. You may tell them that."

Dirk turned to the anxious people whose gaze fixed on him. "The father says he will give food to those who come when the sun rises again."

That meant most of those still scattered over the vast reserve would not collect. It would be impossible for them to get to the agency in time.

"A lot of Shoshones will starve, sir."

"A pity. They know they're all supposed to show up and be counted. If they're off in the mountains, that means they'll have to feed themselves."

The Dreamers. This was Van Horne's ploy to reel in the Dreamers, force them to show up at the agency if they wanted their allotments. No doubt Captain Cinnabar and the army were involved. Collect the Dreamers, who might number a hundred or so. Dirk wondered whether those unarmed blueshirts had plenty of arms just out of sight.

Dirk simmered, but kept his peace. A translator was only that. A schoolteacher was only that. The Dreamers were the prey this time, and when this distribution was done, Van Horne would have a good idea who the Dreamers were, just from looking at the ledger and seeing names with no checkmarks beside them.

Dirk discovered Chief Washakie before him, and many of the Shoshones were eyeing him, not knowing which side he was on or why he had come to the warehouse.

"I am glad you are here, Grandfather," Dirk said to him in Shoshone.

The chief nodded curtly, and turned to the People. "Come. Collect what is owed to you," he said to the silent crowd.

Slowly the gaunt People formed a line that stretched back from the clerks at the table. As each person reached the table, Dirk sang a name in English, and the clerks found it on the ledger and handed the pen to the Shoshone, who drew a careful X where it was required. Many an old woman eyed the clerks fearfully, or studied the chief, or Dirk, or Van Horne, or the warehousemen distributing the foodstuffs from heaps they had built on the platform. A sickening silence enfolded this place, some bleak sadness, the desolation of hunger perhaps, as the People collected sacks of flour and beans, rice and cornmeal.

The women loaded flour and beans onto travois, or heaped the sacks onto the backs of scrawny mules, glancing furtively at the record keepers, who made the magic marks in their books. A few older men received their cornmeal or beans bitterly, their proud stare telling all who watched them far more than words.

An old woman, the elder wife of Walks Along, received her ration and set it on the ground.

"Where is the meal for my man?" she asked Dirk.

"Where is the meal for her man?" he asked Collins, the clerk. "Her man's too feeble to come here."

The clerk shrugged. "You heard the agent," he said.

"Grandmother, they will not give his food to you. He must come for it himself."

She stared at the two clerks, at the orderly script on the pages, and then picked up her sack of cornmeal and smashed into onto the ledger. The cotton sack burst, showering the clerks and the table with meal.

"It is better to die than to eat bad food," she said.

"Take her name down, Collins," Van Horne said. "She'll be docked next month."

The grandmother, her worn skirt dusted with yellow meal, stared at the agent and at the others and turned away.

"Grandmother, stay," Chief Washakie said. He turned to the clerks. "I will give them my ration."

"Very well, sign for it here, my friend," Collins said. The chief slowly scratched a large X on the page, collected his meal and beans, and a sack of flour the old woman had not burst, and carried it away from the line. "Wait here, Grandmother," he said.

She waited, a small stack of cornmeal, beans, and flour at her feet. Others stared, but the line moved slowly forward, each enrolled member carting away his or her own allotment and no more. The pile of food on the planks of the warehouse did not diminish much.

Chief Washakie returned with a wagon drawn by a scrawny mule. He and Dirk swiftly loaded it. To the meager supply of food allotted to the old woman, he had added gourds and melons and squash gotten from his gardens.

"Come sit beside me, Grandmother," he said. "We will drive."

"It is good to sit, Grandfather. It becomes very hard for me to carry these things on my shoulder."

"Well, now, that's a mighty fine gesture, Chief Washakie," Van Horne said to the leader of the Eastern Shoshones. "Let those who receive share with those who don't. Let those who have share with those who don't."

Dirk chose not to translate, but the agent prodded him. "Tell them that."

Dirk did, and the People stared back sullenly.

He watched the chief, dressed in a black frock coat, steer the mule away from the silent line and westward, up the Wind River Valley, where the old woman and her man scratched out a living in a riverside woodland, where firewood was plentiful and held the promise of winter warmth for the very old.

The queue began to move again, each person receiving the allotment due him. Even small children stood in the line, awaiting the moment when their parent would scratch a mark next to their name. It was oddly quiet. The usual jubilation of allotment day was tempered by the new rules, and the presence of grinning soldiers, who enjoyed the sight of Indians collecting white men's flour and cornmeal. The Shoshones stood grimly, enduring the smirky cheer of the soldiers and clerks, the smug satisfaction of the agent Van Horne. Some of them made their mark, collected their sacks of goods, and then stood apart, waiting to see what would happen.

The stacks of goods on the platform didn't diminish much, and the warehousemen scarcely stayed busy. Dirk watched, seeing not charity or benevolence in it, but the subjugation of his Shoshone people by the white men and their army. Was there anyone among those white people who cared whether the Shoshone people lived or died? Prospered or vanished from the earth?

It was Willow's turn, and she put her mark next to her name. Willow was tall, spare, handsome, and the mother of three sons, all of them Dreamers. She was not known to smile much, and seemed to lack the innate humor of the Shoshone people, but her seriousness drove her to take great pride in the People. There was no more beautiful—and remote—woman among the People.

She watched as the warehousemen set the small sacks

and a pasteboard box before her, a miserable dole for a large family. She stared first at the offending little pile, and at Van Horne, and the smiling clerks, and then lifted each miserable pouch and smashed it to the clay, bursting the cheap cotton and scattering yellow meal and brown beans at her feet. Then she proudly walked away, bearing nothing of the dole, her gait strong, her chin high.

"That'll be one hungry family," Van Horne said, amused.

But what Willow started, the remaining people in the food line continued. Next was Hairy Head, an old headman with a proud eye and a lustful way. He was more dramatic. He lifted his little sack of flour high above him, and then smacked it to the ground. It thumped, spraying white flour over the clay, powdering his bare feet, and dusting everyone close.

"Hey!" yelled a clerk.

But Hairy Head was not done. He sprayed beans, scattered meal, and shook the burlap and cotton sacks until the earth had received every last ounce.

The soldiers chuckled. This was sport. Goddamn redskins didn't know enough to feed themselves!

Van Horne, far from being alarmed, was enjoying it. He stood close by, an odd cheer spreading across his face.

"I'll put the agency mules to the feedbag," he said.

The mules would have a lot of chow.

One by one the Shoshone people made their mark on the ledger, received their dole, and slapped the entire month's supply of staples into the stained earth, where the heap of beans and meal and edible food grew minute by minute.

And not one of the Shoshones left. After they had destroyed their entire dole, they stood apart, waiting and watching. Not until the entire nation, at least those who had come to the agency on allotment day, had destroyed their allotment, did they silently drift away.

Dirk watched them go, watched them wearily drag their ponies and travois away.

"What will you say to the people in Washington?" Dirk asked the agent.

"We distributed the goods to all, as usual," Van Horne said.

nineteen

By the time Chief Washakie had returned to the agency, he had heard the story a dozen times from people straggling away. He had sat quietly in his wagon while his suffering Shoshones told him about the flour rebellion. He was not surprised.

"Go find food wherever you can," he had told them.

"Beyond the white men's lines?"

"Yes. I have said it."

And so he gave all his people permission. He would tell the agent.

He drove back, a solitary Indian in a white shirt and black coat, his graying hair loose and held with a headband. His mind was heavy with all that had happened. He felt the whole weight of the People on his shoulders.

The closer he drove toward the bleak structures of the Wind River Agency, the more resolute he became. The time had come to draw a line across the earth. For as long as he had been the principal chief of the Eastern Shoshones, he had seen the white men as assets. His People were not numerous, and they lacked the horses and power of the great plains tribes such as the Sioux and Cheyenne and Arapaho, which waged constant warfare against his People. His alliance with the white men evened the struggle somewhat, and his friendship with these newcomers brought guns and food and peace. They called him a friend, and perhaps he was, or at least he was not their enemy. His contact with them taught him much about the future: his People were doomed to fade away unless they changed. He didn't care much for the change, but there was no other way for his People but to become stock growers and farmers and live on pieces of land, like the newcomers. There could be a good life for his People in ranching and farming. So he had decreed it. But always with his eyes open. The white men came with their own darkness and ignorance and foolishness. Their friendship was as firm as a butterfly's wing. But he saw no real choice. Unlike so many of his People, he had seen how white men lived. And what the future had to be.

He let the weary dray pick its own pace back to the agency. There was no hurry. There never was any hurry. But in time the distant white dots of the agency became small buildings, and then larger ones which caught the late sun of the day, and cast long shadows. And then he was back, his own white house not far distant. But he did not go there, for he had business first, that must be opened and not avoided.

He drew up his wagon before the somber agency building and stepped into the commons, where soldiers had paraded in recent days. Now there were only a few, and he saw they were at the warehouse herding hogs brought in to devour the spilled flour and beans. The soldiers kept a few hogs at the post to eat garbage and supply some bacon now and then. The grunting hogs were busy rooting out every last bit of the white men's food intended to feed his hungry people. He watched for a moment. At least the hogs were getting fat. The soldiers eyed him placidly. The unclaimed food had been returned to the warehouse, and now there were only hogs and blue-shirts.

He entered the silent agency, found no one on hand, and turned to leave. But a voice stayed him, and he found Van Horne at his desk, his feet propped up. A small flask of amber fluid, probably hastily removed from the desk, rested near the office safe.

"Ah! It's the esteemed chief of the Eastern Shoshones!" the agent said, sliding his feet off the desk and planting them firmly before him.

Washakie removed his hat, as was the white men's custom when indoors, and waited for Major Van Horne to compose himself.

"And to what do I ascribe the honor of your company, Chief?"

"My people will starve, Major."

"Now, esteemed Chief, let me see here. I do believe they were handed the staples the government provided for them. I do believe they pitched these wantonly to the earth, and walked away. If they suffer, they can only blame themselves."

"That is what they told me as I rode back, sir."

"Then why are you complaining?"

"They are going to be hungry."

"And is that not their fault?"

The chief thought to drop this line of reasoning. He could do some blaming of his own. The distribution had been altered for certain political reasons connected with the Dreamers. And it would all end in accusations and counter-accusations. They would end up blaming one another and no food would end up in the bellies of his people.

He stood a little straighter, dark and stocky and massive and gray at the temples. "I told them to seek food wherever they could find it, beyond your medicine lines."

The agent, who had been primed for more blaming, took a moment to register that.

"Beyond the reservation? But I did not give permission."

"I gave them permission."

"But you lack the authority."

"I am the chief of the Eastern Shoshones."

Van Horne laughed softly. "That's almighty right, my esteemed friend. But no one leaves the reservation without permission, and I don't give it. Not to anyone."

"I have told them. They will go."

"You could rescind the command, my honorable friend." The agent smiled. "It would halt the trouble."

"I have told them. They will go. They will hunt."

The agent stood abruptly. "Then I'll take measures. Captain Cinnabar will enjoy rounding people up."

"Then let it happen."

Washakie stood, solid and unmoving, determined. "I made the treaty myself. We were given a homeland to possess and enjoy, safe from your people, safe from other tribes. We were not put there by force. Nothing in the treaty says we must stay inside the reservation. We are not a conquered people defeated by your army and put in a prison with invisible lines around it. We are friends. It is our land. These are our ways. I have sent my people to look for meat. They will do it. They will hunt buffalo and deer and elk. They will bring back meat for those who are poor and hungry. They will keep the People alive for one more moon."

"Sorry, my esteemed friend, it's the fathers in Washington who've got the power, and they handed it to me, and

I'm telling you now: tell your people to stay at home. Tell them!"

"No."

Washakie stood quietly, waiting for whatever came next.

"Are you defying me?"

"I am the chief of the Eastern Shoshones."

"And I'm the agent of the government. I could call the guard, you know."

"Here are my arms. Here are my legs. Put irons on them and throw me into the cage at the fort named in my honor."

The Indian agent subsided, stared into the late-hour skies, and came to a conclusion. "I'll deal with you tomorrow," he said. "Don't think this is over."

Washakie nodded. He walked quietly from the office, standing high, making his back large against the white man, and drove his wagon to his small frame house, which sat in bleak subjectivity near the agency. He pulled the harness off his horse, hung the harness on pegs, scooped some shelled corn and poured it into the manger, and closed the gate.

He did not enter his darkened home, but walked the quarter mile to the house of the teacher, and knocked.

The old Crow woman answered, and stepped back at once. "We are pleased to welcome the chief of the People," she said. "Our house is blessed by your presence."

Dirk Skye appeared, surprised by the presence of the chief, and waved him in. "Grandfather, we are honored to open this house to you."

Washakie settled easily in a kitchen chair, and withdrew his tobacco pouch and a small clay pipe, which he filled carefully and then lit with a match he scratched on the underside of the table. He sucked slowly, until the charge glowed orange in his pipe, and then exhaled. North Star joined him at the table, and then, hesitantly, the old Crow woman, too.

"On this day I have told my people to hunt where they will," he said, choosing English as the right tongue here. "When the sun rises I expect to be taken to the soldier camp and held there. Please make sure my will is known to the People. They must go where there might be meat."

"Is there a problem with it?" North Star asked.

"I told the agent that it is my will and command. He said I had no authority. I told him I am the chief." Washakie smiled suddenly. "And he told me that he is."

"He threatened you?"

"I will not undo what I have done."

"What will happen, Grandfather?"

"I believe that when the sun comes up I will be put in the cage at the fort."

Skye looked stricken.

"Sonofabitch," said the old Crow woman.

"Then the blue-shirts will ride out and catch the People and bring them back so that they can starve on our land rather than starve on the land of others."

"The Dreamers," North Star said.

"You speak true words. The white men fear the Dreamers. They turn our home into our prison and send more soldiers to keep us inside of it. Tell me, North Star. Why is this?"

"Grandfather, I wish I knew. They fear Owl and his Dream more than any army. They think that Owl and a few Shoshones are worse than any army."

"I do not see clearly what is happening," Washakie said.

North Star hesitated, and then plunged ahead. "Grandfather, Owl was here. He watched the soldiers parade. He watched them fire the Gatling gun. He watched the pine tree shatter. Later, he made himself known to me. He was amused by the white men. Owl's vision is not about war, not about armies, not about blood. It is about that which has no name."

"Here, was he?"

"Watching from the hills."

"They hunt him as if he was a rabid wolf."

"They won't catch him, Grandfather. He is invisible to them. He walks among them and they don't know it."

"And you did not tell the agent."

"No, Grandfather. I would not betray Owl."

Washakie grunted. "His days are numbered, North Star. I have said it."

"Why do you say so, Grandfather?"

"They think he is the spark that will start the forest fire."

He knocked the dottle from his pipe and stowed it in a breast pocket. "I am tired and my women await me. When the sun comes, I may be taken to the fort. Tell the People Washakie says to hunt wherever they wish; the whole world is their home. Find meat and eat."

"I may join them, Grandfather."

"No, teach the school, North Star. The old ways are doomed. Teach them the new."

With that, he stood, pressed his hand firmly upon the shoulder of the old Crow woman, whom he admired, and slipped into the deepening abyss of night.

twenty

North Star would hunt. He awoke one chill and overcast morning and knew it. This was the right time, when the cottonwood leaves were turning bronze and the aspen made yellow patches on distant slopes. He would make meat for the hungry People.

He had dutifully remained at his schoolhouse post but the students had fled. The girls boarding with Washakie had been returned to their parents. The Shoshone people were shunning the agency and keeping their children away. It had been a dreary autumn, sitting in his empty schoolroom reading.

The Wind River Reservation was slipping into the fall, its starvation scarcely noticed at the agency. If the People were going hungry, the starvation was screened by silence. Dirk knew that the Dreamers, still gathering in the mysterious chasms of the mountains, were supplying a little meat to the People, but where they got it remained a mystery. He suspected it was not the meat of game taken on the hunted-out reservation.

He came to his decision suddenly, put away the geography text, and closed the schoolhouse door behind him.

At the teacherage his Crow mother rocked quietly and watched the clouds lower.

"Absaroka Grandmother, I am going hunting," he said. That was the most formal way to address her. But he might properly call her Victoria, his father's name for her, or Many Quill Woman, her Crow name, or Crow Mother, for she had helped raise him.

She absorbed that cheerfully. "I will go with you," she said.

"But Grandmother—it will be cold and hard."

"You saying I ain't worth anything?" she said. "I'm going, dammit."

"But you—but, Grandmother."

"So, maybe I die. It is good to die being useful. I want to be useful. I can still do a lot of stuff, eh?"

Actually, she could. But this would be hard, and old people had few reserves. But she was determined.

"Good!" he said.

She erupted from the rocker with amazing force, and began gathering what they would take with them. He headed for the barn, harnessed a dray he liked, and drove the agency spring wagon to his house. By the time he returned, she had collected a heap of outdoor gear: two bedrolls, a canvas tarp for a shelter, a block and tackle, Barnaby Skye's converted Sharps, with cartridges, assorted skinning knives, ropes, mess gear, and a few pounds of cornmeal.

She had shed about ten years in the space of an hour, he thought as she clambered onto the bench seat beside him. He stopped at the agency, couldn't find Van Horne, and left a note saying he was going hunting. He was glad the agent wasn't around to heap sarcasm or worse on his plans. And that might include being fired for being away from his post. But somehow Dirk didn't care. If there was no one to teach, then his service as a teacher was meaningless.

But as they drove away, Van Horne waylaid him from the agency garden.

"Hunting, eh? Not a bad idea, Skye. Bring back some bear steaks, eh?"

"More likely a few pronghorns if we're lucky, Major."

"And Skye, keep an eye out. If there's a revolt brewing, I want to know about it."

"The reservation's peaceful, sir."

"Hell it is," Van Horne said. "You'll be my eyes and ears."

"Goddamn Dreamers all over," Victoria said.

"Not so funny, madam," the major said.

Dirk wasn't sure where to go, but decided to ford the Wind River and head into the Owl Creek Mountains, and then the Big Horn Basin. The nights were cold: he could bring fresh meat to the People even if he had to carry it a couple of days.

The wagon was serviceable enough: it would carry two or three deer, maybe two butchered elk. With the block and tackle and some luck, he could load meat without help. A northwest wind snaked the heat out of them as they forded the river and headed into dry foothills, stained red this time of year except for bursts of green in spring-fed gulches.

Dirk knew there would be no game near the reservation. Upriver, the Dreamers were lodged in mountain valleys, drawing their sustenance from sheep and bear and deer. There were few Shoshone north of the river, and North Star steered the agency wagon across lonely reaches so empty of life that even the presence of a crow in the sky seemed welcome.

It was always like this. Around the agency he was Dirk;

away from it, he somehow became North Star. Even as he steered the dray, he felt his Shoshone blood course through his veins, transforming him. He would bring food to the People, if he could.

North Star worried about the ancient woman beside him, but she sat stoically, wrapped in an old Hudson's Bay blanket, cream with red bands. She had been failing for months; her eyesight was weak; she had acquired a tremor. But mostly she had slept and slept and slept away her days.

"This is good," she said. "It is better to hunt in the wind."

He steered the bony dray horse up a draw, leaving behind the slight trail, and headed toward a distant ridge. There was no game in sight. It made the country odd; grasses and brush cured everywhere, untouched by four-footed creatures. North Star saw no sign, either, except for that of an occasional cow illegally on the reservation. He reached the spine of the ridge and paused to let the dray blow, and they found themselves gazing down upon a mysterious ocean of land. Far below, North Star spotted what he thought was a patrol from the fort, making its noisy blue way across the reservation. He saw no wildlife at all, nor any sign that wildlife had been here for a long time.

A dozen miles ahead was a saddle that might take him down to the Big Horn Basin, which was now cattle country. He hesitated. Agency Indians with a gun and a wagon could look a great deal like rustlers to any passing band of drovers. He might be a federal employee; he might speak fluent English. But the cattlemen up that way would see him and Victoria as rustlers and would not bother to get the facts.

It was something to think about.

The real problem was not Shoshones rustling cattle, but

ranchers stealing grass. They sent small herds into the hidden valleys and obscure meadows along the northern edge of the reservation, taking their fill of the grasses that belonged to the tribe. All the agents, including his father, knew of it and tried to stop it, but lacked the resources. And the army tended to look the other way. So the Shoshone pastures had been steadily invaded, especially during dry years, and the several large ranches to the north were never punished. Neither were their transgressions acknowledged in the reports that regularly winged their way to Washington City. As much as two-thirds of the reservation pastures were encroached by cattlemen.

North Star drove into rougher upcountry, between escarpments of red rock laced with juniper. He doubted a wagon had ever traversed this country, and indeed he could be forced to turn around at any time. All it would take would be an impassable gulch or deadfall or a bottom choked with slide rock. The gloomy sky lowered over the distant red ridges, making the place somehow sinister. These were the Owl Creeks, and beyond the great basin of the Big Horn. Surely in a place so remote, there would be game.

He paused to let the dray blow at a narrows where passage was compressed between cream and red rock, some of it in tumbled heaps.

"Want to walk, Grandmother?"

"Hell yes. This is a spirit place."

He scarcely knew what to make of that, but helped her down. She peered keenly at the vaulting stone, and headed at once toward an overhang where rock protected a shallow hollow, a brown shadow fifty yards up a talus slope. She wrapped herself tightly in the blanket to stay the wind, and pushed ahead so swiftly that North Star could scarcely keep up. But then she reached the wide hollow with its red roof, and stood quietly.

"Old ones," she said.

He saw at once the figures daubed on the rear wall, vast numbers of them, some pale and ancient and flaked, but others newer and brighter. Some had been drawn in ochre; others in black, probably employing colored clay mixed with grease.

There were stories here, dozens, maybe hundreds of stories. Some of the figures clearly had been painted on top of ancient ones, destroying the earlier stories. But one in particular caught North Star's eye, vague and faded and higher than others. There were stick figures armed with lances and bows and arrows, and these figures had surrounded a giant beast, a strange beast, with monstrous legs, huge ears, great tusks, and a snake erupting from its head. A mammoth.

"Goddamn," muttered Victoria. "This a bad place."

There were stories of buffalo hunts, wars, fighting. There was a head with a war axe buried in the skull. There were human figures pouring arrows into a giant horned animal, an elk perhaps. Sometimes the stories were easy to follow: some were victory celebrations, memoirs of scalpings, battle stories, bravery stories, but there were other stories more obscure, some in which it was hard even to make out human figures.

They worked their way along the cliffside hollow, and then stopped at a recent image, its paint fresh. It might well be an owl, with round eyes, short ears, a curved beak, peering at anyone who might behold it. It was recent; there was a paint pot nearby, and daub sticks that would permit any passerby to add to the images. And some had. Here were new figures, pumping arrows into a different sort of beast, with small horns. Could these new animals be cattle? North Star stood, amazed, at the sight of scores of these bold new images, so new that they made the ancient figures pale in importance.

"Goddamn Dreamers boasting about supper," Victoria said.

Somebody was doing a lot of painting, North Star thought.

He and Victoria seemed to have stumbled on an obscure artery that took people on or off the reservation. He remembered the times, a few years earlier, when the tribe's own cattle kept vanishing. His father, Barnaby Skye, had made it his first priority to build a herd of cattle owned in common by the Shoshone people. He had begged a few cattle from outsiders, helped the Shoshones guard and feed and water their little herd. But in all the years his father was Indian agent the herd never grew, and somehow cattle vanished. He knew, but could never prove, that cowboys from the neighboring ranch country simply pilfered the tribal cattle; that those cowboys drove their herds onto the good grass in the obscure corners of the reservation, paying nothing for the trespass, and usually nabbed a few Shoshone cattle when they pulled out. In the end, Barnaby Skye's dream had come to nothing, defeated by neighbors, by an army that didn't much care to protect the people on the reservation, and an uncaring Indian Bureau in Washington City. That defeat had filled Barnaby Skye with sorrow and anger, and hung over him until he died.

Now, as North Star stood before this wall daubed with a thousand stories, well above the bottoms of this obscure gulch, he intuited that this had been a great smuggler trail used by the cowboys on the ranches to the north, and now by the Dreamers. It seemed likely that the Dreamers, still drumming through the nights and awaiting their vision of liberation, were feeding themselves one cow at a time, pulled out of the herds beyond these mountains. Maybe the whole thing had been so slow and secret that so far, anyway, the ranchers were unaware of the loss. But that was speculation. What North Star did know was that no ranchers had come storming into the Wind River Agency demanding repayment and punishment of those who were taking livestock.

Maybe there was justice in it, he thought. All those years that the ranchers were stealing reservation grass and beef were being repaid now. But he didn't push that idea far. There was so little proof; nothing to prove that the cattle outfits had stolen Indian beef; nothing tangible now to prove that the Dreamers—if they were really involved—were thinning the herds to the north.

He helped Grandmother down the talus. She had reached an age when she seemed to glide, and so light was her body that she left no footprints behind her. He helped her into the wagon and set out once again, along this obscure gulch that would lead them—somewhere. Two hours later, still under a leaden sky, they reached the saddle, and peered into an obscure world, gray and silent, cold and angry, where three or four ranchers lorded over giant dominions like feudal barons, zealously excluding the rest of the world from their fiefs.

North Star fought off an odd fear, and slapped the reins over the dray.

twenty-one

Cold fog lay over the land at dawn, which made it even more lonely. The western reaches of the Big Horn Basin were as empty as any place on earth, featureless slopes scraggly with sagebrush, arid and dull, a place to hurry past to reach something, anything, more hospitable. A cast-iron sky continued to oppress the land, and occasional mists filtered down from a haphazard heaven.

North Star thought it would be a good enough place to hunt if only because it was so devoid of humankind that mule deer or antelope might prosper there. He wiped the moisture off his father's Sharps, the last of several that Barnaby Skye had owned, and checked the load.

Grandmother Victoria would tend camp. The moist air had set her bones to aching, and now she huddled under a half-shelter fashioned from the tarpaulin they had brought along. She fried up some johnnycakes for breakfast, building a fire of dead sagebrush that lasted just long enough for the task. The dray was finding grass tucked under the sagebrush. A seep provided water enough, though rather alkali.

"Just what an old lady needs for her stomach," Victoria said.

"I'll not go far, Grandmother," he said.

"Hunt," she said crossly.

North Star headed up a shallow draw, his Sharps tucked into his arm. Maybe with some luck he could fill the water-beaded wagon with some antelope and deer and start back to the reservation.

No wind blew; maybe that was good. Wind sent notice far ahead, but this gray day the air was heavy. He crossed one ridge and headed down an anonymous slope, suddenly fearful of losing his bearings. There wasn't a thing to steer him back to Victoria. Not a landmark, not a mountain, not an odd-shaped cliff, not a tree. But there were his footprints in the dewy brush, which might not last long. He realized he would need to be careful about getting lost. Victoria couldn't harness that dray and had no means of going home if they should become separated.

North Star remembered his red bandanna and backtracked to the ridge where he could see their camp as well as the open country where he was headed. He tied the red emblem to the highest sagebrush, which stood glistening and silvery five or six feet above the earth. It wasn't much of a landmark, and he was going to have to be cautious.

Then he headed toward a flat where he thought game might be, trudging through silence. When he descended he saw that nothing grew there; it was a featureless bottom of naked gray clay. But out on that clay were creatures which proved to be antelope when he got closer. Their white rumps were turned toward him. He marveled at his luck. But he still needed another hundred yards, so he edged quietly, a few yards at a time, pausing frequently, alert to the slightest restlessness of the pronghorns. He saw no sentinel on a distant ridge, but maybe that was the fog closing between him and the sentinel. He made his hundred yards and decided it would do, especially if he could get a bench shot. He found a boulder, settled behind it, and rested the octagonal barrel on it, choosing the closest antelope. But he would have to wait until it stood broadside, so he settled quietly. This was good. He wasn't more than a third of a mile from Victoria. It was misting again, and he thought maybe the mist was what muffled his presence to the shy and alert antelopes.

His chance came moments later when the antelope turned. He shot, the boom vanishing in the mist, and the antelope dropped instantly. The rest scattered. He reloaded the Sharps and studied the ground. There were no antelope in sight. He found the dead antelope and tied a rope to its front legs. He would drag it if he could. That turned out to be a good choice. When he drew the antelope onto the thin grass the mist lubricated his passage. He pulled it steadily toward camp, over a ridge and down. In short order he was lifting the pronghorn into the wagon bed and untying the rope.

"The boys will chase the girls," Victoria said, echoing a belief that antelope meat induced lust. "Goddamn, I wish I was young again." She wheezed a little chuckle.

"We may as well break camp here; I've chased away any meat," he said.

He collected his picketed dray and began harnessing it, while Victoria broke camp.

The collar and harness leathers were icy in his hand, but he didn't mind. The antelope in the wagon would keep well if this continued. He slid the bridle over the dray's head, making sure the bit was in place, and then went to help Victoria tuck the bedrolls under the tarpaulin. Sleeping dry was something they both cherished.

He helped her aboard and took the lines, only to realize he was seriously disoriented, with no sun, no sky, no features to guide him. Still, the ribs of land here ran from high country south and west, toward the valley of the Big Horn, east and north. That would have to do. If he headed downslope, he might eventually reach the river, and the bottoms where mule deer abounded. He started that way, driving downslope as much as his instincts permitted, his wagon wheels leaving a silvery trail behind.

The day brightened and the mist and fog began to thin, and North Star began to see the valley. The river was a black streak miles ahead. There should be plenty of deer.

The horsemen boiled out of the mist, four of them, riding wet horses, the dew silvery on their hats and coats. Cowboys. Dirk reined in the dray and waited, as the horsemen swirled close, eventually forming an arc in front of him. Then one rode close, studied the wagon, eyed the antelope.

"Good morning," North Star said.

"Maybe it isn't," the one who had peered into the wagon replied.

"I'm Dirk Skye, and this is my mother, Victoria. We're from the agency."

"I already got that from the wagon," the man said.

"The agency's short of meat, so we've been hunting," North Star said.

"Hunting, eh? I'd call it something else," the man replied.

"We have an antelope and are heading to the bottoms to hunt deer."

"Deer, eh?" The man laughed.

The man's eyes radiated a certain cruel amusement. He

was wire-thin, with an elaborate mustache, and a water-beaded revolver holstered at his side. His craggy face suggested an intimate acquaintance with outdoor living.

"Your name, sir?" North Star asked.

"It don't matter none, since you won't be around to repeat it," the man retorted.

The others, sitting quietly on their water-stained mounts, eyed the wagon impassively.

"I'm the teacher at the agency," Dirk said. "My father, Barnaby Skye, was the agent for the Wind River Reservation for four years."

"That makes it all the worse, sonny boy," the man said. "Old Yardley, he had nothing but grief from your pa, and that's a fact."

So this was Yardley Dogwood's outfit. North Star knew all about the man, but had never met him. His father had clashed repeatedly with the rancher, beginning in 1870 when Yardley had almost strung him and Victoria up just for crossing the range the Texan was claiming.

"Well, talk to Major Van Horne," Dirk said.

The cowboy smiled through the cracks and crags in his flesh, leaned over and plucked the Sharps out of the wagon bed. "Must be your old man's," he said. "Old Skye, he was keen on Sharps. I 'magine a few of us are, too."

"Take it up with the army. Captain Cinnabar's commanding."

"We ain't taking it up with no one," the cowboy said. "Fact is, you're rustling. Now, don't gimme that bunk. That there antelope's a decoy, so you look like some friendly old redskin. Fact is, that wagon's about right to hold a six-hundred-pound mother cow. Fact is, you're off the reservation where you ain't supposed to be. Fact is, we're missing a few beeves and was getting mighty curious where they done disappeared to, and now we know. They been dragged over them mountains and fed to all the redskins yonder. Fact is, we caught you red-handed."

Victoria started cackling. She laughed and wheezed, so the cowboy glared.

"Turn off the cackle, old woman," he said.

"Go to hell, cowboy."

"There ain't a tree in sight, or we'd string you up proper for rustlers. So I guess we'll just drive on down to that river, and string you from a cottonwood."

Dirk stared, unbelieving. How could this be?

"On what evidence?"

"Hell, you being here in a wagon's all we need. Old Yardley, he'll be pleased as punch. A Skye whelp at that."

Dirk felt his fate closing in on him, even as he sensed an eagerness build in these cowboys from Texas. He thought to whip the dray into a gallop, and gave up on that. Bleakly, he sought some exit, some escape, and saw none. They had him.

The cowboy grinned. "You gonna drive that rig peaceful to the hanging tree, or do we drive it for you?"

"You can drive it yourself," he said. He saw no point in cooperating with his executioners.

But the cowboy simply lifted the lines and handed them to one of the others. They would lead the dray, and the wagon.

Thus did they proceed through the fog-patched morn, toward a destiny that North Star could not bear to think about. Beside him, Victoria huddled deep in her blanket, an odd smile on her face, seeming to enjoy it all.

They were flanked by the riders, men with stained slouch hats pulled low, wiry beards, and bright death-lust eyes, who glanced now and then at the doomed, and acted twitchy. Was this the end? Would this mean he'd never see another sunrise? Would this be the last of Barnaby Skye's fragile family?

He felt his pulse quicken with the fear that was eroding his composure, and yet he could do nothing but sit in utter helplessness as the cowboys led his dray down the long shallow grades choked with sagebrush and into the bleak black bottoms of the Big Horn River. Trees arose, giant cottonwoods with good horizontal limbs that would welcome a rope. But this party was not headed toward them, but somewhere else, and that interested North Star. A log line camp, an outlying cabin, rose out of the murk, and he saw horses in the pens, and a handsome buggy.

Even as they pulled up, an enormous man emerged from the cabin, his wavy hair tinged with gray, his black gabardine attire a feeble effort to maintain some gentility. It would be Yardley Dogwood himself. In short order, half a dozen other cowboys boiled out of the small cabin and stared.

"I do believe we've caught the rustlers red-handed," said the nameless cowboy who had brought them here.

Dogwood peered into the wagon bed, observed the antelope, and sniffed.

"Ah declare, you've caught them straightaway," he said. "I guess we'll perform some immediate and final justice."

"What's so pissant pleasant about this, Yardley, is that this pup is no less than old Skye's half-breed brat, and that's his old squaw," the captor announced. "And it ain't over. This pissant boy, he's the property of the government of the United States, the same that had its way with Texas. This pissant, he's the teacher over there at the Wind River Agency, teachin' them red buggers how to steal cows, looks like."

"You don't say. An employee of the damned United States government? Guilty as sin," Dogwood said.

"We haven't rustled a thing. We were hunting!" North Star snapped.

"That there antelope, it's sure dead. Now, boy, that antelope was rustled. Fact is, I own every antelope, deer, elk, bear, wolf, raccoon, weasel, prairie dog, and mosquito on this range. And you've gone and rustled my meat. Everything on my range is mine, boy, all mine."

North Star felt like shouting, but there was no replying to an argument like Dogwood's.

"Speak up, boy, speak up! Yoah lookin' a little pale around the gills, yes sir, even through that Injun face. Must be Skye blood making you pale. What you want? A trial? We'll have us a trial. Ah'm the judge and this here's the jury and you'll get a measure of real Texas justice."

It was best not to speak. Victoria was cackling.

"Old witch, shoulda took care of her eight years ago when she crossed my land without my say-so," Dogwood said. "But now justice knocks twice.

"Now, then, the prosecution'll bring the charges. There's forty beeves gone, give or take, and who knows where they went? Feedin' the nits and lice over yonder, beyond the red mountains. Now we got us a wagon with a dead antelope in it for an excuse. You got anything to say, boy?"

There wasn't.

Dogwood heaved his weight forward a little. "Gents? What's your verdict?"

"Rope!" yelled one.

"Two ropes!" yelled another.

"Yonder's a mighty fine lookin' cottonwood," Dogwood said.

twenty-two

Dogwood hefted himself around to face Dirk and his mother Victoria. He scratched at his chin whiskers and lifted in his vast belly so it would set better over his belt.

"Ah do declare, you've had yourself a proper jury trial, and them jurors, they came up with a conviction, fair and proper. Therefoah, I'm condemnin' you to hang by the neck until expired. Any questions?"

Dirk knew better than to say anything. But Victoria laughed, her faint wheeze sandpapering the assembled drovers and Yardley Dogwood himself.

"You got the funniest sense of humor I ever did see," Dogwood said.

Off in the cottonwoods, the magpies were making a ruckus. Dirk saw scores of them, white-bellied black birds, rowdy as blue jays, insolent as crows. It looked to be a magpie convention over there, with more magpies flying in from everywhere. That was odd; magpies didn't flock, and they wintered in the north. But there they were, collecting among the cottonwoods.

"All right, let's get this here act of justice a-going," the rancher said. "Jason, you git the wagon down there under the limb, and it'll be a handy drop."

Jason grabbed the lines and drew the wagon toward the cottonwoods, setting up an awful cackle among the magpies. Victoria whickered, and Dirk thought the old woman was daft. But Magpie was her spirit helper, and her magpie medicine had been with her all her years. Many was the story she told of the ways Magpie—she always used the proper name—had come to her and Dirk's father in moments of trouble.

Jason led the wagon under a limb of a noble cottonwood and let it rest there. The rest of the cowboys, all still on horseback, collected there, and Dogwood drove his black buggy there also.

"All right now, we'll do this right smart. Someone make some nooses."

The cowboys stared at one another.

"I seen it done," one said, "but I never done it."

"Well, give her a try."

Several cowboys undid the lariats from their saddles, and tackled the noose knot, with little effect. The magpies were making loud complaint, their white and black bodies springing from limb to limb, or sailing around the gathering.

"Maybe we'll shoot a few of them magpies if they get pesky," Dogwood said. "Anyone got a scattergun?"

No one did.

Dirk felt a deepening sickness in his heart.

Two or three more drovers wrestled with nooses, but they all came undone, or wouldn't let a rope slide through.

"I 'magine we'll just have to do her with lassos," one said.

"That would be fine, mighty fine, fittin' and proper," Dogwood said. "I declare they're gonna swing from lassos. Suits rustlers mighty fine."

Two lassos were thrown over that fat limb, which disturbed the magpies even more. Some sailed by, curious about what was disturbing their gathering.

Jason drove the wagon until it was directly under the limb.

"Lady and gent, you gonna stand up for the fitting of the necktie, or do we stand you up?" Dogwood asked.

The rest of the cowboys were crowding close now, most of them on their horses, watching the proceedings with glinted eyes. One of them swallowed hard, and others were licking their lips.

"Well, don't just set there on your worthless asses, help out!" Dogwood growled. Jason was adjusting the lassos higher, but the pesky magpies were swirling around him.

"Damned birds; what's wrong with them, anyhow?"

He yelled and cussed and flapped his arms, but the magpies didn't cease pestering him, dodging his swings and fluttering close, black and white bellies and wings, iridescent feathers, and raucous chattering.

"You don't need to tie up; just roll that rope around a time or two, and it'll hold long enough to bust a couple of necks," another drover said.

"Gotta get the length right. You two stand, you hear?"

There was no escaping this. Nothing left.

"Stand up now, Granny," a cowboy said.

Victoria set aside the blanket that had wrapped her and stood quietly. A cowboy dropped a lasso over her shoulders and pulled it snug. Then he rolled the other end twice over the limb, leaving enough to hang onto if the rope slipped.

"All right now, breed boy, yoah next for the fitting."

The sky turned black with magpies. Hundreds of them, whirling everywhere. Magpies alighting and departing, landing on horses, pecking at rumps, landing on Yardley Dogwood, black on black.

"Yeouch!" Dogwood yelled, flapping at a magpie that had just pecked him in the neck. "Varmints outa hell! Chase 'em away!"

The collected cowboys howled and waved ropes and waved arms, but the magpies only whirled closer. One landed on a horse's head and began pecking the eyes of the horse. It screeched and sawed its head, but another began pecking its rump until the horse began bucking.

A dozen landed on a cowboy's horse and began pecking rump and ears and nose and eyes. Another handful landed on the cowboy, pecking neck and face and hands and shoulders. The horse exploded, and birds whirled away.

"Ow!" yelled the cowboy, lashing every which way.

Another army of magpies descended on other horses, pecking rumps and heads, necks and withers, while still more landed on cowboys' hats and shoulders, splattering white stuff over the horses and men, cackling all the while, until the cackle turned into screams.

Dirk sat in the wagon, agog at what whirled before him, unaware that no bird assailed him or Victoria or the dray or the wagon. Victoria quietly removed the lasso from her neck, and stood watching, while magpies swirled everywhere, wheeling into combined bombardments, assailing one horse and rider after another, until most of the horses were wheeling and rearing and pawing, and cowboys were tumbling off and running away, pursued by still more birds.

"Stop this here wicked business, bloody birds, or ah'll

whup you Texas-style," Dogwood cried, but a magpie landed square in his face, its claws clutching his big nose, and began pecking his eyes and cheeks. He screeched, and tumbled backward, his hands finally flailing the bird off.

Birds sailed to the ground, lashed by horse tails, only to wallow back to their feet and flutter away, regrouping for another assault. Some magpies landed on slouch hats and began pecking at heads, working through felt to rap at skull and hair, until vexed cowboys lifted their hats to shake them off. Other magpies settled on the back of the agency dray, waiting for a chance to enter the fray again.

"Ah declare, death on all magpies," Dogwood cried, withdrawing a small revolver from somewhere in his ample clothing. But a magpie landed on his face again, pecking fiercely even as the revolver discharged.

Another cowboy withdrew his iron, this time aiming at Dirk, but a dozen magpies landed on his face and others on his shooting arm, causing it to spasm, and the shot went wild. Dirk ducked and pulled Victoria with him, but she swiftly clambered to her feet again, joy permeating her seamed face.

No bird had touched her. Or Dirk. Nor had any bird assaulted the dray, or the wagon. Not even the dead antelope in the bed. He stared, unbelieving, at the magpies everywhere. They were no longer darkening the sky, but were ganged up on targets: a cowboy here, a frantic horse there. One cowboy broke for the line camp a hundred yards distant, slapping and howling, and then others broke, too, and then Yardley Dogwood clambered up, lifted his belly over his belt, and lumbered after the rest, chased by scores, hundreds, uncountable numbers of magpies driving them away.

The lassos hung forlornly from the great tree.

Dirk couldn't fathom what had happened but he knew they remained in great danger. There would be rifles in that line camp. He leapt to the ground, gathered the lines, got onto the seat, and urged the dray away, turning the animal directly away from the camp.

"Best get low," he said to Victoria.

She ignored him. A hundred magpies alighted on the walls of the wagon box, and rode quietly with the wagon, and dozens more settled on the back of the dray, swaying with the horse's movement.

Victoria laughed.

"I don't get it," he said.

"There is nothing to get, North Star. Goddamn magpies, they didn't like those Texans."

The magpies rode the wagon as if it were a victory parade, swaying with the wagon as it progressed.

"But Grandmother, this was your medicine."

"I'm too old for medicine."

"But Grandmother, this couldn't just happen. It's impossible."

"Then don't believe it happened."

"But Grandmother . . ." He gave up. There could not be an answer. There would not be an explanation in the white men's texts. No naturalist could explain it. And then he knew all this was something outside of the world of white men. The men huddled in the cabin would blame it on the season, or molting, or hunger, or the approach of fall, or something, anything, else.

"I will be North Star, Grandmother."

"Your father would be pleased, North Star."

"I can never tell this to anyone."

She laughed softly.

"Maybe Owl. Maybe Owl would know," he said.

"Damned boy. He don't know nothing."

They drove around a shoulder, up into sagebrush, and the magpies deserted them. They took off in bunches, abandoning the walls of the wagon box, and seemed to rise as a cloud, and then vanished.

North Star watched, troubled, wanting to see them fly away. But they were gone.

He reined the dray to a stop. Suddenly he felt drained. In the briefest of time, he had gone from life to death to life, and had seen something beyond fathoming. He sank deep in his wooden seat, utterly lost to anything but the fact that he lived. Blood coursed his veins. He saw, he heard, he thought, he felt.

Grandmother Victoria leaned across and drew his hand into the parchment of her own, and held his hand. How could an eternity have come and gone? But it had, and now he was back in the world he knew. The Shoshone world, and the world of his mother, the Absaroka.

He rested, not wanting to start the wagon moving, but just to sit in static wonder in this hollow choked with sagebrush, which smelled aromatic in the moist air. Victoria said nothing, but held his hand in her ancient one, sharing wordlessly what they had seen and felt, and the mysteries of all of it.

"How long ago did Magpie come to you, Grandmother?"

"I was a girl, maybe twelve winters. Who gives a damn?"

"When you had the vision, where were you?"

"Up in the hills at a sacred place. I didn't cry for four nights and days. I just spread a robe and waited, and if a vision would come, I would be pleased. That's all."

"Did Magpie promise you something?"

"I'm too old to remember, North Star."

"Did you foresee Magpie coming into your life?"

"Hell no. I went back to the village and told the shaman I'd had a vision. He honored it, but didn't think much of it. Boys had visions. Girls, well, hell, North Star. Who knows what a woman is?"

North Star didn't understand at all, but that was fine. Maybe no person of two bloods could understand any secrets. He slapped his lines over the dray, and it tugged the wagon westward and out of the bottoms where improbable things had happened, things he would try to forget because they made no sense.

"Lots of antelope where we are going, eh?" she said.

"I hope so. Maybe we can get more." But then he realized, sadly, that his father's fine Sharps was no longer in the wagon.

"I don't have my father's rifle, Grandmother. The cowboy has it, and won't return it."

"Well, hell, boy, we got some meat to give to the People, and that's good," she said.

twenty-three

Death sat beside Dirk all the way back to the reservation. Death was there, coloring his every thought. He could think, see, feel, hear, but Death was smiling at him all the while. He felt very small.

They reached the crest of the Owl Creek Mountains, and dropped steadily into the reservation, the wagon bouncing over a nonexistent road. Victoria swayed beside him, her eyes shut, wrapped up in the old blanket that excluded him from her world.

When they reached the Wind River Valley, he thought what to do. He spotted an encampment of the People, and headed toward it. He saw a headman, old Giver, and drew up near his lodge even as others in the camp flooded his way. Victoria woke up and smiled.

"Greetings, Grandfather Giver. I've been hunting, and I've come to give you meat," he said, nodding to the antelope in the wagon bed.

"Ah! It is a good meat, and the People will have a feast,"

Giver said. "We thank you, North Star. And we greet the Crow woman."

Dirk stepped down, lowered the tailgate, and slid the antelope off the wagon, while the silent crowd watched. They were dancing and drumming in their hearts with the thought of real food, not white men's flour.

Two younger men swiftly hung the animal to a limb and set to work with knives while the crowd watched. Everything would be eaten. And the hide put to good use.

"Where did you find this antelope, North Star?" the old headman asked.

"On the other side of the mountains, Grandfather."

"Ah," said the old one. "There would be meat there, is it not so?"

"A little, but hard to find, Grandfather."

The old headman smiled. "It is a good day when we can have a feast," he said.

Dirk saw about fifteen Shoshone adults and a few children. It wouldn't be much of a feast, he thought. But to them it would be.

"We must go now," he said, and offered his farewells to the rest.

They watched silently as he hawed the dray toward the river. He found a crossing, made his way over gravel until he hit the channel, and water tumbled over the floorboards and the dray was swimming. Grandmother Victoria lifted her feet, and then they were driving up an incline and out. He wished he had his father's skill at crossing a river.

A mile farther he ran into a column from the fort. He halted his wagon and watched the trotting horses approach, by twos, and realized Captain Cinnabar himself was commanding. The column halted before the wagon, forming a wall of bluecoats on this chill day, men with elaborate mustachios surveying him eagerly.

"You, is it?" the captain asked. "With the agency wagon."

North Star didn't feel much like talking. At the moment he'd had his fill of white men, especially those with guns.

"You remember my Crow mother, Victoria, Captain?"

"Skye's woman."

"My father's wife."

Cinnabar grinned. "As you wish, young feller. And what brings you here?"

"Hunting," Dirk said.

"Looks like you had no luck."

"And what brings you with a large patrol, Captain?"

"Rustling, boy. We've had complaints. Rancher up in the Big Horn Basin says he's lost a lot of beef, hundred or more. We're going to put a stop to it. It's those Dreamers hiding out in the hills, and if we catch any with beef hanging from a tree, we'll do some hanging of our own."

"I see. My father devoted a lot of his time driving the ranch cattle off the reservation."

"Yes, and that's caused bad blood with white settlers, boy. They have long memories."

"Because my father tried hard to keep them from stealing grass from the People?"

Cinnabar grinned. "Let's just say your pa was not popular with Yardley Dogwood and some of the others up there."

"It wasn't their grass. The Indian agent is charged with protecting the reservation from outsiders. My father offered to lease reservation pasture to the ranchers up there, with the money going to the Shoshones, but that wasn't in the cards. The ranchers preferred to steal it. And also steal agency cattle."

"Listen, boy. The Indians never got their own herd

together; kept eating it. So all that grass was going to waste. It didn't hurt the Shoshones none to get it eaten down and put to good use."

"Free grass. I don't recollect that any rancher paid the Shoshones for it. I suppose those same ranchers would charge any Indian pasturing animals on their range."

"Well, that's neither here nor there, laddy. We're going to put a halt to the rustling, and if that means stringing up a few red rustlers, we'll do it."

"Without a trial? Without the Indian Bureau having a say?"

"Boy, what's unseen is invisible. It's a big, big land."

"Van Horne approves?"

"You bet your red ass, boy."

North Star wanted only to get back to the teacherage. "Guess we'll go," he said.

"Say, boy, where's your weapon? You been hunting with sticks and rocks?"

"My father's Sharps was confiscated, sir."

"Confiscated, was it? Who?"

"Dogwood."

"Where?"

"Big Horn Basin."

"You were off the reservation!"

"You have any objection?"

"No one has permission, boy."

"I am a free United States citizen employed by the bureau. I will go where I choose and take my Crow mother if I choose."

Cinnabar digested that, but wouldn't quit. "Confiscated?"

"And hanged," North Star said. "Hanged from a cottonwood."

"Confiscated and hanged. I'd say old Yardley Dogwood botched the job."

"Ask him. Good afternoon, Captain."

North Star hawed the weary dray into a walk, and drove past the staring troopers.

"That's sure a yarn, Skye," the captain said, bawling at North Star's back.

He heard the captain stir the column into a trot, and then the sound faded away.

North Star found some pleasure in the confrontation. Just let Dogwood try to explain how magpies ruined his necktie party. Let him talk about stringing up the old woman and the youth, only to be set upon by a thousand angry birds. He laughed. Victoria sat quietly, wheezing joy.

"Goddamn, I want to be there when that bastard talks to that rancher," she said. She tittered cheerfully. He laughed. They chuckled. They cackled all the way back to the agency.

He dropped Victoria at the teacherage and headed for the barns, where he unharnessed the dray, brushed it, and led it into a pen where it would find water and a full manger. He started wearily for his house but Van Horne intercepted him.

"Any luck, boy?"

"An antelope."

"Where was that?"

"Big Horn Basin."

"That was pretty cheeky, going there. Run into trouble?"

"Dogwood. He took my father's Sharps and tried to hang us."

"For rustling?"

"There was an antelope carcass in the wagon. He said it was his antelope and we rustled it. He said he owns all the deer, elk, coyotes, wolves, and mosquitos on his range, too."

Van Horne stared, not knowing what to say. Then, "Glad you escaped. Dogwood must be getting soft."

"Maybe he saw an apparition," North Star said. "Maybe he saw things that can't be, that aren't in this world, and maybe it was too much for him."

"The only apparition that Yardley Dogwood is religious about is the barrel of a gun."

"Well, we're here. It was a hard trip, and we didn't find the game we hoped for."

The agent stared, uneasily. "Dirk, there's something about this I'm not understanding."

North Star shrugged. "Next time you see the man, ask him about it."

"I wouldn't get an honest answer. Of all the people surrounding this reservation, he's the most troublesome. He was cheating the Shoshones out of meat when he had the reservation contract. Your father's daily logs are filled with efforts to drive Dogwood's livestock out of the reservation, or at least charge him for pasturage. He's a whiner. He's sent his men over here to tell me our People are stealing his beef. Cinnabar's looking into it. And he's organized the ranchers into a loud voice in Washington. Truth of it is, this reservation has better grass than he's got in the Big Horn Basin, and he wants it. He's been pressuring Congress and the Indian Bureau to move all the Shoshones somewhere else—anywhere else. Anywhere that white people don't care about." Van Horne eyed North Star and Victoria. "And now you tell me you had some serious trouble. I need to know about it."

"We're back and we're safe."

Van Horne didn't budge. "You were with the Dreamers, maybe?"

"We were alone," North Star said.

"It would have taken a few dozen Dreamers, all armed, to drive off Dogwood and his crew."

"We were alone," North Star insisted.

Van Horne saw how it would go. "The Dreamers are all mixed into this. I'm sure of it. That Owl is stirring things up. I'm going to have Dogwood come in, and I'm going to get this story, the entire story, and we'll see about this," he said, shortly. But then he softened. "I'm glad you weren't hurt."

"We didn't see anyone, least of all any of the Dreamers. We were hunting on a wet morning in fog and next we knew, Dogwood's men surrounded us and took us to the boss. We were tried and convicted in about two minutes of killing a Dogwood antelope."

"And they let you go?"

"No, Major, they tried to hang us."

"Then what happened, boy?"

"Ask Yardley Dogwood, sir. I'm sure he'll be glad to tell you all about it."

"Dogwood's not a man to retreat from anything, Skye."

"He didn't retreat from hanging us, sir. He'll tell you the story."

"You're not talking. On second thought, I'm going to drive over there and talk to Dogwood and his crew myself. I won't have him threatening my agency people. I'm going to listen to his side of it, and draw my own conclusions. I'm as tired of him as your father was."

North Star smiled. "He's at the south end of his range, in a line camp there. And if you go, I want my father's rifle back. They stole it."

North Star felt the agent staring at him as he headed for the teacherage. He found Victoria busy at the stove, nursing a newborn fire and stirring up some johnnycake batter.

"The agent's sniffing around. He knows he hasn't got the story, and I'm not going to tell him," he said.

Grandmother Victoria smiled.

"Even if Yardley Dogwood were to tell the agent exactly what happened, no one would believe him," North Star said. "Magpies? A thousand magpies stopped a hanging?"

"I don't know what happened, either. Goddam magpies, what were they doing, eh?"

"But Grandmother. Magpie's your spirit helper."

"I ain't seen a magpie in a long time. I'm too old, and them magpies, they don't give a damn. Them magpies, they're just waiting to pick my bones." But then she smiled. "Goddamn, I'd like to be there."

She wheezed, chuckled, and poured the batter over the skillet.

North Star was riven, as usual. The Indian in him was hiding a whole universe, an entire cosmology from the white men. The white man in him couldn't begin to fathom what had happened in the southern reaches of the Big Horn Basin, and why that entire flock of magpies flew into a hole in the sky and disappeared.

What could a two-blood man believe?

twenty-four

Beneath a golden moon, Owl trod toward an alpine ridge. The silence was as deep as his loneliness. The boy carried only an ancient robe, wanting nothing with him that was wrought by white men. A few streamers drifted past the moon, but the night was mostly clear and cold.

He came to the ridgetop where he would seek the vision, unrolled the robe, and settled quietly upon it, cross-legged. He closed his eyes, letting the world drain away from his spirit, ignoring his chilled flesh, which puckered in air cold enough to turn water to ice. The suffering was good; his triumph over the suffering wrought by cold was even better. After a while his flesh seemed to fall away from him, and there was only his spirit, at one with the black bowl above him.

The moon transfixed him, a pale orb with none of the sun's warmth. But the moon was the lantern of the Gray Owl. It was full and mysterious and rich with promise this icy night.

Owl lifted his arms toward the moon, but prayed to the Owl, dreaded specter of the Shoshones.

"Owl, you came to me when Mother Moon drove Father Sun away. You told me to take you as my spirit guide. You told me never to cease crying for you. You told me to dream of yourself, the Owl, and to take the name most feared by all my people.

"I have done these things. I have taken your name. I have told my story to the headmen of the villages, and to the warriors and boys. We all dream of you and dance to you. We are Dreamers, awaiting the time of newness, when the white men will leave our land forever.

"I have waited for you. The Dreamers wait for you, and drum for you, and sing for you. We have let the world know that Owl is coming, and Owl will make all things new. When Owl comes, the soldiers will go away. When Owl comes, the ranchers will drive their herds away and the buffalo will return. When Owl comes, the trappers and farmers and white people who live in wooden houses will go away. The earth will shine, and the buffalo and bear and elk will return.

"That is what you showed to me that hour when Mother Moon defeated Father Sun, and the world grew still and dark. I have done all things that came to me in my first vision. I have gathered the Dreamers in the mountains, where we celebrate your coming. I have sent messengers to other Peoples, Bannocks and Nez Perce and Paiutes and Arapaho, telling them of my vision, that all white men will go away where they make their camps, as well as where my People make their camps.

"Now, Blessed Owl, my heart cries for a vision. My mind cries for a vision. I want to take back to the Dreamers what I receive from you this night. I want to tell them that the time has come. That the Dreamers will drum and sing as the white men go away. That the buffalo will return, great black herds grazing where the cattle grazed, our meat, our life, our shelter, even as we had known in the times of our fathers.

"Blessed Owl, we are not far from winter, when the snows will fill the valleys that have been our refuges, when the Dreamers can no longer hide from the eyes of white soldiers. When the Dreamers can no longer find food or make lodges or stay warm, or escape through the snowdrifts to reach better places. The time is growing short. This is the moon of the frost. Any time now, the cold and snow will drive us out of our refuge.

"Owl, please give the word, begin the times when the People will be as they were in the times of the fathers. Owl, I plead with you now. I have come to this place, far from the Dreamers, and await a sign from you. Hurry! Do not forsake your servant, the very one known as Waiting Wolf, to whom you imparted a message in the time of the black sun."

Owl's prayer flooded out of him almost miraculously, drawn from something so deep inside of him that it didn't need rehearsing. It simply rose to his lips, and he cast his words into the air, and stared at the moon as he pleaded for his vision.

They were waiting for him, far below. He had told them he would seek a vision, and was sure that the Gray Owl would hear his pleading. He would return with news. They had watched him hike up an obscure trail, walking closer and closer to the bowl of heaven. They were cold. Food was hard to find. The army was prowling, pushing into places the soldiers had never gone, looking for the Dreamers.

And soon there would be no meat, when snow lay on the earth recording every print of hoof and moccasin, making visible that which had been furtive and invisible all these moons. It was time to plead, and never stop pleading, because the Dreamers were on the brink of dissolving, filtering back to their villages to starve with the rest of the Shoshones, the people of hollow bellies and gaunt faces.

He saw only the cruel moon glaring back at him, and knew he must have patience, though he was wildly impatient, the spirit in his young body aching for news from the Great Gray Owl that had promised him a new world.

He settled back on the robe and stared at the moon, letting himself be transfixed by its relentless glare as it traversed the black sky. He ignored the cold creeping through his limbs, making his legs hurt and his hands numb. If the Gray Owl demanded that he suffer, then he would gladly suffer until the Owl saw that the boy had suffered and proved himself worthy. He would be worthy; he would ignore the ache, the killing numbness.

So he sat on the cold robe and stared at the cold moon and the cold mountains and the cold valleys, and waited. This night the Owl would grant the thing that all the Dreamers waited for. He was sure of it.

Time passed slowly. He stared at the moon and it stared back, and finally it passed zenith and started to slide away, and still the boy waited, so cold he could no longer feel his legs and his arms hurt as if someone were poking his flesh with porcupine quills. Once, when he could not endure longer, he stood, lifted his aching arms toward the black sky, and cried out. "I am your messenger. I am ready to carry the Word back to the People! I am ready to die! I am ready to do your bidding. I am ready and have waited, Gray Owl."

But there was only silence and cold and darkness.

Later he stirred, for he could no longer ignore his body even though he tried, and he stood and paced and lifted his arms. He cried and sang his own songs, celebrating all owls and his new name and his mystical mission. And then he sat again on the frosty robe, and didn't move until the eastern horizon began to blue, and the moon vanished from the heavens.

The boy debated whether to leave. His pleading had gone unanswered. Some youths fasted and endured as many as four days, but he was numb and angry, too. The Gray Owl had not come with the promised word. He dreaded going back to the camps of the Dreamers with no word. He dreaded the things he would see in their faces, the sharp glances. They all followed their own roads. But somehow the boy knew this would be different, after months of dancing and pleading, and night music, and visions of the world they had lost and hoped to regain.

He stood bitterly, seeing the eastern skies redden and turn gold. Finally Father Sun blazed over the edge of the world, and Owl's bitterness turned to hurt. He picked up the ancient robe, wrapped it over his shoulders, and ignored the immediate warmth it gave him. He paused one last moment, doubtful, debating whether to stay on through another sun, or two suns, or three . . . and reluctantly started down the long trail to the valleys below. Owl felt the frost of the morning lace his legs. There would be warmth in camp where small hot fires would burn, their smoke dissipated to nothing amid the towering pine trees. His shame was fierce in him. He didn't know how he would face the Dreamers, grown men, hard and strong.

Then, even as he slid along the trail, a thought came to him as softly as the brush of an owl's wing, a feathered thought that took flight in his mind, a thought that brimmed with power. Yes, the Gray Owl had come after all, the Owl had brought a redeeming message, the Owl was his spirit guide after all. The thought grew large in his heart, and bloomed in his mind, and Owl knew that he had been visited by the feathered one, who had brushed its wings over the face of the boy. His blood danced through his body, his pulse lifted, his eyes brightened, and he danced down the trail, more alive than he had ever been in his short life.

He walked into his encampment, and instantly everything stopped, and the world was gazing his way. The Dreamers were still at breakfast and the smell of boiling beef rose from the black cookpots hanging over tiny fires. They stared. The spring in Owl's gait must have told them something, because they soon gathered at the center of the encampment, along with some runners from the other Dreamers, scattered through the misty mountains. They had all been waiting, and he would not disappoint them.

Owl knew well how he appeared to them. The boy had vanished and the man had risen into his flesh, and that was good.

"I greet you, my brothers," he said.

"Grandfather Owl, we greet you," one replied.

"You are waiting for word. Owl went off alone to plead for a vision, and now Owl has returned alone, and you are waiting for word. Have you eaten?"

"Not yet, Owl."

"Then we will celebrate and I will eat with you."

Eat! That meant that his pleading had ended; he had word. He would take food with them all. They collected closer, wanting not to miss a word. He saw his friends, men with whom he had shared moons in the mountains, and now they watched him sharply, missing nothing, their glances boring into him.

He raised an arm, welcoming them all to hear him, and soon every Dreamer in that remote camp crowded close.

"The spirit guide brushed me with his feathers this very dawn, my friends. The Great Gray Owl, most fearsome of all the creatures on the earth, above the earth, below the earth, and in the waters, has spread his wings over his servant who is one of the People."

He paused. A deep silence ensued.

"The time is coming when all the white men will go away, and the buffalo will run in great herds, and the earth shall abound in elk and deer and wolves and coyotes and sheep and hares. I know this to be true. And there will be a sign. And the sign will tell all the People that the moment has come, and the sign will be known to all the Shoshones, and known to all the tribes in this land, to the north and south, east and west. This sign will signal the end of the white man. He will drive his cattle away. He will leave his houses. The soldiers will march east to a distant place. The missionaries will be stricken, and their false words will vanish from this land. And soon Father Sun will shine for the People, and Mother Moon will glow for the People, and all will be as it once was."

He stopped, letting them digest all this good news, and he would not be rushed.

But then it was time to reveal the great secret, to let them bury it in their hearts and live with it ever more.

"I have the word, and it is good. This time will come at the very moment that Owl dies. When Owl dies, and begins the Long Walk, the People will be freed."

The silence lay so heavily on this group that not even a bird sang in the morning light.

"I do not know when this will be, when life will be taken from me so that the People may be given a new life. But soon. Soon."

This met with even more silence. "The white missionaries have their Jesus. The People have Owl," he said, pointing at his chest.

He stood patiently, letting their gazes probe him. He wished to be probed by all their gazes, so that they might see Owl in his moment of glory.

"Go to your clans, your people now. The Dreamers will disband for now. Return, and wait. Filter back to your wives and grandparents and children, and be among them, and wait. Dance the Dreamer Dance now and then, in the quiet of the night, but wait. Wait for the sign. Wait for the time when Owl is sacrificed for the People. Wait!"

twenty-five

Prescott Cinnabar was determined to put an end to it. He would stop the Dreamers cold, and stop the cattle rustling that neighboring ranchers were howling about. If there was lawlessness on the reservation, he'd mete out whatever punishment was necessary.

Toward this end he had assembled a formidable force, which included cavalry from Fort Laramie, and had divided them into flying columns, one of which he would command. The ranchers were angry. The Dreamers threatened to start an uprising. That brat of a boy, Waiting Wolf, was stirring up an evil stew.

This time, by God, the United States Army would chase every Dreamer out of the mountains. And in the process, stop at every camp and village and settlement and put the fear of the army into the redskins.

It was, he thought, an enjoyable enterprise, and it delighted him to be in the field while the weather held and his encampments were pleasant.

"Whenever you reach a village, look for beef. If you find

hide or bone or beef, we'll have the culprits," he told his subalterns. "Catch the devils red-handed." He laughed at his own joke.

He had formed them into three columns, two south of the Wind River, one north, and when they reached the mountains, they were to probe every glade and glen and hanging valley, and if possible drive the reprobate Dreamers toward the other columns, and then they'd herd the Dreamers like cattle back to the agency for some sharp disciplining.

But so far, there was no sign of anything illicit at all. The starving villagers had no meat and were subsisting on snakes and frogs. In a few lodges there was a little jerky, old and dried, the traditional emergency food of these people. Elsewhere, the soldiers discovered a little pemmican in parfleches. His men hunted vainly for cowhides, hanging meat, fresh leather clothing, new moccasins, cattle skulls or horns, hooves—any evidence at all of recent rustling. But there wasn't any of that.

The rancher who'd complained the loudest of all, Yardley Dogwood, kept escalating the accusation. At first he was missing a few cattle; then thirty or forty. Then a hundred. The last time he sent word to Major Van Horne, he alleged he had lost several hundred.

But that was the way the game was played. Cinnabar didn't doubt that the rancher had lost a few animals, but the inflated numbers were nothing more than a way to lodge a claim against the Wind River Agency for a lot of beef. Still . . . the army must act. And if the Dreamers were eating a cow now and then, the Dreamers must be brought to heel.

But the Shoshone villages seemed innocent. The columns marched into one after another, finding no meat or bones or hides. The one thing they did discover was that many of the young Shoshone males who were supposedly up in the mountains dancing through the nights, were living quietly in their villages. It was a puzzle.

The column rode into one camp on the Wind River and at once the Shoshones stood to watch the soldiers in smart blue coats and forage caps, clank and clatter into the quietness of the camp. This camp, perhaps a dozen lodges and wickiups, was somber. The ancient lodges sagged; even the newer canvas lodges looked worn and soiled. The people looked no better, most of them virtually in rags. They were mostly barefoot. They were gaunt, too, their cheeks hollow, their legs spindled, and their arms like twigs. Slowly, almost fearfully, they collected as the column rode in and stopped smartly. For an odd moment, there was only silence, except for the whispers of the chill breeze.

No headman appeared, and Cinnabar wondered whether the chieftain was sick. But there were a few younger men, their copper chests unadorned, perhaps because they had little to wear. The captain studied the surrounding trees, looking for hanging meat, and he checked each lodge, looking for a cowhide staked to the barren clay. He saw nothing from astride his chestnut mount. Maybe a search of the surrounding bottomlands would yield more. He would think about it.

But the younger men interested him. They stood quietly, their faces masked. They were not welcoming but neither did they seem hostile. Cinnabar studied them; they looked so much alike it was hard to separate one redskin from another. But there was one who interested him.

"Walks at Night, it is good to see you," he said.

Walks at Night nodded.

"And I do believe your friend there is Mare. It is good to see you both," the captain said.

Mare, who spoke no English, seemed to comprehend.

"I see many of the younger men are here in the villages," Cinnabar said. "That is good."

Walks at Night simply nodded slightly.

"I believe that the Dreamers have returned," the captain said.

Walks at Night simply stared. The subchief was known to be among Owl's inner coterie.

"We're here peacefully, my friend, just checking to make sure everything on the Wind River Reservation is lawful. I'm glad it seems to be," Cinnabar said.

"The People are hungry, Captain."

"Of course they are. They threw their flour and beans to the earth and left their rations for the hogs at the post to clean up."

"Bad food, Captain. There is no meat."

"Well, that's what we're here about. The ranchers are saying they are losing cattle and that the meat's vanishing into the bellies of your people. I'm here to stop it."

Walks at Night simply stared.

"We are going to search here for evidence," Cinnabar said.

"The People get only a mouthful each moon," Walks at Night replied.

Cinnabar was growing impatient. "You could be raising your own herd. The Shoshones were given enough to start. You could be growing crops, growing hay, growing grains, growing vegetables, plowing and planting. You could be raising poultry. But where are the planted fields, my friend? Where is the herd? Where are the sheep and cattle and pigs and chickens and geese and melons and wheat and oats and barley? It's harvest time, but what have you planted or grown, eh? Why do your men sit before their lodges and gamble or stare at the sky, or talk about hunting when there is no game?"

The Indian simply stared, not wanting further conversation.

"Where are the Dreamers? Where is Owl, eh?"

"They are gone, sir."

"Gone? What do you mean?"

"Owl pleaded for a sign, and word came to him to wait. He returned from the mountaintops and told us that he had no sign. Go back to your people and wait. That is what he said. Wait for the sign."

"And you did? There are no Dreamers hiding from us?"

Walks at Night drew himself up. "We did not hide. We pleaded for a sign, and we heard none. So we left the mountains. That is what Owl told us to do, and we have done it with a heavy heart."

Well, this was news after all, Cinnabar thought. "One last question, Walks at Night. Where is Owl?"

"I do not know, Captain. No one knows. He is alone."

"Ask your friend Mare, please."

Mare listened, and shrugged and shook his head.

"We will find Owl, no doubt about it."

"Maybe he will find you," the Indian said.

Enough talk. Captain Cinnabar turned to his column, which seemed to glow. Light shattered off of metal, sun glinted on steel. The sleek horses glowed from the brushing and grooming they received daily. Their hooves were freshly shod.

"All right, we'll search these lodges and the bottoms. Look for hanging meat, cowhides, bones, and report to me. Sergeants, divide by fours. Parsons and Bailey check the lodges. The rest scour these bottoms. We'll collect upstream a mile."

Cinnabar sat easily as his sergeants took over, directing groups of dismounted blue-dressed soldiers into the bottoms. The Shoshones stared bitterly, but were helpless to do a thing about it. The grinning soldiers probed every lodge and wick-iup, taking their time, but found no food.

"Nothing, sir," one reported.

There was no meat here. It probably would be found in other camps. The captain, with his adjutant, rode briskly west, while the Indians watched silently. They were a wretched lot, and it was all their fault. Well, mostly their fault, he thought. He liked to judge matters fairly.

"Just because one camp's clean doesn't mean others are," Cinnabar said to Sergeant Wolfe.

"They et it all, sah. It's in and out of their bellies. Looks to me like they're living on snakes and birds."

"Revolting," Cinnabar said. "Meadowlark stew."

The column reassembled upstream, and rode west, a blue snake coiling through the river valley. They pounced on three more camps, and found no evidence of rustling. In one shabby lodge they did find a parfleche filled with jerky, but there was no evidence it came from rustled cattle. It could have been jerked from the agency meat ration.

Behind them, they left Shoshones of all ages and estates staring bleakly as they rode away.

When they were skirting a long root of a mountain, a sergeant pointed to distant horsemen far up the long grassy slope. Not even a spyglass helped Cinnabar identify this group, but there seemed to be about a dozen, and they were heading obliquely away.

"Sergeant, divide the command and we'll flank those riders. I'll work forward; you keep them from turning tail," he said.

In a moment the command had stretched into two arms working at a fast trot on the soft grade. By then the two columns had been spotted, and the distant horsemen milled, argued, and finally stood their ground on a naked hogback.

Cinnabar felt his mount gather its muscle for the uphill dash, and saw that his men were crouched low over their McClellan saddles, plainly making themselves a small target. But there was no evidence that the horsemen above were arming themselves. One in particular seemed to be mounted on a draft horse of formidable size, and the captain began to fathom who was up there—and maybe why. As he got closer, he saw there were half a dozen unmounted horses in that cluster of horsemen.

The two arms of cavalry and mounted infantry swiftly engulfed the horsemen. They were cowboys, sitting nervously on cow ponies, their hands carefully on the pommels of their saddles. And on that dun draft horse sat Yardley Dogwood, massive, still in a black outfit, with a formidable hat shading his red face.

"Good mawnin'," he said.

"You, Dogwood," Cinnabar said.

The cowboys were being very careful with their hands, which was good. In the middle of this group were half a dozen gaunt Indian ponies, one or two of them with a US brand on the flank, horses given the Shoshones by the government. The rancher and his men had no business on the reservation and were violating law.

"It's not like it looks," Dogwood said.

"Then explain," Cinnabar said.

"We're looking for strays, and thought maybe a few of our missin' cows sort of drifted this way."

Dogwood smiled. Cinnabar laughed.

Encouraged, Dogwood continued. "Ah reckon three to

four hundred of mah mighty fine beeves sorta drifted over heah, and we're of a mind to fetch them back to the home range."

"A few days ago, it was a hundred or so."

"Well tempus does fugit, don't it? Every passin' hour, a few more of them beeves of mine seem to hanker for this good grass heah, and it is my bounden duty to round 'em up and take 'em home."

"And before that, it was thirty or forty, Dogwood."

"Well, upon my honor, Captain, I'm suffering a hemorrhage of beef of late, and it's threatening to strip me clean."

"And so you've got a rope around half a dozen beeves there," Cinnabar said. "And a rope around a few necks up in the Big Horn Valley."

"Well, they sure look like beeves to us, Captain. They got hooves and four feet and we think it's a proper trade for four, five hundred cows."

Cinnabar eyed a gold-colored stallion that was wild-eyed and restless surrounded by a hundred horses and men in blue. The stallion yanked back on the rope about its neck, and trembled.

"That cow there, the gold one, looks like it needs some milking, Dogwood. Now here's what you're going to do. You're going to get off that plow horse and you're going to grab that gold cow by the handles and milk her."

"She ain't likely broke to the milk-pail, Captain."

"Well, you Texans don't lack for trying, Dogwood. Now you fetch yourself to the ground and you milk that gold cow."

"That one there?"

"That one."

Dogwood looked sorrowful. "I gotta fess up, Captain.

That there stallion looked like a good enough trade for some of the beeves that got took."

"You're taking Shoshone horses. You're illegally on the reservation. You're in trouble."

"I never did like you blue-bellies none," Dogwood said, "but I smile alot."

"Free those Indian ponies," Cinnabar said.

Dogwood motioned, and two cowboys released the ponies, which whirled free and soon vanished upslope.

"Dogwood, get this straight. You're going to get off the reservation and stay off. If there's been rustling—and so far we haven't got any evidence—we'll deal with it. It's the business of the Indian Bureau and the army, and we'll take care of it our way. If we catch you or any of your men, or any other rancher, on the Wind River Reservation without permission, you'll spend more time in the post lockup than you care to think about."

"Wrong side won the damned war," Dogwood said.

"We're taking you to the boundary line, and you can count yourself lucky," Cinnabar said. "Don't push your luck. And next time you try hanging a government employee, consider your own neck."

twenty-six

Owl huddled in a blanket, but the bitter wind cut through it and chilled him. He waited where he always waited for food, at the shattered pine tree on the slope above the agency. His friend Tai pe, Sun, brought him vegetables and sometimes meat culled from the agency's kitchens or root cellars whenever she could. But it was always hit-or-miss, and many was the time when Owl simply went hungry because Sun could not come. She was one of the serving women who found employment from Major Van Horne to cook and clean and launder.

Now as the sun faded on a wintry autumn day, it appeared that Owl would miss another meal. He was a man; he would endure. But it angered him. He only wanted food. He stared bitterly upon the agency below. A lamp glowed in the agency window. Another glowed at Chief Washakie's clapboard home. Another glowed in the window of the teacher's house. And off in the hazy distance, a few lamps glowed at the soldiers' fort.

They would be warm and safe in their buildings. He

would endure another freezing night, a lost youth who could not go home, who had no lodge, who was hunted by the white men. He didn't know what they would do with him if they caught him, but many of the People had warned him that the white soldiers were looking for him, wanted him badly, and would take him away.

So he dug deeper into his miserable blanket and waited for Sun to bring him something, and watched the smoke curl from the chimneys and light glow from the windows of glass. Someday soon it would snow, and he didn't know what he would do then. He would not let them catch him. He felt safe. The bluecoats were all marching across the reservation, and hardly any were at the fort. The settlement below him was as peaceful and quiet and empty as if no one were there.

For a moment he closed his eyes and dreamed the settlement away, dreamed of empty fields below, with nothing but grass on them, just as they always had been before the white men came. He wanted the buildings to go away, and the soldiers to go away, and the agent to go away, and nothing but wandering buffalo there on that flat, buffalo and quietness. He did not want a bugle to sound, or a flag to flap in the wind, or a wagon to rattle, or the metal of the soldiers to clink. He wanted only the silence that was a true sign of peace and freedom.

He did not know what to do. He was alone, cut off from his people, unable to see his friends, except for Sun, who shyly slid a little food to him. No one on the reservation had any food to give him. All the game was gone and even the snakes and prairie dogs were hunted out and eaten. Only a few fish remained, but that was unclean food. And dogs. He might yet eat a dog if he were dying of an empty belly or an empty heart.

So he waited bitterly. The Great Gray Owl had betrayed him. The Owl had come to him the day the moon stole the sun, and gave him a mission and a new name. But when? An icy gust whipped his blanket open and numbed his leg. He would have to walk to restore his warmth. The nights grew longer now, and the days shrank, and with each day Owl grew more bitter and desperate. He stared at the house of the agent, wanting to kill the agent. He stared at the house of Chief Washakie, who betrayed the People and led them to starvation. He stared at the little house of Skye, North Star, filled with loathing for all the white men's ideas that the young teacher was teaching the People. Maybe he hated North Star most of all, because he was teaching them foreign ways, and burying Shoshone ways deep into the hard clay of the past.

He waited a while more, and it became clear that Tai pe, Sun, was not going to walk up the slope to the shattered pine tree. He choked back his hurt. Why didn't she come? Where else could he find food? Bitterness wormed through him as he sat resolutely yet a while more, while twilight faded into harsh blackness.

He was fifteen winters, and maybe that was all the time allotted to him. He told himself he was not afraid of death. A prophet could not be afraid of the Long Walk that would come to him. He had seen many of his age die; some as children with diseases. Some of accidents. Some of carelessness. He had seen Shoshones die for nothing at all, as if they knew their race was doomed and so they sat down and died because it was the time of the white man, and the People would be no more.

Sun was not coming. He stood, feeling the hurt of his muscles, not knowing what to do. There were caves far away where he might shelter alone and forgotten; but he would need to eat. He stood, arms upraised, and pleaded once again to the Great Gray Owl who had given him a vision.

"I do not know what to do. I do not have your wisdom, and I am not far from going away forever on the Long Walk."

He listened to the silence.

"You have abandoned me. Where is your wisdom? Why have you gone away? You made me your brother. Am I your brother? I took your name. I am Owl! Now it is dark, the hour of the owl. Whisper to me."

But Owl heard no word, saw nothing in the cold sky, glittering with icy stars.

"I want to help the People!"

This time he received an answer. "I am the creature the People fear most." Yes, the thought leaped into him, and he wondered at it. The People feared the Owl. The Owl was evil, tricky, and a harbinger of doom.

And then the silence returned, cold and dark and cruel.

Owl wished he were still Waiting Wolf. He stood on the ridge, high above the agency, but there was nothing more. The Owl had glided off into his nether world, and Owl stood alone and cold.

He saw the light in Chief Washakie's window. The restless air made it glimmer, brighter, softer, unsteady. Owl wrapped his blanket tight and started down the long slope into the darkness. He reached the flats and trudged across them, alone on a lonely night, unnoticed by those sheltered in the clapboard houses. He passed the agency buildings, the school and the teacher's house, and continued to the house of the chief. There he stood, bitterly, until cold and raw hunger drove him up the three wooden steps to the porch. He saw the lamplight within.

He knocked softly, as one would scratch on a lodge cover to announce one's presence, but no one opened. So he rapped harder, and heard footsteps within, and the door opened, spilling light and warmth over the boy.

"It is you, my son," said the chief. He stood in the lamplight, huge and stocky, his hair loose about his shoulders, his gaze gentle.

"I seek your wisdom, Grandfather."

"Come. We are eating. I will have Leeta bring some."

Warmth struck Owl. He found the women in the kitchen, along with the chief's son, who was older than Owl. Owl could scarcely remember the names of the chief's women. He could not remember if Leeta was the older wife or not. But it was an older woman who rose at once and filled a bowl with steaming stew and found a white man's spoon for the boy.

They were not at table, as white men might be, but were sitting on wooden chairs, their bowls nestled in their laps. Owl felt the heat of the stew through the bowl, warming his numb hands. He stared bitterly at the stew, feeling defeat if he sipped one spoonful. He was Owl, and he would not eat. But he did, angry with himself as he wolfed down the savory stew, with its beef, potatoes, and some vegetables he could not identify. He ate and then Leeta filled his bowl and he ate more, bitter at himself, bitter at the kindness. Bitter at the man who called Owl a son.

When at last Owl had consumed the two bowls, he sat quietly. No one spoke. Then, with a slight nod, Washakie set things in motion. The women collected the bowls. Owl watched a thin girl, rather pretty, younger than himself, and he watched the older boy, who looked ashamed, and he watched the older women, their hair braided and shining, in their blousy dresses, drop the bowls into a pail of water.

Washakie nodded, and headed for the parlor. Owl followed, and settled on the soft couch. He preferred to squat. No one true to the ways of the People would sit in a chair. But now he sat in the couch, even more bitter because he was being robbed of his own nature.

The chief reached for his pouch and a clay pipe, and tamped the cut tobacco into it.

"A smoke, son?"

Owl had barely smoked in his life, but he nodded. All this was ancient ritual, and was a mark of peace. For now, he would smoke the pipe, even if the Owl's beak was clawing out his heart. And there was the chief calling Owl son. It tore the boy apart.

Placidly, the chief lit the pipe with a lucifer, drew on it a few times, and handed it to the boy.

It was a peace offering. Bitterly, Owl drew on the pipe and coughed the pungent smoke away. Hastily he handed it to the chief, who drew again.

And the pipe passed back and forth until the charge was burned, and Owl was nauseous from the fumes. But a great tranquility was passing through him even as the chief tapped the dottle out and set the pipe aside.

There was peace. Off in the other part of the house, Owl heard the women busying themselves, but here there was peace. He hated the peace. He wasn't here for peace.

"You cried for a vision," Washakie said.

The boy remembered his lonely night on the high ridge beneath a cold moon, and chose his answer carefully. "The Owl came and told me to wait. I sent the Dreamers away."

"The Dreamers are in their camps?" Washakie said.

The chief knows that, so why does he ask? Owl thought.

"I sent them away. They will wait."

"They honor your vision. They would follow you."

"Yes. Whatever I said, it was done."

"And they dreamed and danced the dream that the Owl gave them, but now the Owl has said the time is not ready. When will it be ready, son?"

Owl had a sense that the chief knew exactly what had been prophesied; that Owl would need to be the Christ of the People before the white men would leave, and that his death would be the sign.

"I think Grandfather knows."

"It would be good to set me straight so that it is not a whisper in my ear."

A rage boiled through Owl. Was he a child to be ordered about? And by a chief who had betrayed his people and was now destroying them?

Still, Washakie was the chief of all the People. "The Dreamers watch and wait for the sign, and the sign will be when I begin the Long Walk, and then the People will be free, and the white men will go away forever, and there will not be so much as one wooden building standing; and buffalo will graze the grass where this post is."

"This is what the Great Owl gave you, then," Washakie said, but it wasn't so much a statement as a question.

"Yes!" The young man simmered. "Yes, the Owl gave this vision to me."

Washakie stared into the gloom outside of the windows. There was nothing to be seen. The post was wrapped in darkness, and only one lamp remained, in the house of the missionaries.

"Then it is so. You have received the gift of vision from the one creature the People fear most of all, the harbinger of bad news, and the one trickier than the coyote."

"He was true! He came when the moon hid the sun!"

Owl was seething again. No longer did he use the polite term of respect, Grandfather.

"He will save the People from the white men!"

"Is there anything else, son? You received word on the ridge, and the word is good, and you took the word of the Owl and gave it to the Dreamers. And do they still dream?"

"They wait, and sometimes they dance, in the quiet of the night when all sleep, and they wait for the time when I will go upon the Long Walk, and all the white men will fall away from here."

Owl was angry. Was the chief questioning his vision? Was the chief wondering whether Owl had received a true vision from his spirit helper? Never had Owl received such an insult. And this from a leader who was working every sun and moon to destroy the ways of the People and bury their heart. He was a friend of those white men. A friend!

The boy stood abruptly. "I will go," he said.

"Go in peace, then, son."

"Don't call me that which I would not be!"

"You are treasured by the chief of the People."

It was too much. Owl whirled away, glancing only once to see the chief standing quietly, a great sadness caught in the lamplight.

Then the boy bolted into the cold night, where silence and peace pressed him from all sides. There was only one lamp lit, in the cottage next to the mission.

twenty-seven

An ill wind was blowing. It cut cruelly through Owl's blanket, reminding him that he was poor, that he had nothing, that he was a castoff, an outcast, a waiting wolf. The agency slumbered in gloom. No moon shone.

The only lit window was in the cottage of the missionaries, the Partridges, across the empty fields, aglow in thick darkness. Beside the cottage loomed the chapel, an oblong structure painted tan, with a steeple and a cross. But the night was so black Owl could not see the steeple.

Wind whipped through his blanket. It would not cover him this night. Icy air eddied around his neck and back, and sawed at his legs. He walked toward the mission chapel, the wooden box that held all of the secrets of white men. Out of the black book of the white men sprang all their mysteries. Gunpowder and iron and glass and cloth. Out of their black book came all the laws, all the things that robbed the Shoshone people of themselves, of their own beliefs. The church was a robber, stealing his heart, pecking at his soul like an eagle pecked at carrion, tearing his flesh with its rules.

"Not true, your things," said the missionaries. "Try our way. Try the real God, not those animals or superstitions. Do not do this. Do not do that. Live in peace!"

The missionaries had robbed him of his self. Robbed his parents and his kin and brothers and sisters of their selves. Told them they could not be Shoshones anymore, but must be just like white men. Told him . . . when did they ever stop telling the People to be different?

And those missionaries never stopped telling the white men the same things. They told the soldiers what to do and think. They told the agent what to think. They told the teacher, Dirk Skye, what to think. They told the big chiefs in Washington what to think.

Almost without knowing why or how, Owl headed that way, tried the door of the mission and found it unlocked. He stepped into darkness, a faint candle scent catching him. It seemed even blacker there than outside, if that was possible. He had to feel his way around. At least the wind didn't cut through his blanket, even if it was no warmer there.

This was their holy place and he should respect it. But all he could feel was rage, because they had stolen everything from him, and from all the People. Stolen it, and no one could have it back. It was whispered that even Chief Washakie was one of theirs now, that they had come into him and cut out his spirit and taken it here, to this church, and now the chief was nothing more than a white man in dark skin.

The wind hummed, robbing Owl of silence.

Now his eyes were used to the gloom. A little starlight filtered through the windows on either side. He groped toward the altar, found a heavy brass candelabra and coiled his hand over the cold metal. The brass felt good in his hand. He carried the candelabra with him, out of the sanctuary and out of the mission church. He carefully closed the door behind him to keep the spirits locked up within. He did not want the spirits following him into the night.

He felt cold. The Great Gray Owl was watching him from some distant limb. The Owl, with its big unblinking eyes, could see through the night and see into the hearts of all Shoshones, and was peering into Owl's own heart.

Owl filtered silently across the sward, and peered into the lamplit window. The man, the Reverend Thaddeus Partridge, sat quietly reading. An oil lamp burned on a side table. On the other side of the lamp sat his woman, Amy Partridge. Their boy was nowhere to be seen. Owl stared at the pair, knowing they were absorbing more of their dark knowledge from those books. Owl could read a little, and knew some alphabet, because North Star had taught him these things. But reading was hard, and in his heart he didn't want to learn those things in the books, and he knew that reading those things would eat the heart out of the People and put them in their graves, so he didn't. He had become a Dreamer so that he wouldn't ever have to learn the secrets of the books.

Owl hefted the cold brass candelabra, and it felt good. It was heavy and that was good. The woman, Amy, paused and stared out the window directly at him, but he knew she didn't see him in the dark. And that was good.

He slipped around to the door of the cottage and opened it and stepped in, with a rush of cold air. A parlor stove was heating the room where the two Partridges read.

They both looked up at once, and saw him standing there, beholding them.

Owl knew what to do. He didn't wait. He raced toward the white shaman, the candelabra high in his hands.

"Oh!" said the woman.

The shaman didn't wait, either. He bolted upward from his chair, his blue stare fixed on Owl, and then slammed into Owl even as Owl's arms swung downward with the massive brass war club. The shaman was inside the swing, bowling Owl backward even as the brass club glanced off his back and tumbled to the floor.

Owl careened backward as the white shaman bulled into him, and then toppled to the plank floor, writhing against the shaman's thick arms.

The woman rose suddenly, knocking the lamp off the table. It fell to the floor, shattered, spreading lamp oil in a pool. Blue flame lit the pool, a circle of blue flame, growing outward. She cried out, clapped her hands, and retreated.

Owl fought but the shaman weighed more and fought harder.

"Thad, fire!"

The shaman paused briefly, saw the ring of flame, clawed his way to his feet, even as Owl rolled aside, sprang up, and raced for the door. He escaped into the night and as he passed the window, he saw the shaman and woman smothering the flame with a thick rug. Owl's arms hurt. His shoulder was torn. His ribs ached from the blows the shaman had landed. His neck was twisted. He limped, but ignored the limp.

He dared not stop. He had lost his blanket. It was cold. The Great Gray Owl had betrayed him. Owl was only doing what he knew he must do, but it had gone bad.

Owl ran past the darkened agency, hulking black in the night, passed the agent's residence, ran into a clothesline, found himself in a tangle of clothing, he couldn't say what, and grabbed some of it. One was a union suit, thick and white. Another was a shirt. He collected these and continued, his heart thumping, into the coldness of exile. He had to go away from the People, leave the reservation behind forever, run forever, never stop running, run until he starved, until he fell into a heap of bones somewhere, someplace.

He glanced behind him. The house of the white shaman was not aflame. Everything had gone wrong. Now they would laugh at his vision, the Dreamers would scorn him, the white men would chase him. The cold nipped at the tears on his cheeks.

In the safety of the dark, he paused to let his heart slow. He felt out the union suit, until he mastered the legs and arms and buttons. He stripped swiftly, got into the suit, which was too large, and buttoned it up. Maybe Major Van Horne was contributing to his comfort. That would be good. He put on his own shirt and pants, and then Van Horne's shirt over these, and he felt warm at last. He had layers of white men's clothing to warm him.

He was disgusted with himself. Why had he waited too long in that room? He should not have paused even for a moment. He knew exactly what he would find; he had seen them through the glass. But he had paused, blinked at the lamplight, and that had been his undoing, and now all the Dreamers would heckle him and tell him he was no warrior, no hunter, no chief, no shaman, nothing but a foolish boy who received a false vision he should have ignored, and from the Owl, too, most tricky and treacherous of all creatures on earth and in the sky.

He would go back and do what he must. He would drive the missionaries away forever. He would redden the earth with their blood. He would be Owl, feared by all. But it would do no good now. The white shaman was stronger and quicker than Owl imagined, and now the shaman would be spreading the alarm, getting the soldiers. Owl knew he had failed, and that rubbed his heart raw, and he bounded through the black night scarcely knowing where he would go. He must leave the reservation. He would never see his people again.

He hurried north toward the Wind River, cloaked by night, and no one pursued him. He trotted alone, ignoring his hurt leg, trotted steadily until he reached the river, and trotted along the bank until he came to a gravelly ford. There he stripped, bundled his clothing, and waded across the icy stream, quaking with cold. On the far side he felt safer, though he didn't know where the soldiers were. He dressed and continued north, a plan gradually forming in his head.

At dawn he was in a gulch of the arid Owl Creek Mountains, a gulch that took him straight north, through sagebrush and naked rock and juniper, until he began a serious ascent up tan and red rock, climbing toward the sky. He was hungry but never paused, and somehow his body did not fail him. He was energized by the rising sun, as if its pale warmth was bathing him with new life and heart.

Beyond these mountains was the basin where the white cattlemen had their herds. There would be meat, horses to steal, saddles, maybe a weapon. What more could he ask than a horse and saddle, meat everywhere, and a gun? These things would be available at any camp, where the herders picketed their horses and left their saddles and guns lying about. Then he would have what he needed, the means to ride straight to the worst of them, the one named Yardley Dogwood, and pay him back for all the times he cheated the people, stole their pasture, delivered cattle that were sick and gaunt and had no meat on their bones. Yes, Owl would settle that score, and Owl would show the white man what justice was.

He found a spring and drank and rested briefly. When Father Sun was high in the blue void, Owl started up the last, steepest wall of rock, and by dusk he stood near the topmost ridge of the mountains. The valley ahead was hidden by ridge after ridge, but even so, the trail of justice would take him downslope. He found a spring on the downslope just as dark loomed, watered there, and settled into a red-rock hollow out of the cold wind. It was his first rest since he had fled the agency, and now hunger gnawed at him. It was hard to quiet himself with his body howling for food.

He subdued himself through the night, and somehow felt his spirit floating away from his miserable body, above himself, looking down upon the boy lying on a gravel shelf, his owl heart larger than the whole universe. Much time had passed since he fled the agency.

He greeted first light by rising and lifting his arms to the glow in the east. He scarcely noticed his body; it was as if he was disconnected from it. As the light quickened, he seemed almost to float, to be free of his body. He would continue toward the valley ahead, which lay shadowed beneath the Big Horn Mountains to the east.

There on the wall of this cavity he discovered images painted by the ancient ones. Thousands of images, and most of all, images of the Owl, with big eyes, small horn-ears, a curved beak, and a square body. Owl marveled. Here was the very home of the Owl, celebrated by the ancients. Here were hundreds of images, all with big eyes, all waiting for him. He knew at once that he was destined to come to this place, and destined to receive this vision, destined to rise out of his body and float above it because it was all part of his vision, the vision he had cried for, the vision he had told the Dreamers about. He stood dizzily, scarcely aware of the body that contained life, for now he was melded into the Owl. It was as if the Owl and Owl had merged into a great spirit that he could only feel and not describe.

He sat suddenly and waited, and felt the silence and felt the truth and felt that his life had only just begun.

twenty-eight

Dirk had six students that morning, all boys. These were drawn from the surrounding countryside, and ranged from adolescents to small children. They showed up now and then, all according to whim, or maybe for reasons he didn't fathom.

The erratic attendance made instruction difficult. He could scarcely remember where each child left off, nor had he any idea what had been absorbed and what would have to be taught again. Still, he was delighted to see them file in.

Had Horse Whipper learned some English? Did Biting Bear master some arithmetic? And where was Yan Maow, Big Nose, in learning the alphabet? Dirk kept careful attendance records, but they did little good. So this morning, he resorted to telling stories in the Shoshone tongue, but stories about the white world and the people in it. He didn't know if it amounted to a schooling, but it might prepare these boys for the changes in their lives that would be forced on them.

It seemed a strange morning. There were armed soldiers

scattered around the agency, most of them wearing sidearms. The sight of all those blue-shirts disturbed the boys. They stared out the schoolhouse windows, and didn't listen as Dirk told them about how he had been schooled in a great city of the white men called St. Louis. He sprinkled English words liberally through his teaching, knowing that at least the boys would gradually become English speakers, which is what the government wanted. Still, until there could be regular classes and a boardinghouse for the students, not much would be achieved.

He stared at Otter Beard, and his friend Tindooh, and then at the earnest lad Tissidimit, and wondered what good he was doing. Was he helping them or leading them to perdition?

Halfway through the bright fall morning, he had a visitor, Pan-sook-a-motse, who was Major Van Horne's factotum.

The graying man smiled, and motioned. "Chief, he want see you quick quick."

"I'll be along, thank you."

The Shoshone left, closing the door carefully against the sharp breezes.

"I'm going to give you a recess. I'll be back after I talk to the agent," he said.

The boys would head for the schoolyard and play one of their games with a ball or some sticks, or just sit in the pale sun and take the air.

Dirk threw on his woolen coat and headed for the whitewashed agency, once again aware that there were a dozen soldiers lounging here and there, to no apparent purpose.

He passed two soldiers at the door of the agency, and found the Indian agent and several other people, including Thaddeus Partridge and Lieutenant Keefer, the newest shavetail at the post.

The agent turned at once to Dirk. "Well, what have you to say?"

"About what?"

"The murderous assault."

Dirk realized he was missing something important. "I don't know what this is about."

"I'll tell you what!" the reverend said. "Waiting Wolf is what. He walked straight in while Mrs. Partridge and I were studying, and tried to brain us, is what!"

"Brain you?"

"With a candelabra from the altar. Sacrilege on top of murder!"

Van Horne continued the story: "It's a good thing that the reverend was alert and in fine shape. He leaped out of his chair straight into the boy, so the blow came over his head and caught his back."

"Yes, and I tumbled him, and Mrs. Partridge tipped the lamp, and we had a fire and she smothered it with a rug whilst I chased that wretch out of the house. He got away, the miserable cur."

"And made off with my long johns and a shirt," Van Horne added.

"Waiting Wolf? Owl?"

"I don't care what his name is. He can change it ten times if he wants and he'll still hang. And all the Dreamers are going to hang, too."

Dirk absorbed all that slowly. "Was he alone?"

"Alone, skulking about here, knowing that Captain Cinnabar's in the field, hunting down rustlers and Dreamers."

"A perfect moment to strike!" Partridge said. "But I know my history, Dirk. The Whitmans up in Oregon. Marcus Whitman, Narcissa Whitman, slaughtered by treacherous redskins they'd brought into the fold. Doctor Whitman, who'd given over his life to helping those savages. Oh, I knew my history and didn't think twice. It was save Amy or perish."

"I somehow missed it," Dirk said.

"How could you miss it? The place was in an uproar."

"I did see the soldiers this morning."

"You must be a deep sleeper, or else you think you're not vulnerable," Van Horne said.

There was something in the observation that Dirk didn't like, but he let it pass.

"Why me? Why Amy and me and Bobby?" Partridge asked. "Why not a soldier, or the agent, or the schoolteacher, or one of the civilians at the post? I'll tell you why. Because I'm a priest, and everything I say and believe and preach is a threat to the savages. They know it. That boy knows it. He started up the Dreamers, with a vision of getting rid of us. And it's clear that he's after the church. Drive the missionaries out, and the rest will collapse. And it's true. Belief marches ahead of all else."

"Well, Thaddeus, I think you're putting a little too much emphasis on religion," the lieutenant said. "The army's here and it's going to stay here, and it's going to affect the lives of the savages."

"Owl attacked the church," Partridge said. "He attacked God. He knows. He's bright. He knows that it's us against the heathen. It's our beliefs against their superstitions. So he struck where it counted. That's why I'll need protection, Lieutenant. He's decided who's his enemy, and while I wish it weren't so, that is how he's thinking. I ache to lead him toward the light, but he's committed to preserving the Shoshone animism and hoodoo. Owl, dreaded creature of those people, owns his heart, and as long as the boy's thinking that way, my family and I need protection."

"See to it, Lieutenant," Van Horne said.

"Yes, of course. We'll post a guard every night, or you can stay at Fort Washakie each night," Keefer said.

"I'd like a guard, sir."

"Where's the boy?" Dirk asked.

"No one knows. Gone. We've sent a dispatch to the captain to hunt him down, but this is a big country, and the boy has friends," the agent said.

Dirk supposed that Owl probably was close at hand, which was how he had fed himself. Owl lingered near the shattered pine above the agency, and confederates supplied his needs. But Dirk didn't feel like saying it. For some reason, he still liked Owl, or at least felt some connection with him, and wished that the youth would simply vanish, maybe head west to the farthest Shoshone bands, close to California. He'd be safe there.

"Well, Skye, you know the boy better than anyone else. Where do you think he'd be?" the lieutenant asked.

"I don't know."

"How far did he get with his schooling?" Van Horne asked.

Dirk didn't mince words. "He was the brightest one I've taught. He blotted up everything, asked questions, challenged me, and had an amazing curiosity about the world of white people. I'd say, even at age fifteen, he knows more about Europeans and white civilization than any other Shoshone, including the chief."

"Well, I didn't mean that. Could he do arithmetic? Could he read and write? Does he know English?"

"All of those things."

"Then he knows we'll hang him."

"For what?"

"Rebellion, mutiny, attempted murder."

"He hasn't killed anyone and he's only trying to preserve his nation," Dirk replied.

They stared at him, and he knew the stare all too well.

"He's a boy of fifteen," Dirk added.

"What did you teach him, Skye?" the lieutenant asked.

There it was again, a little more open this time. "I taught him that the Shoshones are a fine people, a nation led by a fine chief."

"Well, yes, but didn't you tell them that they needed to abandon their old ways?"

"Yes, I told them that there won't be more buffalo, and the old ways won't work."

"Well, Dirk, you didn't get it across to Owl," Van Horne said.

"I'm here to gather intelligence, Skye. You know the boy better than anyone else. What's he going to do next?" the lieutenant asked.

"I haven't any idea, sir."

"Those Dreamers, dreaming of driving us out. Is he going to summon them? Has the time come that they're dreaming about? Is that why he tried to murder the Partridges?"

"His dream, as I understand it, is that the whites will leave peacefully. That's what the Dreamers are waiting for. The army will go; the agency will shut down. The private citizens will pack up."

"Why?"

"Because their God failed them. Because they will lose heart and go away."

"But no rational person would believe that," the lieutenant

insisted. "That's propaganda, but what's real is the boy's little army, the Dreamers."

"They are poorly armed, starving, and know they haven't a chance, Lieutenant," Dirk said. "This is a spiritual matter. They walk a circle, beat a drum, and sing a song of hope."

Keefer stared sourly, and smiled. "Well, I suppose you would know all about that," he said.

Dirk felt their distrust and condescension again. "Yes, sir, I do," he replied.

"This reservation's in a state of anarchy. There's a rebellion brewing. The boy's out there, calling the Dreamers to arms, and then this place will be knee-deep in blood," the lieutenant said.

"I think not, sir. This is about belief."

"I don't understand this rubbish and don't need to," Keefer said. "This is a military matter. I've sent a dispatch to Captain Cinnabar, and he'll contact the other columns in the field, and we'll put a lid on this reservation. If the savages want a fight, we'll give them a fight. If they try sneaking up in the night, we'll be ready. If they try to flee, we'll box them in. They have no place to go. They'll be spotted and reported. They haven't any food, and if they try to take some, they'll find every militia man in the area armed and waiting."

Dirk absorbed that bleakly. "He's a boy with a vision, sir. It'll all die away."

"No, Skye, Owl is a public enemy, a menace to civilization, a murderer, an organizer of sedition and rebellion. And we're going to snare him one way or another, and we're going to make a public example of him before the entire Eastern Shoshone nation."

"You'll find the people living quietly in their villages, Lieutenant."

"Yes, for the moment. Until they get the word. And then they'll take up the weapons they've hidden from us, and burn and rape and kill until no white man is left alive."

"That won't happen, sir."

Keefer stared. "How would you know, eh? How would you know?"

"I understand their religion, sir. I learned it from my mother and my kin."

"Yes, you would know, wouldn't you?" the lieutenant said. "Major Van Horne, we'll need to make some plans to prevent an insurrection. We'll need the utmost privacy. I'm thinking perhaps your teacher should return to his schoolhouse and teach his minions about the world of science and civilization."

"Why, yes, of course. Thanks for coming over, Dirk. We'll take it from here."

"Have you talked this over with Chief Washakie?" Dirk asked.

"No, this isn't his business, Skye," the lieutenant said.

"Not his business? He has the authority to prevent armed conflict. He's their chief. His word is law. He's also one of the most persuasive men in the Shoshone nation. They'll hear him."

"Well, young man, this is for the Indian Bureau and the army to deal with," Keefer said.

Thaddeus Partridge looked relieved. "Dirk, my boy, you just teach them the religious fundamentals, the Sermon on the Mount, Ten Commandments, the ways of redemption, and you'll be worth your weight in gold. Once these Shoshones see the light, things will go a lot more smoothly. You can help us here."

"I'll leave that instruction to you, sir. That's your mission, I believe?"

Partridge stared long. "It's my mission; I'd hoped it was yours, too, my young friend."

They stood around Van Horne's desk, waiting.

Dirk saw something in their faces, something in the waiting, that excluded him.

"Good day," he said.

They nodded silently. Whatever they were planning, they would not include Dirk Skye, the two-blood teacher, in on it.

twenty-nine

Owl scarcely noticed his hunger for a while. His spirit was detached from his body. He floated above the starving boy and didn't feel the faintness that stole through a body no longer his. He tumbled down the mountains, finding little to eat. The birds had devoured the last berries, and all the earth was brown and silent as it waited for the cold.

Still, he was one with his spirit guide, and didn't need his own flesh. So he walked down gulches toward the Big Horn River, where the white men had vast ranches and thousands of the four-foots they raised and slaughtered. He discovered knots of the four-foots in the groves along the river, where there was still an occasional patch of green grass.

All that day he walked along the river bottom, seeing the arid mountains to the west, and the misty Big Horns jutting high on the east. He passed cattle but had no weapon, not even a knife, nor the means of making a fire, so the meat meant nothing to him. Here in the bottoms he did find cattails, and borrowed the wisdom of his mother. He pulled the cattails from the swampy ground, collected a heap of roots, ground them to a pulp with rocks, and began masticating them. They were thick and white and starchy, and made an emergency food. They should be boiled, turned to a paste, but he had no fire and no pot and no knife. Still, the pulverized roots were ambrosia for his belly.

All that day he saw signs of the white men and their herds, but he saw no one, and slid quietly along the river, scarcely knowing where he was going. Twilight found him far north of the reservation, in country he had never seen. Then, just before dusk, he spotted light, and discovered a log building with men inside, sometimes visible through windows. And in the pen nearby were half a dozen horses, and several saddles perched on the top rail of the pen over their blankets, along with some tack, including bridles and one saddlebag.

Ah! He settled in a copse of cottonwoods to watch. He would be patient. Sometimes the men moved about. Sometimes they came out to piss near the river. One came out and went to a bin, opened the lid, and took a bucket of grain, oats perhaps, to the mangers and fed the grain to the horses.

Ah! This was all just fine. Dusk came slowly, but it came, and then darkness, and the tired men blew out their lamp and fell into silence. Still Owl waited. It would take them a good while to slip into a deep sleep. He studied the sky, anxious that no bright moon appear, but none rose, and he remembered that Grandfather Moon would be only a sliver this night.

He studied the horses. One had spotted him, and stared at the copse where he sat in blackness. That would be tricky. He decided to move about, let them see him and smell him for a while, so he padded near the corral until they all saw him, their ears pricked forward. But they did nothing. He slipped closer, walked around the corral while they eyed him, taking time to examine the saddles. Most of them were empty, without so much as a bedroll, but one had a sheath for a weapon, and he saw the butt of a gun poking from it.

Ah! He didn't disturb the horses at all, though he was choosing which one he would take, and settled on a buckskin mule that seemed almost friendly. Mules were his brothers, and he had always wanted one. He slipped over to the bin and opened it, discovering half a burlap bag of oats. Ah! Food for man and animal. He could grind the oats between smooth rocks, let it soak, and eat the oats. He filled the saddlebags with oats, and decided he wanted the scoop, too. So he took it and gently lowered the lid.

The horses were used to him now, but still they watched intently. He eyed the silent cabin, not knowing whether one of the men was peering out of the black window. He couldn't help that, and slowly opened the gate to the pen, letting himself in. He plucked the bridle off the rail and headed for the mule, which stood quietly and let itself be bridled. He led the mule a little to see if it was an obedient one, and then stopped where the saddle was, the one with the weapon, and soon he was yanking up the cinch and buckling it.

Then he opened the gate and left it open. It would be good to let the horses out. He led his mule into the deep shade of the cottonwoods, away from the pale moonglow that had begun to brighten the land. There was more moon than he had expected, and it gave the men in the cabin good vision.

The mule tried to return to the herd, but Owl swiftly tugged it away, and somehow kept the mule moving. He let the buckskin poke its nose into his chest and sniff, making acquaintance. He checked the stirrups, which were a little long for him, he thought, but he would not do anything about that for now. Changing their length involved a lot of work, lacing and unlacing the straps.

He was ready. He mounted easily, and settled himself in the white man's saddle, and felt the mule accept him and await commands. He glanced back, and saw the horses drifting out of the pen, but not going anywhere in particular.

The odd thing was he didn't know where to go. But he thought to go to dry ground, where the hoofprints would vanish in the hard clay, so he headed west until the land rose and the bottoms gave way to sagebrush-dotted slopes. No one followed. When he was well above the bottoms, he looked down on the cabin and saw no movement. The horses had drifted toward the river and were grazing.

Now at last he drew the weapon from its sheath, and found he had a repeating carbine. It was loaded with fifteen bullets. He thought he knew how to lever another shell into the chamber, but wasn't sure. He would find out how it worked once he put some distance between the men and himself. Ah! He was a warrior, for the moment. Owl felt a flood of kinship to his spirit protector, the Gray Owl that glided silently through the darkness.

He drifted aimlessly, not knowing or caring where the mule took him. He passed some cattle, and thought to shoot one, but he didn't. He had no knife to butcher with, and no flint and steel or match to ignite a fire to cook it. And perhaps the loaded carbine was intended for better things. It could kill every government official at the agency, and an army officer or two as well.

But when he reached a hogback he paused, confused. He had no plan. He didn't know where he was going. He hadn't given it a thought. The mule stood restlessly under him while he pondered. But there was nothing to weigh. His life was not in his hands. His spirit creature would take him wherever he was destined to go.

He surrendered to fate, wondering what would become of him. He eased the reins and felt the buckskin move slowly, and he turned the mule south, back toward the reservation.

He rode easily toward the Owl Creek Mountains, and found his way up the same gulch that he had descended, and found the sacred spring where the ancients had filled the cliffs with owl images. Here he dismounted and fed the mule some oats. He wasn't very hungry, but he hammered some oats between two rocks, and then left them to soak in the can, and in the morning he might have something to sustain him.

Now, though, he climbed the cliff to a high place and knelt under a sliver moon, letting the frosty air cool his body.

"Spirit guide, now I must do what I must do," he prayed.

There was no response.

"Now I must free my people," he said.

Silence greeted him.

"Now I must accept my fate," he said. "The Dreamers are dreaming, and every Dreamer is pleading with you to set my people free."

He felt numb, and it was time to descend into the hollow, where the wind would not seek him. He had a saddle blanket now for warmth.

He didn't sleep, and knew he wouldn't sleep again. But he watched the stars slide across the canyon and disappear, like mortals who slid so briefly into the vision of many eyes, and soon were forgotten.

In the morning he tried his oat mush, and it was edible but full of grit. It didn't matter, for it needed only to sustain him for a while. He shook himself free of the frost, wiped it off the back of the mule, and saddled the animal once again. By day, the mule was the color of gold.

He saw no one as he topped the arid mountains and began his descent to the reservation. He was on the loneliest road of all. He dropped into a gulch that showed signs of passage. Shod hooves had peppered the clay with prints. The soldiers had been there, but not recently. The manure was brown and dry.

Late that day he entered the valley of the Wind River, and saw many more prints of shod hooves. The soldiers had been everywhere, in thick columns, patrolling for rustlers or Dreamers or whatever it was they were hunting. But now they were not here.

He reached the upper end of the reservation, snugged against the mighty mountains, and there he found the farthest of the camps, a dozen lodges where the People struggled to survive by hunting when there was nothing to hunt. He knew there were some Dreamers living among them, and he was eager to see them.

As soon as he rode close, the Shoshone people swept out to him and greeted him with great joy, and smiled up at him. They studied his golden mule, and the fine saddle, and knew where these had come from, and laughed softly. The People were gaunt from hunger, and so ill-clad he scarcely knew how they would survive the winter. There were no more buffalo to turn into robes and greatcoats and moccasins and hats and gloves.

He discovered Mare in the camp, and greeted his old friend, one of the first of the Dreamers, and one of the most respected. He stepped off the golden mule to greet his friend with a clasp.

"Ah, Mare! It is good you are here," he said, even as the Shoshones gathered. He saw other Dreamers, too, boys and men, standing quietly, perhaps quizzically.

"I have a gift for you, Mare," he said, and untied the rifle sheath. He handed the sheath and carbine to Mare.

"Use it well, Mare. There are fifteen cartridges in it."

"You would give this to me?"

"Use it well, and dream. The time is coming now."

This evoked a deep silence, for all the People heard him say the time was at hand.

He unbuckled the saddlebags and handed them to the village elder, a man he knew who wore his hair unbraided, under a headband.

"Tindooh, here are oats. Make a meal for your people," he said. "Make tea and eat the oats."

"You have blessed us, Owl."

"Do that to remember me, Tindooh."

"We will eat and remember, Owl."

"And on this night, let the Dreamers dance."

"They will dance, Owl."

"The time has come, and you will know it when it happens, and you will be free. All the white men will walk away from here."

They gazed at him silently, almost in rapture. The gray-haired ones studied him sternly. The children edged close, so they might touch him. He gathered the children to him, and blessed them with a hand on the head of each one. The worn mothers collected their children then, and watched shyly.

It was time. He smiled at them, stepped onto the gold mule, and crossed the river. The water at the ford was shallow, and soon he was headed down the trail to the next camp, farther toward the agency. There were prints of many shod hooves on the trail, and that was good.

He found many Dreamers in the next camp, and they swarmed around him as he rode the golden mule into the center of this place, which was very close to the cold river. They studied him and his mule, and the shirt and the union suit poking through, and they remained silent, even as the people collected there.

He had no gifts to give these people except the greatest gift of all.

"I have come to tell you the time is at hand," he said. "Soon the white men will walk away. Soon the People will be free to go anywhere, hunt anywhere, and all the earth will be our home again. This night, let the Dreamers dance. And when the time comes, you will know it, and you will be free."

They stared raptly, knowing that Owl's words sprang from someplace beyond the ken of most persons. These were messages from the world beyond the living, so they listened with respect and never missed a word that Owl said.

Then he steered the golden mule away, and they smiled at him, and rejoiced at the things that would happen soon. Some followed him out of the encampment, wanting to share some of his long journey with him. They flanked him as if they were his guard, walking proudly beside the golden mule as they traversed the trail along the sparkling river. Then, after a while, he paused, nodded, clasped the hands of those that were offered to him, and went ahead alone. They didn't turn back, but watched Owl until he was out of sight and walking through the silence of a cold day.

There would be many more camps to visit, many more Dreamers to contact, before he was done.

thirty

Good times were coming. Wherever Owl went, the word preceded him. In some mysterious fashion, the People knew he was coming and stood at the edge of their camps, awaiting him and his glad tidings.

Many camps lined the Wind River, where the Shoshones could find firewood and a little food, and one by one, Owl visited them through the moon of first frost. He marveled at the greetings he received.

"Greetings, Grandfathers and Grandmothers," he said, as he rode into an encampment.

"Greetings to you, Grandfather Owl," they replied.

"Good times will come soon," he said.

"How will we know?"

"You will know when it happens. My spirit guide has told me of this. Wait for the good times."

"What will this time be like, Dreamer?" one old woman asked.

"There will be meat in every kettle, and the People will be fed, and there will be hides to make lodges and coats. Every man, woman, and child will have new moccasins to warm their feet. There will be elk and deer and buffalo and coyotes and wolves and antelope."

"And when will this happen, blessed Dreamer?"

"When the white men leave. Soon the white men will load their wagons and go away. Soon the soldiers will march to the east, from whence they came. Soon the settlers will give up, because they don't belong here, and drive their oxen away. Soon the fire wagons to the south will stop riding the iron rails. Soon the world will be as it always was and always will be, with meat enough, and the People will sing, and dance the Dreamer Dance, and take gifts to the other Peoples so that all may know that the white men have gone away."

Often they stared raptly at him, absorbing his words with hope in their faces.

"Where did you get that mule, blessed Dreamer?" an old man asked.

"My spirit guide led me to the mule and gave it to me. It was in the corral of a white man, and when I saw the mule I knew at once that the gift was given me by the creature that has entered into my heart. It is a beautiful mule, with hair the color of the sun, and when I am done with the mule I shall return it to the white man."

Sometimes some older people stared at him, unconvinced, or at least in sharp silence. He ignored them. Everywhere, the People were expecting good times, and the Dreamers dreamed.

"When will this be?" they asked in each settlement.

"Soon! Before the snow flies, before the last of the birds flies south."

"But most have flown south, Blessed One."

"Soon, soon, for I have said it, and my word is true."

"What does our chief say of this?" one asked.

"Our blessed chief awaits the word, and is silent. When the word comes that the white men are gone, he will lead us once again, and the People will be great among the tribes, and we will dazzle the other Peoples with our meat and our weapons and our strength in battle, and our warm lodges, and our good moccasins."

In one camp, where some old and powerful headmen and shamans had pitched their lodges, Owl sensed that they stared at him darkly.

"The soldiers are looking for you," said one.

"Where are the soldiers? They are not here! They marched from one end of the reservation to the other, where the Arapaho people are, and they did not find me. And now they are back at their post."

"This is trouble," another said.

"Only for a moment, and then the good times will come. Some things are destined, and all must come to pass before the good times come, Grandfather."

"And what is destined?"

"That is only for Owl to know, but you will all know when the good times begin."

An old woman came close to touch him. "You are the Beautiful One to come," she said.

"Grandmother, you have seen me wisely," he replied, touching her cheek.

"Aie! He is the Beautiful One! I have said it," she cried.

"I am what was given to me, and nothing more, Grandmother. I am nothing, but my word is true, and the word is the promise, and the People will enjoy the word."

"You are not nothing; you are everything, Blessed One."

"I came into this world with all the gifts given to a

Shoshone boy-child, and soon I will leave the world with nothing at all."

"You are leaving the world?"

"When the time has come for all to happen, it will happen, blessed Grandmother. All the People will see and hear and celebrate."

He left that camp with the mark of a prophet upon him, for he could see into the future, and he could awaken the People to the times that would come.

There were many camps to visit, and he went to them all, riding his mule the color of the sun, and he was greeted in every village with great joy, for his message has speeded ahead of him, so that the People were waiting. They brought him water and bits of meat, and he refused the meat but he took the water, and proceeded on his way, drawing closer and closer to Fort Washakie and the agency.

And nowhere was there a bluecoat soldier, for the columns had all gone back and the whole reservation belonged only to the People. He rejoiced, and steered the friendly mule downriver, and let it eat the brown grasses, and let it water at the riverbank, and was in no hurry, for time didn't matter, and all was ordained to happen the way it was ordained to happen.

And so, in the middle of a sleepy afternoon, he rode the golden mule straight into the agency grounds, and no one stayed him. He saw no one about. A thin stream of smoke rose from the schoolhouse stove, and more smoke rose from the chimneys of the agency, because the weather had turned sharp. He rode the mule to the agency, and tied it to the hitch rail, and saw no soldiers and not a soul was stirring.

He pushed open the outer door, and then walked through the antechamber to the office of the agent, Major Van Horne, who was slumbering with his feet upon his desk, and his beard buried in his chest.

The agent awoke with a start, squinted at the youth, and lowered his legs.

"Yes, what?"

"I am Owl."

"Who, who?"

"The one you seek."

"Go away, don't bother me."

"I will wait."

Owl settled in a chair while the agent stared at him.

"The boy? The Dreamer?" the agent said.

"I have heard you want me. I am returning a mule to its owner."

"Owl!" The agent yanked open a drawer of his desk and extracted a revolver and waved it at Owl.

"Guard, guard!" he bellowed, but no one was about.

"Don't you move," he said, and rumbled through the agency, looking for a soldier or two. He came back much riled up.

"All right, you, we're going to talk."

"My words are not very good in your tongue."

"We'll get the teacher," Van Horne said.

At last a sleepy clerk showed up.

"Get Dirk Skye. At once. To translate."

The clerk eyed the boy, the waving revolver, and the agent, and vanished.

They sat quietly, but light and joy were building in the eyes of the agent. Then, after a commotion on the porch, blue-shirts boiled in and swarmed around Owl. The big chief himself strutted in, eyed Owl, and barked an order or two. Soldiers patted down the boy, and then stepped back.

"You got him," the big chief, Cinnabar, said.

"I caught him sneaking around here," the agent said.

"Well, you caught the most dangerous savage in the West," Cinnabar said. "I was ready to post a reward for his capture."

"We'll defuse all that now," Major Van Horne said. "This does it."

"What are we waiting for, Major?"

"We're waiting for Skye to come translate."

"Hope he's up to it," Cinnabar said.

"Oh, he's good enough when he wants to be," the agent said.

The teacher arrived, glanced at Owl and the rows of soldiers forming human walls in the office. Owl glanced back. The teacher looked unhappy, unlike the rest. Owl smiled at him.

"All right, ask him why he was sneaking around here, Skye."

Owl understood the English. "To give myself to you," he said.

"And why?"

"It is what I must do to make the vision come."

"What vision?"

Owl smiled. "The People will be free, and the buffalo will return."

"There, you see? Insurrection from his own lips."

Dirk Skye hadn't translated a word.

Owl addressed him in Shoshone. "This must happen for all things to be. Soon the white men will walk away. They will fill their wagons and their oxen will take them away. Then the People will live as they always have. But for this to happen, Owl must give himself to them."

Dirk Skye, North Star, hesitated, glanced at the white men, and slowly translated.

"Give himself to us?" the agent asked.

"I must die," Owl said, in English.

"Well, you'll die all right, just as soon as a tribunal can convict you."

Owl smiled.

"He is fulfilling his vision, given him the day of the eclipse," North Star said. "It is not a vision of war against white men. It's a vision of the heart going out of white men, so they turn away from here."

"How do you know that, Skye?"

"The boy has shared it with me."

"You've been in touch with him? Eh, Eh?"

"Yes, sir."

"And you didn't report it?"

"That is correct, sir."

They stared at North Star, who stood resolutely.

"Ask him whether he tried to kill the Partridges."

Owl listened, and replied in Shoshone. "The shaman brings a false vision to my People, and if the false vision goes away, and white men have no faith in it, and stop believing, then the white people will walk away."

North Star translated reluctantly, as if he did not want to give these words to the white men.

"Does he or does he not admit he attempted murder?"

Owl pondered the question. "I wished that the bad message of the white man might die and so I attacked the bad message."

The agent was amused. "With a heavy candelabra," he added. "I'll take it for a confession. You think that's a confession, Prescott?"

"Sounds like a dandy confession, Sirius."

"You figure the little devil was fixing to lead an insurrection, kill us off and kick us out of our turf?"

"Sure sounds like the little devil was planning it," the captain said.

The agent turned to North Star. "Ask him if there's more of those Dreamers lurking around here, waiting to pounce."

Owl raised himself high in his chair. "I came alone."

"Alone, eh? But you've got a bloody army ready to jump. Is that it?"

"They are singing tonight, dreaming the dream this night."

"Sure sounds like an old-fashioned revolt to me, Captain."

The captain leaned over. "Ask him what happens next."

The teacher asked, and Owl pondered his reply. "This is the beginning of the end of white men's times. It was given to me by my spirit guide, who talked to my heart, who told me some things must happen, and now these things are happening, and now the world will change, and my People will rejoice and sing and dance, and lift up their arms to the sky."

The big chief was impatient. "We've got the brat. We'll triple the guard and take care of things around here. I'll convene a tribunal to convict this little bugger, and then we'll string him up. That should solve a lot of problems around here."

"The golden mule. I was given the mule, and now you must give it back. It belongs to the one who has cattle north of here. Owl is done with the mule," Owl said.

The teacher translated.

"Why a mule? The things can't run fast," Cinnabar said.

"It was given to me. The voice said, take the mule. It is the color of the sun, and I rode the sun to this place."

The agent, Major Van Horne, chuckled. "All for show," he said.

"I'll start my carpenters on the gallows," the captain said. "Right here, in the commons, that'd be a good place."

"Perfect place, Captain. Two days from now is Distribution Day, when they all come in for their monthly dole, courtesy of Uncle Sam. Now that's fitting, isn't it? We'll have us a hanging on Distribution Day."

thirty-one

They summoned Dirk as translator. At ten sharp he made his way to the post, passing officers' quarters, each a whitewashed duplex with a broad porch. Old Glory flapped in the November wind, sometimes snapping hard.

There was no chamber at Fort Washakie to convene a trial except the mess, so the tribunal would meet there. Two guards outside the door in dress blues snapped to attention as he walked in. He was on time, but the last one.

Seated at a table were Captain Cinnabar, Lieutenant Keefer, and Lieutenant Wigglesworth, all spit and polish with their long mustachios combed and waxed. A porky recorder sat at one side, pen poised. Six armed guards watched the exits. The boy sat on a plain wooden chair, surrounded by dark space, awaiting his fate. He was dressed in the rags he had worn from the beginning.

Cinnabar rapped hard with a gavel. "This tribunal is called to order. We will try one Owl, formerly Waiting Wolf, a Shoshone. He is charged with insurrection against the government of the United States, attempted murder of American citizens Thaddeus and Amy Partridge, and theft of a mule from a United States citizen off the reservation. He is further charged with inciting to riot on the reservation, the theft of cattle off the reservation, illegal hunting by an Indian off the reservation, threatening the Indian agent with death, and threatening the chief of the Shoshone people with death. How does the defendant plead?"

Dirk translated.

"I plead whatever it is that is wanted from me."

"You need to plead innocent or guilty."

Owl smiled. "I will let them decide. I have no words for them."

"He declines to plead, and says he will let you decide, sir."

Cinnabar turned to the clerk. "Enter a plea of nolo contendere. He does not dispute the case against him nor does he plead guilty."

The captain turned to the boy. "In that case we can find you guilty without contest."

Owl shrugged.

"Before we sentence you, tell us in your own words about these events," Cinnabar said.

To Dirk's surprise, Owl agreed to. He stood, and in his own reedy voice he told his story.

"Grandfathers, the People are starving. They were given a home, but they are prisoners in their home, and cannot even hunt beyond the invisible lines. I grieve for the People, for my mother and father and the children who go hungry. I grieve that the buffalo were taken away, and that we cannot hunt them. I grieve that we don't get good meat, as was promised us."

Dirk translated that, even as the youth seemed almost to

expand as he stood there in that austere room, surrounded by soldiers. His eyes lit as he began his next recitation.

"Grandfathers, on the day when moon darkened the sun, there came to me a vision, a gift from Owl, the creature we Shoshones know to be the worst of all creatures, a trickster that flies in the night. Grandfathers, Owl entered my heart and told me about good things that would lift the hearts of the People. It was time for us to dream of the good life to come, and he gave me a dance to dance, and told me to seek out Dreamers to dream the dream I was given, and so I did.

"Grandfather, we received good news. Someday, at a time still hidden, the white people would walk away from here, their hearts heavy, because this was not their home. And this would not be caused by fighting but because their hearts were heavy. We would not take up bows and arrows and guns and lances; we would wait for the white men's hearts to grow heavy, and then they would go away, and the buffalo would return, and we would have enough to eat, and all the world would be as it was."

Dirk translated faithfully, yet feeling that he could not convey the joy and hope that underlay the boy's thoughts.

The tribunal listened impatiently. Cinnabar was steepling his fingers. Keefer was tapping his fingers on the tabletop.

But still the boy continued, his reedy voice somehow turning all this into a song.

"Grandfathers, we danced and waited in the mountains, but no vision came. I pleaded with the Gray Owl for a vision, for word when all these good things would happen, but Grandfathers, no vision came to me, and the Dreamers were growing unhappy with me. I told them I am not a leader, just a young man who was given a vision, and all I could do was wait, and cry for a vision."

Dirk translated, but he could not manage to turn it into the song that was pouring from the boy's heart. His English made it all blocky and matter-of-fact, while the boy's words were flowing like a river of music.

"Grandfathers, then the word came to me, and I rejoiced to receive word from my spirit guide, and the word was that I must give myself to the soldiers, for only then, with my passage to the Long Walk, would the new world come. Then all things would be restored to the People, and the soldiers would pack up and walk away, and the men who herd cattle would go away, and the missionaries would go away, and the schoolteacher would go away, and all things would be as they were ordained from the beginning of the world. The People would have buffalo and elk and deer and antelope to eat, and a place to live beside the river."

"Skye, tell him to hurry up. We don't need to listen to all this."

"He was saying, Captain, that upon his death the vision would be fulfilled, and the white people would leave."

"Yes, yes, but get on with it."

"Grandfathers, once I heard the word, I began my long journey here, and urged the Dreamers to dance. And now the Dreamers know I am here, and they are dancing, and they know that the time has come, and that the moment I begin the Long Walk, the hearts of the white men will sicken and they will go away."

"Skye, haven't we heard enough?"

Dirk turned to the boy. "He asks if they have heard enough."

"I have said everything, Grandfathers."

"Does he want to talk about attempting murder of the Partridges?"

"Grandfathers, it was not the shaman but the bad spirits he was forcing on us that I thought to destroy."

The tribunal listened incredulously.

"This is nonsense. Has he anything else?"

"They say your talk makes no sense, Owl. Have you anything else?"

Owl's eyes glowed. "I am ready."

"Ready for sentencing?"

"When Owl dies, that will be the time when the white men's hearts fail them and they will go away from our land."

"He says that with his death the vision he had of white men leaving here will come to pass, sirs."

"Eh! The boy believes that foolishness?" Cinnabar asked.

"With his life, sir," Dirk said.

Keefer laughed, and the other officers smiled broadly.

"Anything else, boy?"

Owl stood tall, on his tiptoes, and lifted up his hands until his arms stretched high above him, as if in supplication.

That made the officers uncomfortable.

"Well, let's get on with it, gents. This fellow's not pleaded innocent, and we've heard him describe his role in plotting an insurrection, and he's admitted his attack on the Partridges, so what's there to discuss, eh?"

Cinnabar looked at each officer.

"I think we have a verdict, sir," said Wigglesworth. "It hardly needs discussion."

Cinnabar rapped his gavel. "Very well. Owl, you are sentenced to hang by the neck until dead for the crimes of insurrection against the government of the United States, and for attempted murder of white citizens of the aforementioned country. The sentence shall be executed at high noon, tomorrow."

Dirk started to translate, but the boy waved him off with a small gesture.

"It is as I was told in the vision," he said in English.

Dirk sprang forward. "Don't do this! This boy didn't start an insurrection! He never did. He didn't raise an army. He didn't question your authority. He didn't lead a mob. He didn't fight you. He didn't murder anyone, even if he started to."

"Skye, you're out of order."

The gavel cracked down.

"He's not guilty of these things. Show me his army! Show me his weapons! Show me!"

"Skye! Stop that."

"This boy had a vision. He gave his vision to his people, which is their custom. You haven't proven a thing. You haven't proven that he stole anything, or hunted outside the reservation. You haven't proven anything. Reconsider. Or let him appeal."

"I'm warning you, Skye! You are out of order."

"Take this case to the Indian Bureau! Let them review it! Don't do this!"

Cinnabar's gavel cracked down like a gunshot, and it shattered.

"Guard, take this man from here."

The guards sprang toward Dirk, who felt their hard hands clasp his arms.

"Any more from you, Skye, and I'll throw you in the brig."

The guards dragged him away. He saw Owl watching him impassively, and understood what the boy was thinking: you cannot change what is to come, which is what was given to me in a vision.

They dragged him not only from the mess, but through the outside door and ejected him at the steps.

He watched the two bluecoats, both corporals, smile at him.

The flag was snapping and cracking like a Gatling gun in the stiff cold breeze.

He headed for the Wind River Agency office, off in the distance. Sirius Van Horne had not attended the proceedings, but maybe Van Horne could do something. The army was required to heed an agent in any emergency on the reservation. Maybe, maybe, the agent would listen.

He hurried into a bitter wind, walking across a commons where the post carpenters were building a gallows. They had the uprights and crossbeam in place, and were starting on a platform and trap. They seemed to be enjoying their work, in spite of the wind.

He bounded into the agency, knocked decorously on Van Horne's door, and was summoned in.

"You, is it?"

"I have an urgent request, sir."

"For you, Skye, everything is urgent."

"They've condemned the boy to hang tomorrow. For crimes he didn't commit. He never started an insurrection. That wasn't his intent. He was only waiting for his vision. His Dreamers were inviting the future to arrive. They danced to welcome the future."

Van Horne sighed, as if he were dealing with a child. "That's nonsense. The boy is a subversive influence. He was bent on overthrowing me."

"His vision is that when he dies, the whole thing will come true. The white men will pack up and leave because they don't believe in themselves."

A malicious glint lit the agent's eyes.

"I suppose you believe that, too, Skye."

"I believe that a lot of Shoshones believe it, and will see in the hanging the beginning of a new world."

"I asked you if you believe it, I think."

"No, I don't. But I see bloodshed and sorrow if you let that boy hang. I see my people suffering, dying, all because of an unjust sentence."

"Oh, fiddlesticks, Skye. You're as silly as the redskins."

"You have the power to stop it, sir. On the reservation, you have the power to override the army. Ask them to delay this. Ask them to submit the evidence for review. Ask your bureau to look at this first."

"My oh my, Skye, and you half white, too," Van Horne said. "I'm intending to let the army do exactly what it intends. And before a good crowd of Shoshones, too."

thirty-two

A bitter wind sliced through the agency. Dust and grass and leaves fled before it, seeking refuge in calmer corners. The wind cracked and whip-sawed Old Glory, and rattled windowpanes. The wind stabbed through the ill-clad Shoshones who had gathered at the ware-house for Distribution Day. The wind would whistle through their paltry allotment of flour and beans, small parcels that would stave off starvation yet one more month.

The wind hurried around the uprights of the gallows on the commons, but the structure did not quake before the arctic air. Its crossbeam rested solidly on its posts, and below, a hinged platform awaited its sole passenger. A manilla rope shuddered in the whipping air, and at its end was a curious noose, the rope snaked around and around and around, forming a perfect cylinder.

At the warehouse, clerks told the collecting Shoshones that distributions would begin after the sun had reached its zenith, and meanwhile the People should gather at the struc-ture in the commons. The People surmised what they would witness, and gathered reluctantly, curious about the white men's ways to begin the Long Walk. Old and young collected, their backs to the wind, their shoulders hunched against the cold, their faces bleak. They watched impassively, having surrendered themselves to whatever fate was deemed proper for them by the white men. Younger men, lean and muscular, some wrapped in blankets, some in white men's jackets, gathered, too. Some carried a drum, scraped hide stretched tight over a wooden ring. Some mothers stared at the brooding uprights and platform, and chose to lead their children to a place in the lee of the wind and out of sight, where the little ones could settle on the clay and wait.

Old Glory cracked and barked in the wind, like a scolding father. Dirk waited bitterly, wondering whether he could endure the sight that would soon unfold. Victoria had squinted up at the gallows, smiled, and headed back to the warmth of the teacherage. At the opened doors of the warehouse, clerks leaned into the walls and watched. Dimly lit within were sacks and bags of provender, to be doled out to the people, a mark in a ledger for each Shoshone who claimed his food from the government. But on this Distribution Day, all of that was delayed.

The People drifted in, old couples walking, families dragging a mule or horse that would soon be burdened with sacks of flour and sugar, beans and coffee, a ration of beef and some tobacco. It was never enough. Single men stood silently, ignoring the cruel air, their gazes on the noose. No one spoke. It was not a time for speaking.

From his cottage in the distance, Chief Washakie emerged, wearing his tribal clothing, a thick blanket protecting his body, beaded moccasins, a fringed buckskin tunic, and a red band over his forehead, pinning his gray hair against the gale.

He carried an insignia of office, which he handled like a bishop's staff. His face was seamed and flinty. He looked at no one, his eyes never resting on his People, but gazing intently at Indian Agent Sirius Van Horne, who stood at the stoop of the agency, as if ready to duck inside at any moment.

Dirk watched intently. Often, these times, Washakie wore a black suit and a white shirt. But not now. Was the chief saying something? The chief walked steadily toward the gallows, all alone, a wall of space surrounding him. He was a proud and powerful man, and his gait reflected what was in his mind. Washakie glanced at Dirk but didn't acknowledge anyone's presence.

Then, around noon, a commotion rose from the distant post, and a double line of bluecoats began a march toward the gallows, their pace measured by the rattle of a snare drum. At the forefront was Captain Cinnabar. Barely visible between the two lines of soldiers was a thin, short Shoshone boy, in the rags he was wearing when he surrendered himself.

Dirk could hardly bear the sight. Owl was like a rabbit caught between walls of wolves. The boy walked of his own free will, without quaking. When the ever-growing crowd of Shoshones saw the youth, they stared silently. Dirk heard scarcely a murmur among them. But he knew that these people were finding all this strange and disturbing, and wondering why they were invited to a public murder.

Even as the column approached, Dirk fought the impulse to walk away. He didn't want to see this thing. He didn't have to endure it. He hated his own helplessness. His most ardent appeals had been shrugged off. Why were they killing this boy? What had he done but tell his people of a vision?

The column marched into the whipping wind, the force

of it flapping their coats and threatening to lift their forage caps off their heads. And yet they came, smartly in step, the snarl of the snare drum disciplining them all, except for the boy, who walked lithely without the slightest obeisance to the rhythm of the drumsticks.

Then at last the column reached the gallows, and Cinnabar found himself blocked by the presence of Chief Washakie, who stood like a mountain of granite in his path to the rude ladder that would carry the boy up to the platform.

"Chief, may I have the honor of passage?" he said.

"I will stand here all of this day, and all of this night, and all of tomorrow, forever."

Dirk sensed suddenly that the chief had reached some new understanding.

Cinnabar had the good sense to halt the column. The boy stared at the chief disdainfully, almost as if the chief were interfering with destiny. But Washakie ignored him, and began talking in measured tones.

"Grandfathers," he said, with a nod toward the agency stoop where Major Van Horne stood idly by. "Grandfathers, I have words for you. Some winters ago, your nation offered a forever homeland to my Shoshone people, from that day forward to the end of the world. Your nation offered this valley to us, and the hills beyond, to the very ridges of the mountains, for us to enjoy. And you told us that we would govern ourselves. My people would continue as before, protected from our enemies, protected from white men, too. And your agency would help my people become herders of cattle and growers of grain.

"I was made the chief of my people by their common consent, and so I am now, and so do I govern my people, and all things on this land of my people are subject to my rule. This was guaranteed in the treaty with us, my Fathers, and so I come to you with powers guaranteed by the treaty between the Shoshone people and your chiefs and fathers, to which I made my mark and you all signed.

"Now, Fathers, it is my will, in the exercise of my power as chief of the People, that you release this boy at once and let him go. That is my will, and I command it, and I have the right to insist on it according to your words on paper. I have weighed this matter in my mind, and I have decided that this boy, Owl, Waiting Wolf, has done absolutely nothing to merit taking his life away from him. This boy has seen a vision given him by his spirit helper, and he has shared his vision with the People, and his vision is that someday the white men will walk away and the People will be free.

"He shared his vision, and urged us to dream his vision, and there is no crime in it, no evil in it, no hurt in it." He loomed over Captain Cinnabar. "Release this boy at once into my custody. It is my command."

"Oh, now, Chief, this is none of your business," the captain said. "Your powers are confined to matters among your people, but this boy's committed a crime against the United States of America. So, no, I have no thought of releasing him."

The chief rose to his own massive height, and seemed to tower over the captain. "This young man will be freed. He has committed no crime. Where is his army? Where are his weapons? Who has he killed? What has he desecrated? Eh? Eh?"

"He attempted murder against white people, and that suffices."

"It is the custom of Shoshones to let the victims seek their own justice. I have commanded it. Let the Partridges seek what they will of Owl. That is the way of my people, and I require it now."

For a moment, it seemed almost as though Washakie would have his way. The captain paused, glanced at his two lieutenants, at the column, at Owl, and the gallows.

"The answer is no. You will now step aside, Washakie."

But the chief didn't budge. He folded his arms and stood resolutely in front of the fatal steps.

"Grandfather, what will be, will be," said Owl.

But Washakie stood stonily in the path.

Dirk found himself riveted. Would Cinnabar ride roughshod over the most powerful and most friendly and most far-seeing chief they had ever known?

The captain hesitated. Dirk could virtually read the man's mind. Manhandling a chief, any chief, and especially Washakie, would reverberate through the military, through the Indian Bureau, through Congress and the bureaus and the newspapers. It could cost the captain a rank or two or three.

Cinnabar bowed elaborately, hat in hand.

"Have it your way, Chief Washakie. Stand there forever if you will."

He turned to his lieutenants. "Move the ladder."

Swiftly, the command was passed along to two sergeants, who broke formation and lifted the ladder to the rear of the scaffold.

"Column, left and around," Cinnabar snapped. The bluecoats wheeled left and around, pausing at the undefended ladder.

The people stared bleakly. Now some Shoshones turned their faces away. They had come for food, and instead would feast on death.

Dirk wanted to turn his face away, too, to blot out the

next minutes, to flee. But he stood, engulfed in his own helplessness, filled less with anger than despair at a world turned so bleak that life made no sense.

The boy didn't hesitate. Owl climbed almost eagerly, as if the Long Walk were something he ached to begin, something that would free him from all the desolation he had known since childhood.

But then, from that wall of silent Shoshones, a man and woman hurried forth, the woman wailing softly, the man stern and intense. Owl's parents. Dirk barely knew them, but saw at once that they sought clemency for their son.

They reached Cinnabar, who whirled defensively to stay them.

"Why, why must you do this?" the woman asked in Shoshone. "He has done no wrong. He is good. He was given the gift of seeing."

Cinnabar, who understood not a word, said, "No, I won't."

"Let me die in his place," Owl's father said. "I will stand in the noose."

But Cinnabar had had enough. "Remove these people, arrest them. I won't have a riot here."

He did not even grasp that these were the boy's parents.

On the platform, Owl addressed them. "Blessed Father and Mother, what will be will be, for it is foreseen."

The woman, Dirk thought her name was Bitterroot Flower, groaned softly. Soldiers collected around them and led them away.

"Secure a perimeter," Cinnabar said.

At once, the soldiers posted themselves into a square at some remove from the gallows, and kept their carbines in hand. But the Shoshones stood silently, and the threat of riot was nowhere but in the minds of the white officers.

"Get on with this," the captain said.

The executioner, a certain master sergeant who plainly was enjoying his task, tied Owl's hands behind his back, lavishing a lot of cord for a small task. Owl stepped out upon the fatal trap and waited. The sergeant lowered the noose, thick and snaky, over Owl's head, turned it slightly so the knot was off center, and drew it tight. The rope was too long, so the sergeant unwrapped it from the crossbeam, drew it tighter, and anchored it.

Now there was fear in Owl's face.

"Boy, you are sentenced to die for insurrection and attempted murder of United States citizens," Cinnabar said. "Let the world witness your punishment."

He nodded to the sergeant, who peered about in triumph, and then pulled a chock. The trap swung down. Owl dropped hard, and when his feet were still a yard over ground, the rope snapped his neck, and his head jerked crazily to one side. His body flailed once, again, and then slowly sagged into resignation. The body swung gently, to and fro, twisting slightly as the rope oscillated. Dirk was sure Owl's last glance was directly at himself, and it sickened him. A youth filled with a vision had perished.

Not a sound rose from the spectators. They stared, transfixed, at this strange example of white men's justice. This was beyond fathoming. Death for no reason. Was it a crime to receive a vision from a spirit helper? Owl's parents, surrounded by troopers, slumped into each other's arms, and Owl's mother lost tears in her husband's shirt.

"Get your food now," Cinnabar said. "The clerks are ready."

But no Shoshone moved toward the warehouse. They simply stood and stared at the body gyrating on its rope, whipped by the wind.

thirty-three

Dirk found Aphrodite Cinnabar in the shadow of the schoolhouse. There were tears on her cheeks.

"I shouldn't have watched. Father told me not to, which is why I did."

"It's not something to watch."

"Now I can't take my eyes off of it."

The wind-whipped body careening on its rope had a mesmerizing effect. Owl's parents, sitting in the clay below the gallows, drew the eye also. It was plain that Captain Cinnabar had no intention of lowering the body or giving it to Owl's parents. And so they sat and waited even as the Shoshones slowly worked through the distribution line at the warehouse.

"It will be with you a long time," Dirk said.

"Yes! And I prayed it would never happen!"

Dirk wanted only to return to his teacherage and be alone. "Maybe it would be best if you went back to the post," he said.

She stood bitterly. "No, I am in the middle of this." She eyed the swinging body. "The middle!"

She eyed him bleakly, grief and stubbornness in her oval face. "Come with me," she said. "I'm going to the tree."

She meant the shattered pine tree, massacred by the Gatling gun, the place where she and Dirk had talked with Owl; the place where Owl's spirit might be.

"Aphrodite, it's cold. The wind . . ."

"I want it to be cold. I want the cold to numb my bones!"

Reluctantly he followed her away from the agency, into a gulch that rose toward the foothills. In moments they were alone, as if the agency and its grief didn't exist there. He watched her walk, her young body encased in gray gabardine, a severe skirt and severe jacket over a blouse.

She didn't speak, but hiked fiercely upward, braving the bluster of November winds that reached even into the gulch that hid them from the eyes of the world. The cold numbed him; he was poorly prepared for this.

He glanced behind, and saw the small white agency buildings, and something light as a feather waving from the gallows. The boy's body seemed to weigh nothing at all, now that his soul had left it. The food line was moving swiftly. The people were gathering up their sacks and fleeing this place where the earth had been violated. He could see them fanning out, racing away to their miserable wickiups and lodges and cabins. The agency was cursed ground, a bleak scar upon their world.

They reached the pine tree, the needles brown, the wood shattered and gray, and she found a pocket that hid them from the wind and settled into it. He joined her, marveling at the strength of her, the firmness of her jawline, the tightness of her hair coiled into a bun at the base of her head.

The dead pine shivered in the gale, the cruel wind peeling away needles and debris and bits of bark.

She didn't talk, but stared there at the place where she and Dirk and Owl had talked to one another. He knew she was thinking of that, of Owl's fierce visions and temperament.

He thought to comfort her. "Owl is free now," he said.

"I don't want to talk," she said, but she thrust her hand into his and pressed.

He had never held her hand or touched her. A half-blood couldn't do that. A breed could only stand apart, acknowledge nothing, and pretend.

Her clasp was warm, and she eyed him now, not talking but with a flood of meaning even so.

"I know," she said.

The wind seemed to ignore this hollow, or was the warmth rising from something else? He could not say.

"He didn't deserve to be hanged," she said. "He just didn't."

"He was an Indian," he said.

"But what difference should that make?"

"He tried to kill white people."

"But he didn't."

"The missionaries were messengers. It was white religion he wanted to kill."

"He had a dream, that's all."

"Of you leaving," Dirk said.

"Yes, of us leaving. He saw it. Sometimes I feel him saying that to me. 'Go away. This is not your land. You don't belong here. Go away and let us be.'"

"He awaited the vision," he said. "A promised time. The Gray Owl's promise to him. He died for it. Turned himself in for it. He showed up here. No one caught him. He simply walked in, to his death. When he walked in, he knew what his fate would be, but he did it. He knew the future, in ways that I certainly don't. And if his vision is true, his death will begin this thing he saw, this exodus of white men away from the sacred land."

She clasped his hand warmly. "It's hard to believe," she said. "I don't understand these visions. But I do wish we'd pull out. I wish my father would load up his wagons and go away. It's as if we're the aliens here, the violators. I feel like, well, an invader."

"It won't happen, you know."

"I know. It's all hoodoo."

"Yes. We are sitting next to a pine destroyed by a Gatling gun."

"Guns are the reality? Nothing else?"

"That's where I'm torn by my bloods," he said.

"Is there nothing more than gunpowder and iron?"

"I was schooled by Jesuits in St. Louis," he said. "And now I don't know anything."

"I don't, either," she said, softly.

He found himself peering into her eyes, discovering hurt and fear in them, and something else. He found himself slowly leaning toward her, even as she was waiting for him, her lips parted, her eyes an invitation.

He kissed her, his lips touching hers in a wondrous way. His arms slid around her and drew her to him, and hers responded, her fingers tentatively crossing his back, until she and he clasped each other tightly, and he felt the rise of her breast against him, and her lips finding his.

She clung to him, and her arms searched his back, and he responded with wonder and joy. They stopped kissing, and simply clung, and he felt that he wasn't alone now. Not now. At last. Grief had brought them together. They were sharing loss and desolation, and maybe love, too. It felt right to share loss with Aphrodite, to feel her cling, for her to solace her sorrows in his arms. They had found a way to grieve for Owl, and now, in their small hollow on the hillside, they took full measure of what each could give the other. He felt her cheek against his own, and felt her tears melting into his collar, and felt her sighs. And also felt their communion, for in grief they were finding forbidden love, a white woman and a breed, walking up small steps, step by step, by step, to wherever the steps might take them.

The wind shifted and burrowed between them, and tried to bite through their embrace, but no wind could push its way through, and the wind fell helplessly away, and they still clung, desperately, with a need that could not be slaked. Then, finally, she tugged free, and turned a little, so that her head could rest in the hollow of his shoulder.

"Thank you, Dirk," she said.

He wondered why she was thanking him, when in fact he ought to be thanking her. For a little while, the sorrows and griefs of the world had vanished. They sat a while more until the chill air finally triumphed, and then she stood.

"I must go."

"Will I see you again?"

"Yes, if my father doesn't send me east."

"Send you?"

"He says this is no place for a white woman to be."

"Where would you go?"

"To a finishing school."

Dirk had barely heard of such a place. "What do they finish?"

"Me," she said, a sudden smile on her face. "I am unfinished on the reservation."

"When?"

"I don't know. He and my mother tell me what they will do with me. And then I do it."

"Have you been given any choices?"

She laughed, a slight bitterness in it.

"I'll walk you home."

"It'd be best if you stayed here until I am on the post."

"I see," he said, saddened.

But she leaned over and kissed him, gently and firmly and with lips that sent messages. He returned her ardor. Then she stood, faced the bitter wind, smiled, and started down the slope, soon disappearing into the gulch. He watched quietly, knowing she would reappear below, and that in a few minutes she would be walking across the agency and toward Fort Washakie and her father's billet.

He felt bewildered. They had shared grief, mostly. They had found comfort when they reached for it. But there had been more, something that bloomed through the sadness and wrought something that would write itself on their hearts. She was the first white woman he had held in his arms. The first white woman to kiss him. The first white woman to share anything of herself with him. And she was the captain's daughter.

Below, the commons at the agency had cleared, but for the gallows and its burden twisting on manilla. Not even Owl's parents stayed; the wind had driven them off. The food line was empty, and a few clerks were stowing things in the warehouse. Van Horne was nowhere in sight. The blue-coated soldiers had returned to the post. He saw Aphrodite slip onto the parade and angle across it.

He felt the presence of someone there beside the shattered pine, but there was no one. He was alone. And yet he felt it, this ghostly presence, this spirit of Owl resting there before he began the Long Walk into the heavens.

"Yes? Yes?"

"You see, soon they will go," Owl said.

Dirk didn't believe it. The white men were here to stay; it was their world now.

"It is a good dream, Owl," he said aloud, into the emptiness of the afternoon.

"All things pass, North Star."

"You did not have to turn yourself in to the agent. You did not have to sacrifice yourself, Owl. There are many Shoshone Peoples, stretching far to the west. You could have joined them safely and lived out a good life among them."

Owl laughed softly. "The time of the white man will pass, and then the blessed mother will be as she was, and the People will remember," he said.

Then the spirit vanished. Dirk could only sense it, but somehow he knew it. Owl was gone.

Dirk started down the slope and soon emerged on the flat that shouldered the agency and fort. Owl swung in the wind.

Old Victoria had boiled up some gruel for their supper, and they spooned it down. Dirk wasn't very hungry.

He avoided the north window, which looked past the schoolhouse toward the commons, where the gallows stood in the twilight, its burden spinning in the arctic wind.

"He is not there," she said. "He is with the People."

"With the People?"

"They will remember him forever," she said.

"I don't think the People will survive," he said.

She grinned. "Goddamn, you don't put much stock in redskins, do you?"

"It's the whites I don't have faith in."

"Your father and I lived with joy for many winters, North Star."

Later, when he lay abed, unable to sleep, he heard a rhythmic drumming, slow and steady, the sound of a heartbeat. He sat up swiftly, knowing he was hearing the Dreamers. The Dreamers were dancing this night, dancing their Dream Dance, their dance of pleading for a new world, a world like the one that was lost, Dreamers dreaming the promise of Owl's prophesy, that the white men would go away, and the People would live peacefully on their own land.

Sometimes the drumming seemed close at land, as if the Dreamers were circling the commons. Sometimes Dirk swore the drumming rose from the post. Sometimes the Dreamers seemed to dance before the agency buildings. Sometimes the Dreamers drummed a circle around his schoolhouse. Sometimes the Dreamers faded into silence, only to return. Sometimes the drumming rose from Chief Washakie's house out a ways.

He heard shouts, and knew squads of soldiers were hurtling this way and that, hunting down the Dreamers as if they were elk to be shot. But he heard no shots, no scuffles, no sounds other than hurried hooves clattering by. But the dreaming had stopped, and the night fell still, and a quietness returned not long before dawn.

Dirk didn't fall into sleep again. He lay abed, listening for the Dreamers, but with the dawning in the east he knew the Dreamers were gone, far away, off to their miserable huts and lodges and cabins.

When the light had quickened, he peered out upon the commons, and discovered that Owl was gone. And that the gallows had been dismantled and lay in pieces on the hard clay. The People had Owl.

thirty-four

Once again the schoolhouse was empty. That morning, Dirk opened the doors and admitted no child. What parent would send a child to the agency at such a time? From the school windows, a child could see the commons, see the dismantled gallows lying on the clay. No doubt the mothers and fathers of those little ones thought the children might see something else dangling in the wind.

In fact, there wasn't an Indian in sight at the Wind River Agency. The winds swept over the clay, scouring it of horror. But Dirk supposed it would take a lot more than snow and rain and wind to purge the commons of its memories, now scorched into the minds of the Shoshone People.

The school seemed hollow, and exuded a sense of failure. For years, he had struggled to teach the few children who did show up the knowledge they would need to survive in a new world. But he hadn't thought to teach them that the penalty for failing to learn white men's ways and beliefs could be death.

He built up the fire against the cold, and waited for some

student, any student, to pull open the door and slide into the warmth. Often, Shoshone mothers had sent their children without a lunch, knowing that Dirk and old Victoria would somehow feed the child. And somehow the schoolmaster always did, finding room in his salary to supply some oat gruel or a few boiled beans to the hungry child. He thought maybe it could be considered a bribe: send your child to school and a hot lunch will be waiting.

But on this cruel November day, not one student appeared.

He fought off melancholia with dreams. If the students couldn't come to his schoolhouse, maybe he could take school to the students. Take a wagon out and spend time in each settlement, gathering students around and teaching what he could. That was an old dream he had nurtured ever since he learned that the Indian Bureau lacked the funds to build a boardinghouse for students. There would not be much education on the Wind River Reservation until the Shoshone young people could be housed right there at the agency.

But it was an idle dream. His contract required him to be present daily, to open the school every weekday morning, and to maintain the building. Many an idle day there was naught to do but read, but he was always in peril of running out of books, and had borrowed what few of them he could scrounge from the officers at the post.

Live students were such a prize for him that he had taken delight in them, nurtured their curiosity, worked swiftly back and forth in the two tongues, encouraged them, fed them, listened to their joys and sorrows.

But not this day.

There were no books at hand this day. The seven-day clock ticked slowly. The woodstove consumed its fuel and started to cool, but he threw another log into it. He would write, then, as he sometimes did to blot up time.

Letters. There were things that needed attention at this melancholic post so far from Washington City. Yes, write letters about the demoralization of the Shoshones, their near starvation, their lack of support from the bureau. He could write of Chief Washakie's efforts to bring his people into a herding and farming way of life. He could write of the problems posed by deeply felt beliefs, vision quests, the glory of hunters and warriors, the role imposed on women, the need to help these people into different worlds.

He wished Aphrodite would come to help out in the classroom, as she sometimes did. She didn't know Shoshone, but she could show them numbers and lead them through arithmetic and give them English words, and help to feed them when Victoria showed up with some beans or soup. But this day she was nowhere to be seen, and who could blame her?

Still, he yearned for her to arrive, with her usual smiles. They could while away the day, as they often did, and it would be good. He always felt himself melting into her sweetness when she was there, and now he wanted that all the more, especially after they had clung to one another up at the shattered pine tree, sharing a sorrow that deluged both of them.

Letters, then. He unstopped his ink bottle and collected pens with good nibs on them. Letters, but to whom, and about what? Who was he, to send missives to distant bureaucrats? He gazed out the window toward that sorry commons and discovered a work detail from the fort gradually loading the murderous timbers into two wagons. They were simply bluecoats, doing the task assigned them. The two draft horses yawned and waited. The men, working under that executioner sergeant, whose skills had just snuffed a life, were nonchalantly lifting the uprights and settling them onto a wagon bed. Then came the crossbeam, with a severed rope still wrapped to it. Other men were knocking apart the platform planks and loading them. The trap was intact, and the soldiers lifted it onto the planks. Thus did they remove the engine of death from the agency. Soon a Shoshone could walk into Major Van Horne's lair without being reminded of the powers that white men held over him.

Dirk discovered Chief Washakie standing at the far edge, watching, watching, as the death machine was turned into timbers.

He thought to write the Indian Bureau about all that but decided against it. Not just yet. The mails would be thick with messages to and fro, from the agent, from the captain, from the ones in Washington City who presided over flour and sugar and beans and death.

Where had the Dreamers taken the body of Owl? Surely to some secret place well hidden from the eyes of white men. And what would they do with it? And what would they think about it? Every one of them had heard Owl's prophesy: when Owl began his Long Walk, then would the white men be filled with doubt and they would leave.

Would the body be placed in a sepulcher, like the body of Christ? Would it vanish, its whereabouts known only to a few beloved brethren? Dirk ransacked all that he knew of his mother's People, and couldn't say. But he felt sure the final resting place of the boy, forever known as Owl, would be kept utterly secret, and utterly sacred.

He would write the men in Washington City about food—or the lack of it. And how the agent kept the People imprisoned; they could not leave the reservation to hunt without special permission, and that permission was rarely forthcoming. The People needed meat. And he would write about a tribal herd of cattle, one that could supply the People with meat each month once it was built up. And about the theft of pasture and cattle by surrounding ranchers, and about the bitter reality that little was done about it, and the People suffered.

Yes, it was time to write about that. Owl's death had stirred not only the Dreamers to dream again, but it stirred Dirk to do what he must to better things on the reservation, no matter what the risk. So he settled down at his desk, nib pen in hand, and addressed his first letter—there would be many, he thought—to the commissioner in distant Washington.

Dear Sir—

A clatter on the steps halted that. He discovered Agnes Throw Dog, one of the clerks over at the agency.

"The major, he wants you quick," she said.

"I'll be along."

She stared at him, as if she were privy to something bad.

"He's lit a cigar," she said.

That was bad. Whenever the agent fired up, things were bad.

She fled, and he watched her hurry through a gloomy morning and vanish into the agency. He had never been sure of Agnes's office over there, and suspected there wasn't any.

He stoppered his ink and set aside his letters. There would be time for all those, and he wanted to weigh carefully every word he set to paper.

Somehow, he didn't like this. He pulled a coat over his stocky frame, and plunged into the cold, reaching the agency moments later. The agent was waiting, his cigar chomped at one end and pointing upward at the other.

"Sit, Skye," he said. "There's bad news for you. The bureau's canceling your teaching contract. You're done."

He hadn't seen it coming. He thought he had done a good job. It hit him right in the heart.

"Out? But why?"

"Well, they think you're not adequate."

"But why?"

The agent smiled slightly. "You know as well as the rest of the world that you've hardly advanced a student. You haven't put a single student though. The whole lot are as dumb as the day you opened your doors."

Heat built in him. The school had no boardinghouse. "That's not the reason, Major."

"It's one of the reasons. Young man, you've got a lot going against you, and the bureau thought to do something about it."

"Such as, sir?"

Van Horne sucked hard on his cheroot, until its end glowed orange and crackled.

"You weren't following our goals, boy. You're supposed to be giving 'em a white man's education. You're supposed to be turning them into farmers and ranchers—and believers in what we believe in: democracy, religion, the United States of America." He eyed Dirk. "Some think you're not even a citizen, not even a true-blue Yankee."

"Half-Indian?"

"Well, no redskin's a citizen, you know. And you're no more than half of one, and your pa, the Londoner, he switched pretty near at the end of his life. So, no, boy, you weren't in there promoting the best interests of the Indian Bureau."

"Then why was I hired?"

"Favor to your old man, I imagine."

"Who—"

"Wires have been heating up twixt Fort Laramie and Washington City for some while, boy."

That was as much an admission as he would get out of Van Horne.

"Was this because I schooled Waiting Wolf—who turned himself into Owl?"

"That came up, yessiree."

"Owl's vision was peaceful, sir."

Van Horne's cheroot wiggled violently.

"He started a coup. That little brat was fixing to overthrow the government of the United States, and it was pure luck that we caught him in time."

"Caught him? He walked through your door."

Van Horne straightened. "I'm not here to quibble, Skye. Pack up. You've got forty-eight hours."

"To go where?"

"You're an enrolled Shoshone, but that don't mean I'll hand out chow to you. Next thing I know, there'd be another rebellion around here. You'd be the next lightning rod, Skye. You and that old crone, you fetch yourself out of here and don't come back. I'll take the schoolhouse key right now."

Dirk handed it to him.

"And don't go in there. Leave the records."

Dirk stood, shaken. His world had collapsed.

"You have some cash of mine in the agency safe, sir."

Wordlessly, Van Horne opened the black enameled strongbox and handed Dirk his greenbacks, the paltry savings from years of teaching Shoshone children. It didn't come to much, but any cash would help him now.

Then, oddly, Van Horne relented a little. "You'll need to take the old woman off. She can enroll up at Crow Agency. I imagine they'd put her on. She's a card, Skye."

Dirk rose, nodded, and stepped into a different world. The only home he'd had since his schooling in St. Louis was no longer a home. His mother's people were suddenly beyond his reach. His uncles and cousins were severed from him. His mother's grave and his father's grave would no longer be near.

A fierce heat stole through him. This was not about teaching. This was about the other things, and especially about Owl, and that dream of a world restored to his People, the world they dreamed of. Dirk knew what it was. His dark skin, his mother's cheekbones, his mother's ways and beliefs. They had hanged Owl and cashiered the half-blood young man who had once schooled the youth who had started the People to dreaming.

And now young Skye would merely be frontier riffraff, the same as a thousand other breeds, a man who would swiftly be forgotten.

It was a chill November day. He stepped into a different world, and crossed to the house he shared with his Crow mother, wondering what she would think, and what they would do and where they would go, and whether she could survive a long cold trip. It would soon be December, and she was as ancient and frail as papyrus.

thirty-five

Never had Dirk spent so restless a night, one haunted by dreams, regrets, loss, and mysterious terrors that lay beyond any reason he could summon. Several times he rose, peered into a misty night, swore he heard whole ghostly choruses singing, and then tumbled into his bed no more comforted than before he rose.

His old Crow mother had simply smiled at the news that Dirk was no longer the reservation's schoolmaster. Sometimes he didn't fathom her, and he thought she was getting a little daft. But her eyes were always keen, her comments often sharp, and he sometimes thought she was simply strange.

"Now we are free, North Star," she told him.

"Free and penniless," he replied.

"Many lodges would welcome us."

But these night phantasms that were discomfiting him as he lay wrapped in his blanket were a wolf howl rising out of his Shoshone roots, and not his English ones. He could see nothing amiss outside. A cloud cover obscured even starlight, and there was nothing in the walls of black outside his windows to suggest unrest.

He was annoyed with himself. He wanted to be a modern white man but his Shoshone blood spoke to him of other, older, things. The chasm went deep. Aphrodite had seen it, but he didn't think anyone else had.

With the quickening of light piercing the overcast, the restlessness outside quickened, too, and he resolved to dress and patrol the agency, because there was something, a force or spirit, alive there. He poured water into a bowl and splashed his face and wiped it with a towel, and that would suffice. He hurried into his cord britches and a green woolen shirt, and then into the soft moccasins he usually preferred to white men's shoes, and opened the door.

It was hard to see what was seething there, small movement all across the agency commons, things disordered, out of place, wrong. He peered into the murk and discovered that the agency swarmed with people. He saw entire families, grandparents, mothers, fathers, infants. He saw old couples sitting side by side on blankets. He saw young men congregated into silent cohorts. There were women collecting in knots, settling on cold clay. The air was so chill that their breaths were visible. Old ones wrapped themselves tightly in striped blankets. No fire warmed these people, and for a while Dirk could not fathom why they were present.

These people were not chattering, not shouting, not engaged in activities such as cooking or fire building or raising lodges. They were waiting, waiting, waiting, their gazes shifting from the agency buildings to the distant Fort Washakie. They were calm and yet expectant. They studied Dirk as he stood in his doorway, but mostly they watched the fort, and Van Horne's darkened house. As the light quickened, so did these people, and they moved about for warmth. Dirk thought there might be two hundred of them, a significant portion of the Eastern Shoshone people, and they were waiting for this momentous day.

Waiting for what Owl had said would come upon his death. They were waiting for the white men to pack up and leave, for that was what the young prophet had announced would come to them now. The prophet had been sacrificed; now the great exodus of the whites would begin. If not this hour, or even this day, it would be very soon. And they would be witnesses.

Dirk watched, absorbed. These were people with their own vision of heaven before them. Had not this vision come from the most sacred source, the Gray Owl, speaking clearly to the boy who had taken the bird's name? These people would wait, and wait, and wait. They would wait through this day, maybe the next, maybe the day after that, until cruel reality sent them back to their camps and settlements.

By some means, they had gotten Owl's word, and the word was that this would be the great day, and so they had filtered into the agency all through the night, and that was what had made Dirk's night so restless. The Shoshone nation had arrived. There seemed to be almost a physical force in their presence, as if hundreds of hearts and minds were all focused on the inevitable. There was something grand in this, for he was witnessing the fruits of faith. Some of these people had come a dozen or more miles through the darkness to greet this special day in this sacred place. This would be a sacred day, the most holy day in all the history of the People, and now they were waiting for this magical thing to begin. They were not dancing, nor singing, nor shouting. Instead, they were spectators, gathered to witness a change in their world.

For a moment, he wondered whether it would all come true; the soldiers and agent would go away, their lives fallowed. There had been mysterious power in Owl's prophesy, which tugged at Dirk's soul. But he knew that would not happen. He wondered whether he should walk among these spectators, he who was half-white and half-Indian, and perhaps caution them. He decided not to. As the day wore on, they would see for themselves that the soldiers were not packing up, and the agent was not loading his worldly goods in his wagon and driving away. Let them see the white men living their daily lives, and maybe then the People would drift to their villages.

Still, this was a large crowd and a volatile one, and he sensed there could be trouble. So he wandered through the multitudes, addressing many by name, greeting them kindly. Here was Elk Hoof. There was old Feather Falling. Here were the families of the Dreamers, those who had dreamed and danced, and whose beliefs had spread among their kin. Here were watchful young men, thinking of good times ahead.

They were waiting for the dawn. When Father Sun came, their world would shine.

"Skye!" yelled Van Horne, who was standing on his front stoop. "What's this? Come here."

The agent, dressed in a gray woolen robe, stood barefoot on his porch, astonished at the throng spread across the agency commons.

Dirk hurried to the man who had fired him.

"What is this? I demand to know what this is. An insurrection?"

"They're waiting for the sun, sir."

"Why? Why?"

Dirk wondered whether he could even explain this event to this alarmed man.

"They are waiting for their world to be restored, sir."

"Restored? Make some sense, Skye. None of your mysterious red superstitions!"

By now, the throng was ignoring Major Van Horne, and staring eastward at a pink streak across the horizon, heralding the arrival of Father Sun.

"They believe the prophet, sir. That's all there is to it."

"Is this a rebellion?"

"Look closely, Major. Do you see warriors? Do you see bows and lances and rifles? No, you see families. You see old men and children."

"They could have arms hidden in their blankets, Skye."

"I suppose they could. Maybe the children have Gatling guns in theirs."

"Which side are you on, Skye?"

There it was again.

"I will be leaving tomorrow morning," Dirk said.

"Tell them to disperse, and right now."

"They are doing no harm. By nightfall, they will leave on their own. When they see that Owl's vision wasn't true they'll quietly go back to their lodges."

"I want them out of here right now."

"Tell them yourself, sir."

"I'll put it in your record that you've defied me, Skye."

Dirk grinned.

Van Horne glared at him and paced. He was plainly growing more and more alarmed. He shot glances at the tranquil crowd, which was now watching intently. He glanced at the bronze men in their worn blankets, where weapons might be concealed and death might await for the agent.

"This is rebellion. And I'm going to stop it," he said. "These savages are about to start a slaughter. I will not be their sheep."

"Owl's prophesy was that the hearts of the white men would grow heavy, and they would leave because their spirits were heavy, Major."

"That's savage nonsense. This is trouble, Skye. And you're not helping me."

"I just did help you, sir. You have killed their Christ; they're waiting for their salvation. What more is there to say?"

"Killed their Christ? That rotten little rebel? Killed their savior?" He cackled at the sheer novelty of the idea.

The Wind River agent whirled into his quarters and slammed his door. Moments later he emerged wearing a topcoat over his nightclothes and brandishing a revolver. Then he strode purposefully toward Fort Washakie, under the thoughtful gaze of the Indian families.

The sun was peeking over the rim of the east, bathing the agency in a pallid light. Some of the Shoshones greeted Father Sun with uplifted arms, and sang a morning song of praise and joy for the new day. The natural world was quiet, and the breezes had not yet built. Now, with dawn, the slumbering fort came into view.

The quickening day promised joy to the people, and they gathered to gossip, watch the world, make jokes, and enjoy all the good things to come. Children drifted from group to group, while their mothers told jokes and smiled. Grandparents, wrapped tightly in tan and black blankets against the relentless wind, watched keenly, awaiting the moment when the whole world would be changed. For if Owl had said this would be, then surely it would be.

Dirk eyed the shadowed post, wondering about all this,

and supposing that nothing much would happen. But he was wrong. About an hour passed, and then a blue column emerged from the military compound, soldiers on foot, marching by twos, heavily armed. The agent hiked alongside, with several officers. Captain Cinnabar was at the forefront, a shining sword slashing at the breezes.

Now the Shoshones watched with fascination. Was this the great moment when the white men would depart? So they sat on their old blankets, watched, and waited as the blue column marched straight toward the agency and the festive Indians there. When the column neared the crowd, the captain shouted, and the bluecoats trotted into a battle line, over a hundred armed soldiers evenly spaced, their carbines at the ready but not aimed at anyone or anything.

Now, at last, the Shoshones gazed silently. This didn't look to be a departure of the white men. Far from it. Dirk felt a certain dread creeping through him. How could this be? What madness was this?

Chief Washakie appeared at his front door, wearing a collarless white shirt and a red headband and dark pants. He stared at the advancing troops, and then strode purposefully toward Captain Cinnabar, and engaged in some sort of confrontation with the post commander, all out of earshot. For once, Washakie seemed agitated, while the commander stubbornly stood stock-still.

The wide blue line stood at the ready, soldier after soldier poised for battle.

Then the line advanced, a slow, measured pace that brought it close to the idle throng, which watched curiously. It had not yet occurred to the people that the white men regarded them as a threat, and now they watched with cheerful curiosity. Who could say what white men would do or believe or say?

Dirk raced suddenly toward Cinnabar.

"What is this? What are you doing?"

"Out of the way, Skye. You're in the line of fire."

"Line of fire!"

"We deal death to rebellion, Skye, now get out while you can."

The line stood at the ready.

"These people are here to enjoy the day! What rebellion?"

"Under every blanket there's a gun, and you know it, Skye."

"Women and children? Old men? This is crazy!"

"I'm warning you, Skye."

Major Van Horne rushed up, waving his big revolver.

"Your last chance. Get out or face the music!"

The bore of that revolver looked large to Dirk.

"This is no rebellion. This is a holiday. As soon as they see that Owl's prophesy was false they'll leave. They'll drift away. They'll go back to their villages. They mean you no harm. Don't do this."

Van Horne simply chuckled, something anticipatory lighting his face.

Washakie raced forward and stood between the soldiers and the people, his gray hair whipping in the stiff wind.

"You will kill me first," he said, standing his ground, arms crossed.

The Stars and Stripes cracked and snapped in the wind.

Behind him, the people were stirring now. The festive morning had suddenly turned dark, and some of the Indians were fleeing as fast as they could, dragging children with them. Dirk saw mothers dragging children. Fathers pointing away. He saw old men and women clambering to their feet.

"Yes!" Dirk cried, taking his stand beside the chief.

Now the whole tribe was up and running, abandoning blankets, and lunches and shawls. Fleeing in terror, fleeing toward the distant meadows, where bright tan grasses awaited the snows and the world was clean and sweet, and no bullets would fly.

Cinnabar finally paused and stared at Washakie. Kill the chief for whom his post was named? Kill Skye, until yesterday the Indian Bureau's teacher?

"They're leaving," he said. "No need to use force."

"But you already did," Dirk shouted. "This was their home."

"Well, you'll be off the reservation soon enough," Van Horne said.

"Not soon enough for me," Dirk said.

He watched as the grandfathers and grandmothers, the most lame and slow, trailed along behind the fleeing crowds, even as the bluecoats grinned.

thirty-six

Dirk stood in the ill wind, wondering what he had done. The American flag chattered in the breeze. The soldiers dispersed, except for a squad Captain Cinnabar left behind to guard the agency against further insurrection and treason.

Chief Washakie stood beside him, his face granite, watching his beloved people vanish from view, fleeing the dark bores of carbines just as fast as they could. They had left their debris on the frost-browned grass, a desolate tangle of old blankets and robes. There was no weapon in sight. The post slid into silence. The agent, Major Van Horne, meandered back to the agency office. He was whistling "Yankee Doodle." Dirk had never heard him whistle. A few people stood and stared.

The quiet clank of armed men walking away disturbed the deepening quiet. The agency was safe; there would be no challenges here to the world of white men, their faith, their civil order, and their possession of every inch of soil.

"They will not stop at their camps," Washakie said.

"But they are safe now, Grandfather."

"Safe, North Star? Many will slip over the mountains before the storms stop them. In a few suns, many will join the People at Fort Hall."

He was speaking of the Northern Shoshones, settled there on a similar reservation.

"They will leave you, Grandfather?"

"I am old," Washakie said.

"The army will only force them back here," Dirk said.

"Death there, death here, death somewhere else," the chief said.

The old chief stared into Dirk's face. "You stood with me, North Star."

"I had to."

"Then you are a chief. After I begin the Long Walk, you will be chief."

"I am leaving here, Grandfather."

"I know. I have heard. And you will return."

Dirk knew that he would return. His mother and his father were buried only a few yards away. Their graves would tug him back to this patch of earth for as long as he lived. And so would this valley, which he called home. He remembered the first time he saw this valley after years of school, and knew that this was his ancestral home, this place of his people, this land and water and ridge and meadow where his Shoshone people had found their peace.

"Yes, Grandfather," he said. "I'll return."

"When I first saw the white men, I wished to know what they know and be what they are. They are clever and make things from metal. We did not have a wheel or an iron arrowhead or a gun until they brought these things to us. We did not have blankets or cloth. We did not know of the one great

God who made all the world. And they were kind. Your grandmother, Sacajawea brought the captains who came here, and we have been friends of the white men ever since. I have been a friend of them all. It became plain to me that they could give us a better life. We needed their iron, and wheels, and the marks they put on paper. We could grow grain, herd cattle, plant gardens and orchards, as they do. These things are better than starving in winters. So I became their friend, and begged them to teach the People."

He stared at the post. "Come with me, North Star."

The chief strode purposefully toward the distant army compound, whitewashed frame structures around a parade ground. The flapping flags chattered like Gatling guns. Dirk fell in beside Washakie, sensing something important in the very stride that took them swiftly over naked ground. Ahead, soldiers were returning carbines to the armory, heading for latrines, collecting in the mess. Sergeants prowled everywhere; officers had vanished.

"We will find the captain," Washakie said.

He steered Dirk straight toward the headquarters, easily distinguished by the chattering American flag and regimental colors.

"You will do two things," Washakie said. "You will witness. And you will put the marks on paper, just as I want them."

"I will do that, Grandfather."

A sentry at the porch halted them. "State your business," he said.

"I am Washakie."

"Do you have business here?"

"I am Washakie."

The force of the chief's gaze won the day. "Proceed, Chief. The captain's in."

They passed an adjutant, Lieutenant Lawrie, and found Captain Cinnabar lounging at his desk, staring placidly out the window.

"Ah, it's you!" he said, waving the chief into his lair.

Cinnabar seemed uncommonly cheerful. "Now, what may I do for you, my friend?"

"Fort Washakie is named in my honor. I decline the honor."

"What? What? We've honored you as a great friend of the United States."

"You will not use my name. Give the post another name."

"But what's done is done, Chief. We're proud to honor you. This is the only post in the whole country named for a chief."

"I will not give you my name."

The lanky captain rose, stared at the granitic chief, and shook his head. "Not in my power to do that, my friend."

"I will take back my name now."

At last, Cinnabar seemed perplexed. He didn't need or ask for reasons. "Well, my friend, I think if you just let this ride a few days, you'll come around to know that we've tendered our highest esteem in this. Just give it, oh, a couple of months. That will give us all some perspective, eh?"

It seemed for a moment that Cinnabar had triumphed, even as the old chief stood quietly. Then, "I will ask Mr. Skye to record my request with your marks on paper. Then I will submit the paper to you."

Uneasily, Dirk glanced around, looking for a nib pen and a sheet of paper, and saw only an empty blotter, ink bottle, and pen on the captain's desk.

"The adjutant will have the paper and pen, Grandfather," Dirk said.

He stepped into the outer office.

"A paper, ink, and pen, sir," he said.

The adjutant glanced sharply at Dirk, and then produced the necessary items.

Dirk returned. Cinnabar, preferring to stay civil, simply watched as Dirk laid his paper on the captain's utilitarian desk, along with the writing tools.

Dirk dipped the nib into ink, and tapped it carefully because he lacked a blotter, and sat, poised.

"I think, Chief Washakie, that you may prefer to go through channels," Cinnabar said. "I'd suggest you take this matter to the agent, Major Van Horne, and he will accommodate you."

"You are the army," Washakie said, standing unbudged.

He turned to Dirk. "Make the marks. I do not give my name to this post. I do not permit this. It must not be Fort Washakie. My name is a good name, and I will keep it for myself. It is not for others."

"I'll request the change," Dirk said.

"It is not a request. I take back my name. It is a good name, and it is given to an unworthy place."

Dirk wrote slowly, formulating the chief's thoughts, and finally read his letter to the chief, while Cinnabar stood, bemused. "To the United States Army. Dear sirs. Fort Washakie was named for me. It is my wish to take back my name and not give it to this post. Herewith, I do not agree to giving my name to any military post. It is a good name, and doesn't belong on a military post governing the Shoshone people. Washakie is not a name for the army."

"If that is a good way to say it, let it be said. I will make my mark."

Washakie took the pen and drew an X at the bottom of the letter.

Dirk added, "His witnessed mark," and signed his own name.

"Now make another like it, for me to keep," Washakie said.

Dirk copied the first letter, and Washakie marked it, and kept the copy.

"Now, Captain. It is done. I take my name back. Call this post whatever you will."

"I'm afraid, Chief, it's not that simple, but I will forward it up the command."

"I will do this. If you do not take away my name, I will choose a new name, and the old name will lie in the dust, gone from me."

Cinnabar eyed the paper as if it were a lit firecracker. "I'm going to give this some time, Chief. I think you might come to reconsider."

"You will not send it to your commanders?"

"I think you'll want time to rethink this, Chief."

Washakie turned to Dirk. "I will send the duplicate, then."

Cinnabar recovered whatever aplomb he'd lost. "Well, sir, I'll mention it to Colonel Brackett, at Laramie, and leave the matter in his hands. Meanwhile, we're honored to be at a post named for a great chief, and great friend of the American people."

"An hour ago you were on the brink of slaughtering your friends the Shoshones."

"Stopping a redskin revolt, yes. But we're all grateful it didn't happen."

"Are you?" asked Dirk.

Cinnabar stared, and in the stare were manacles and leg irons and jail bars. "I gather you'll be off the reserve tomorrow. Let us say, away from here before sundown. After sundown, you will be subject to whatever discipline I wish to impose, in order to preserve the peace, and for as long as I choose to impose it."

Dirk smiled suddenly. "You just keep on preserving, Captain."

Washakie took his time departing, and stood in innate splendor, his steely gaze resting on Cinnabar, the adjutant, the headquarters, and at last at the letter withdrawing his name from the post. It was not a petition.

He nodded to Dirk, who followed, and soon they stepped into biting wind, and the flags rattled like a rifle volley.

The sleepy post and agency of Fort Washakie slumbered. Dirk doubted that the chief's message would achieve anything. It would be handed up the command in a plain "for your eyes only" envelope, and then quietly die. Not one officer would understand Washakie's reasons, and it would all be dismissed as Indian hoodoo. Not one would question what had been done to the Shoshones, starved and virtually imprisoned on a barren land, as a reward for their allegiance and friendship with the government in Washington City. They would shake their heads, smile, gossip about this bizarre frontier episode, and talk of it over drams at the officers' clubs. And Chief Washakie would see his people die away, powerless, hopeless, and lost.

"It was Owl who caused this trouble. His vision was false, and his boy-heart was too eager," the chief said. "He brought death on his wings. He shot black arrows at me, at you, at the People. He did not hear what he said he heard. His tongue was not true."

"Grandfather, somehow I reached out to him. He only wanted to give the People what they once had."

"No, North Star! He was a bad one, and bad ones make themselves important. He took us to the cliff and we looked over the edge."

"You stopped a disaster, Grandfather," Dirk said, hoping to lift the heavy heart of the old man striding beside him.

"I stopped a quick trouble, but not the slow trouble. And you joined me; two Shoshone men against a hundred guns. You have a great heart, North Star. You will be the leader of the People."

Dirk felt uncomfortable with the praise. "We will go to my Crow mother's home in Montana Territory," he said.

"The Absaroka are good people. Go with my blessing, North Star. And think kindly on an old man who spent all his years trying to keep his people safe and well and at peace."

They had come to the true parting point, where trails divided. Washakie embraced the younger man, his worn hands pressed upon Dirk's shoulders. "I will not see you again. But someday you will return to the Wind River, and you will lead our people toward a better place. Remember me."

Dirk fought back the tears welling in his eyes. "You are my grandfather, the grandfather of blood and bone," he said.

The chief took his solitary path toward his cottage while Dirk stood in the wind, watching the man who had devoted much of his life to preserving his people.

Dirk hurried to his teacherage, even as the flag snapped at him. Old Victoria would be waiting, ready to help pack, ready to laugh at the whole world, ready to slip her ancient hand into his and hold it tight.

thirty-seven

Then came the hard moment. The wagon was loaded. The dray in its harness. The teacherage emptied of Dirk's few possessions. Clothing, books, bedding, utensils, and some beans for travel. The horse stood placidly, head low. No one else stirred. The windows in the dim white buildings were black holes.

He helped his Crow mother to the wagon, but she pointed, and led him in another direction, toward a grove of cottonwoods and a fenced graveyard nearby. Barnaby Skye's son and widow walked over frosted grass, when the air was still cruel with night. They entered the silent grounds, finding it coated with silver. There was a crystal coating over the stones and wooden markers, and the brown clay shone with ice.

Barnaby Skye and Blue Dawn, or Mary, lay side by side, with mounds of earth over them. The sacred ground on Skye's other side lay flat and undisturbed and was intended for Victoria when her hour came. It was quiet. The morning birds had not yet greeted the sun.

Victoria stood a moment, and then slid to her knees at Skye's grave, and then lay down in the frost beside him, her old arm outstretched over Skye, her cheek in the frosty grass. Dirk watched her, saw love, and sat down beside his mother, Mary, of the Shoshones, and remembered his birth mother when her eyes were bright and that sweet smile caught her lips. He felt a strange attraction to the very earth there, felt it draw him toward it, felt that if he should abandon that place he would be torn inside, shredded, an alien wandering an alien land. This would always be where his spirit lived.

Time stalled, and he sat quietly while Victoria whispered things known only to herself. She struggled to her feet and approached Mary's grave, and stretched herself beside Skye's younger wife, her arm caressing the frosted grass, making patterns in the crystal ice. Victoria's spirit was wherever Skye was, wherever Mary was.

The eastern sky lightened a little, a layer of salmon along the edge of the world. Dirk helped his Crow mother to her feet. She wiped her hands on the woolen skirts she chose to wear this bitter day, and nodded. He offered his arm to her, and she took it, and together they padded back to the teacherage and the wagon waiting there.

He looked at the load; all he possessed and not much at that. Much of his salary had gone to feeding lunches to his students. He had a few double eagles hidden there, and a few greenbacks, but that was all he had to show for his years in the classroom. His reward had been the few who learned a little, who might be better equipped to prosper in the new world of the white men. But those were half a dozen, and as he stood at the wagon, he was engulfed with a sense of failure. It had all come to nothing.

He helped his Crow mother to the seat in the wagon, and

drew a robe around her. He was about to climb up beside her when he heard his name, softly and sweetly.

It was Aphrodite, hurrying toward them, a shawl over her shoulders against the bitterness.

"Dirk! I'm so glad I caught you. I've come . . . I've come to wish you Godspeed . . . Godspeed to you both."

She was lovely standing beside the wagon in the salmon light. Her face was gentle and her lips soft and he discovered sadness in her eyes.

"Aphrodite. Thank you. I've enjoyed knowing you," he said, staying away from more dangerous ground. There had been the blossom of love.

"I've enjoyed you, too, Dirk."

"I guess you're going east soon," he said.

She nodded. "It's been arranged."

"I guess we won't be seeing you again," he said. It was safer to include Victoria.

A fleeting sorrow crossed her face. "I wish it could be otherwise, Dirk—and Mrs. Skye."

He wanted to hug her. He knew she was forbidden to see him. But there she was.

"We had good times together," he said.

"Yes! And we accomplished things together. We taught. We helped these people. And you stopped a slaughter. That's where it was heading. You are one of the blessed."

That must have been hard for her to say. She was talking of her father's blue line of soldiers.

Reveille sounded at the distant post, mournful in the frost.

"I must go!" she said.

She slipped close, folded her hands upon his cheeks, and kissed him. He started to hug her, but she slipped away.

"Good-bye Dirk!"

And then she fled. He watched her hurry back to Fort Washakie.

Then he climbed aboard the wagon and settled himself next to Victoria. She eyed him sharply, and then reached across to kiss his cheek.

Twice this dawn, he had been kissed.

"I want to visit my people," she said. "Take me to the Absaroka."

He pulled on gloves, lifted the lines, and slapped them over the croup of the dray, which jerked into motion. He drove toward the Wind River, not turning back, not permitting himself a last look at the cluster of quiet white buildings, their eastern walls pink in the long light. The iron wheels ground over clay, leaving twin streaks through the frost as he drove away from his only home.

He didn't know where he would end up. First to his Crow mother's country, but then what? He was a two-blood, and there was little room in the world for people of two bloods. He wasn't a white man; he wasn't a Shoshone. Even less was he a Crow. He was not welcome at the Wind River Reservation. He might not be welcome other places. He was not welcome at Aphrodite Cinnabar's home. He remembered her farewell with a sigh. He remembered the few quick hugs and tender kisses that had comprised their starved intimacy. He remembered the sound of her voice, and the tug of her hands. Now she was gone.

He felt low. He had failed to school the Shoshone children. He had failed to stop Owl, or prevent his hanging. He had left nothing behind him, no improvement among the People, no skills that would help them ranch or farm or enter business—or deal with the new world imposed by distant people in Washington.

"You'll show those bastards a thing or two," Victoria said. Her seamed face was wreathed in smiles.

He wasn't so sure, but he liked her approach.

All that long day the wagon creaked and pounded over frost-hardened ground. The going was easy because the earth was firm, and there were no mud holes or heavy grasses to slow their passage. He rested the dray now and then, not wanting to lame or weary their only source of transportation. The draft horse was old, but sturdy, and seemed tireless as long as it could move at its own slow pace. So Dirk let it.

They forded the river and Dirk steered the dray toward the Owl Creek Mountains, the route that would drop them into the Big Horn Valley once again, and past the ranches there, filled with men who had no use for people of any color.

Victoria must have attuned herself to his thoughts.

"I got Skye's revolver right here," she said, "and I'll put a hole in anyone gets in our way, especially that Yardley Dogwood."

"You read my mind."

"I have medicine. And I have many years."

That night they camped in a wind-sheltered hollow. The weather held, and the camp seemed pleasant enough. The next day they descended through red rock country into the Big Horn Basin, which stretched into the northern haze. And not far beyond that would be Absaroka country, Yellowstone country, the other home of the Skye family.

Those rocky slopes had some mystical quality that resonated in Dirk. They passed ancient picture drawings, brimming with strange images, sometimes painted over the images underneath. What was there about being a mixed-blood that tugged him in two directions?

They reached the arid basin of the Big Horn the next day,

and Dirk immediately headed for Owl Creek. The iron tire on the left front wheel was dangerously loose. They made camp among naked cottonwoods. As soon as Victoria was comfortable, Dirk blocked up the wagon, pulled the wheel, and rolled it to a sandy bank and settled it in the cold water. By morning the felloes would swell and pinion the tire.

"You want to soak in the hot springs tomorrow, Grandmother?" he asked.

"If I get in there, I'll never get out," she said. "Skye and me, we went there a few times. It sure started his juices flowing." She wheezed her delight at the memory. "But I was young and damned good looking."

"You still are, Grandmother."

"I remember all the boys who wanted me. Who played the flute. Who threw their blankets over us. Ah, North Star, I remember the Absarokas. To see them again—that is my dream."

They faced a long drive through Dogwood's range, or at least what he claimed was his, enforced mostly by six-gun and threats.

"Grandmother, we have some choices to make. We can drive straight up the river or we can go far around."

"We're Skyes, North Star."

That was answer enough. The next dawn Dirk pulled the wheel out of the creek and slid it onto the axle. The tire was tight. They started in a silence so profound that not even the wind whispered. There were streamers across the sky. For miles, the only sound was the clop of the dray's hooves and the grate of wagon wheels over clay and rock. Victoria seemed uncommonly bright, and Dirk wondered at it until he realized she was going home. Her Absaroka people were her home, wherever they might be. Now, at great age, she would be reunited with them, and that was as much as her heart could ever want. He glanced at her now and then, marveling at the transformation. It was as if she had shed thirty years and buried all her sorrows.

They struck the brushy valley of the Big Horn at midday and turned north, following a well-worn trail furrowed with wagon ruts. But they saw not a cow or steer or calf, and no game, either. The world seemed uncommonly lonely. He saw a few ravens, but no magpies, and wondered at it.

Toward the end of the day they found cattle sign, none of it green, but much of it recent. They were approaching the holdings of Yardley Dogwood, the fat Texan who staked a claim to the whole area, and would have snatched pasture from the Shoshones if he could get away with it. It took an army to seize and hold so much of the good earth, and Dirk knew that this rancher's army could be deadly. And yet he drove straight downriver, passing occasional pens and line shacks.

It was well nigh dusk when they raised the cottonwood log ranch house off on the horizon, which already had buttery light slipping from its windows.

"You sure?" Dirk asked Victoria.

"This'll be goddamn fun," she said.

There still were times when the old woman startled him. He hadn't seen her so gleeful in years.

The ranch yard was as large as Texas, it seemed. There was a log bunkhouse spilling light, a whitewashed board and batten foreman's cottage, and the main building, with massive cottonwood logs notched with gun ports and bulletproof window shutters. Off a way were pens and a barn and some rude outbuildings.

"Wasn't long ago he tried to hang us," Victoria said. "Goddamn, that was funny."

Dirk couldn't quite fathom where some of her notions came from. He remembered only the terror and the strange sick sensation of his imminent strangling.

No one stayed them as he drove the wagon into a loop that would take them to the ranch house. Maybe they were all eating, he thought.

At last the rattle of the wagon drew notice, and several rough-dressed men spilled through the massive door to see what was causing the commotion. Dirk circled his wagon around and parked it at the front door, while assorted Texans gazed first at him, then at the wagon, and the old dray, and finally at the brand, which was US. Dirk's horse was a condemned army dray he had purchased.

All of this sufficed to draw the rotund master of this empire to the door, where he was silhouetted by lamplight. Yardley now sported a goatee, a sure sign of status, at least in Texas. He peered into the gloom, registered Dirk and Victoria, and approached.

"Ah do believe it's young Skye off the reservation, and the old woman who commands all the magpies west of the Mississippi. Well, ah say, welcome. You defeated the Confederacy. You're just in time for dinner, but we haven't decided which of you to cook first."

thirty-eight

"Gents," said Dogwood to his cohorts, "these heah guests are my nemesis, my embarrassment, and my betters. This lady commands an army of magpies, and these miserable pests halted a good hanging and drove my entire command to disgrace. This heah gent, Dirk Skye, is the progeny of Barnaby Skye, the Indian agent who made me deliver prime beef to the reservation, and to watch my tally, because if I was one beeve short, he'd string me up by the privates. These heah are my archenemies and conquerors who have come to sup at my table and enjoy my misery."

The gents were smiling. They wore trimmed beards of all descriptions, especially elaborate mustachios, and were well manicured even if their clothing was rough. Dogwood introduced them all, saying they were his Texas cohorts during the late unpleasantness, and now ran the ranch. There were another thirty in the bunkhouses and camps round about, and a few "yellow dogs"—which Dirk took to mean non-Texans.

Dirk couldn't remember all their names, but there was a

Pickens and Smithers and Bannister and McGinnis and Peck. In turn he introduced Victoria. "She was born Many Quill Woman of the Absarokas, and was captivated by my father soon after he quit the Royal Navy and entered the fur trade in the twenties. I owe my life to her, because my father was a one-woman man and only her insistence that he take another wife resulted in his finding the Shoshone who became my mother."

"Goddamn, I was stuck with all the work until he got another woman, and then I had someone to boss around," Victoria said. "I wish he'd gotten half a dozen more, so I could be lazy, but Mr. Skye had all the women he wanted."

"Well, sah and madam, you'll see none around heah," Dogwood said. "I don't much care for 'em. Now, come set. We've a slab of beef out of the stove, ready to slice—prime rib, medium to rare, sprinkled with salt, to be specific, that being all we've got to eat around here, which is a bore. So grab a plate, slice off what'll fill you, and hit the grub."

Dirk and Victoria each sawed some juicy meat, and added a boiled potato, and settled at the trestle table, while the rest followed suit.

"Is that meat suiting your belly?" Dogwood asked. "It's a damn bore, but we got nothing else to offer guests of honor."

"It comes close to buffalo tongue," she said.

"There, you see?" Dogwood said. "I am defeated. We get whipped by magpies, whipped by blue-belly soldiers, whipped by stray redskins, whipped by old Indian agents, and whipped by buffalo tongue."

"My people lived here. We wintered here. We found buffalo here. Now it is yours," Victoria said. "How could you feel defeated?"

"Yes, ma'am, I'm defeated. I wanted to own Texas, with

New Mexico tossed in, and got stuck with this miserable patch of cold ground somewhere north of the North Pole."

Dirk wasn't quite sure where this conversation was leading, but the rib roast tasted just fine.

"My pa jumped ship in Fort Vancouver with nothing but the clothes he wore and a belaying pin, and somehow he survived," Dirk said. "He was a Londoner and made it to one of the early rendezvous."

"I've done a little research about that bozo," Dogwood said. "This fella's old man, Barnaby Skye, he was right up there with Jim Bridger, Tom Fitzpatrick, Will Sublette, and all the rest, back in the beaver days. There was no man his match, they said. He could lick a dozen Blackfeet, subdue a grizzly, bury a rival fur brigade, and whip any man that tried him."

"He was gentle to the last, sir. He avoided fights."

"That don't tally, boy."

"If you imagine he was a big, tough mountain man, sir, you'd be quite wrong."

"What are you tellin' me, boy?"

"That he was a man of peace. He'd fight if he got forced into it, and only if he couldn't escape it."

Dogwood masticated beef, glanced sharply at his cohort, and chewed steadily, digesting food and information.

"That don't tally," he said. "But never no mind. What's happening on the reservation? You hang that little firebrand yet?"

"I tried to prevent it, sir. So did Chief Washakie."

"Then they should've hanged the pair of you along with the boy."

"They came close, sir."

"I'm missing a story here, boy. Tell the whole thing square and true."

Dirk set down his knife and fork, knowing he wouldn't be eating for ten minutes, and plunged in. "You see, sir, Owl wasn't a rebel. He was a seer, a boy filled with a vision."

Dirk talked quietly, straight into the mounting skepticism of the Texans. Only it wasn't skepticism. They didn't understand. They knew nothing of vision quests, the guidance of spirit helpers, and the world of auguries. They couldn't imagine a bunch of redskins believing all that hoodoo. They couldn't fathom the Dreamers, dancing in the night to evoke the blessings of the Gray Owl.

"You and the chief, you stood against a line of blue-belly carbines?" Dogwood asked at the end. "You faced them guns, did you?"

"It gave the people time to flee, sir."

"You should've pulled out a hogleg and shot that captain plumb dead. Fight to the death, like Crockett and Bowie at the Alamo. They're heroes, boy. They're three-ball roosters. They fought to the last man. They're Texans. But you stood there unarmed? I don't fathom it. What did it win you?"

"It made them think twice about shooting us, Mr. Dogwood."

"Think twice about shooting you? No man in his right mind thinks twice about shooting anyone. He just does it."

Dirk smiled ruefully. "It cost me my welcome, sir. Major Van Horne didn't like it. We're on our way to the Crow Reservation."

"I hate the bluecoats, boy. Eat up and slice some more beef. Any enemy of the bluecoats is a friend of mine. I wish I knew what was cooking down there. I'd've armed the whole Shoshone nation, just to kill off some federals. A Winchester repeater for every bloody redskin. By God, that Owl fella had some sense."

"It never was about that, sir. It was about seeing the future, the world returned to what it was before white men arrived."

"That's like sayin' the Mexicans should have kept Texas."

There was no explaining anything to Yardley Dogwood, Dirk thought.

"What's on your platter, boy?"

"Crow Reservation. I'll start a school for them, if I can."

"With what?"

"With nothing. My father arrived in the American West with the clothes on his back and a belaying pin."

In truth, Dirk hadn't known what he would do until that moment, but once Dogwood had elicited it, he had an inkling where his future might lie.

"Go claim some land up there, boy. I'll send a few beeves to get you started."

"You, sir?"

"Anyone faces down them Federals, he gets what he needs from me. You get yo'self some land, boy. You do as I say, now. You put some beef in the belly of the Crows. Maybe they'll quit stealing mine."

Dirk couldn't fathom it. The meal progressed quietly after that.

"You two, you sleep in the barn if you want. No colored folks bed in the house, boy, but there's hay in the barn. Your nag, give it some oats. Me, I'm going to pour three fingers of Kentuck, and go to bed."

With that, the massive host rose abruptly, and lumbered off. The others soon followed.

It certainly had been the strangest encounter Dirk had experienced. Not a one of those Texans had grasped what the crisis on the Wind River Reservation had been about. But what did it matter?

He and Victoria made splendid beds out of hay, and took off at dawn, when the ranch was just stirring.

"Goddamn, that was fun," his Crow mother said.

Dirk found himself wishing his father could explain a few things to him about white men. About people like Yardley Dogwood, who tried to hang Dirk one day and offered him a few cows on another.

He drove north, leaving wheel tracks in the heavy frost, and soon they were engulfed by silence once again, as the world poised itself on the edge of winter. This route, laid out by old Jim Bridger, would take them around the southern reaches of the Pryor Mountains and into Yellowstone country. With each passing day, old Victoria seemed to bloom. Dirk swore that a decade and fallen away, and then another decade. Her eyes brightened; her gaze was more keen. A flock of magpies discovered her and erupted in hilarious gossip. She beamed at Dirk, assumed more responsibility for setting up each camp, and sometimes remarked on old, familiar landmarks as the wagon pierced into the heartland of the Crow people. She was going home. She would soon be talking in her native tongue to her relatives and friends. She had been one of the Kicked-in-the-Bellies, and a member of the Otter Clan, and soon she would be among them. Her crinkled face was wreathed in joy.

She had endured on the Wind River Reservation happily enough as long as Skye was there, but she had failed since his death—until now. The joy exuding from her affected Dirk in an odd way, and he pressed the old dray to move along faster as they passed through the desert between the Beartooth and Pryor Mountains and rolled into the still-green foothills of Yellowstone country.

They reached the river and its multiple trails one chill

afternoon, and paused only a moment. The new agency had been located at Rosebud Creek, off to the west, in some of the sweetest country the human eye could ever see, a land of foothill slopes, clear creeks, good bottoms perfect for crops, jack pine hillsides, and above, the bold blue Beartooth Mountains, already crowned with white. The original Crow Reserve had encompassed a vast homeland south of the Yellowstone River, but gold discoveries at its western perimeter had resulted in the loss of its westernmost reaches, and now the homeland embraced a tract that extended into the high plains as well as these majestic mountains and foothills. Shrinking reservations were already an old and irritating story to Dirk, but maybe the Crows, ancient allies of the white men, might fare better than some tribes. But even as he thought it, he sensed a rising cynicism. Who could say what the Crows would end up with?

Where the ragged two-rut road reached the Yellowstone, Victoria stepped to the earth, walked to the bank, ritually held her hands in the sweet waters, and then ritually cleansed herself, baptizing her hair and face and breast with the icy water. Something magical was refreshing them all. Even the old dray lifted its ugly head, let the breeze riffle its mane, and waited restlessly to start pulling the wagon west.

They traveled under gray bluffs dotted with cedar and pine, and encountered nothing but a few mule deer in the lush Yellowstone valley. On the north bank there were signs of settlement; but there on the south bank, in the Crow Reserve, the valley was as it always had been, and perhaps always would be.

When they reached the valley of the Stillwater River, old Victoria started humming, and as they ascended the valley, she began exclaiming at the occasional evidences of her people. Sometimes it was a cabin with a thin line of smoke rising from it; other times a lodge erected on a distant plateau. Once they saw a small herd of horses with saddle marks on them. Once they encountered a youth on a stubby pony, and Victoria chattered with the boy, in a tongue Dirk could barely grasp. But the smiles said more than the outpouring of strange words.

"He says the agency is a hard day's travel still, but we will find the people there, and everywhere," she said. "He is Bull Tail, grandson of Walking Duck, whose kin I know well. Walking Duck is a clan brother of my friend Ice Walker. His father is a friend of Whistlers."

Dirk was rapidly losing track of the relationships and generations, but Victoria was recording them all in some sort of ledger in her head.

As they progressed up the river toward the agency, they encountered more and more Crows, most of them snug in blankets or capotes against the numbing air. But it reached the point where they could hardly move a hundred yards before being hailed by various people, some of whom knew the old Crow wife of Mister Skye. They chattered, sometimes on horseback as Dirk steered the dray toward the distant adobe-and-log post. He knew some Crow, but this flood of words between his old Crow mother and this crowd came too fast, and he finally settled on keeping the dray moving to get out of the harsh cold of early December. There were patches of snow in tree shadow and gullies, and ice-sheeted puddles on the road.

Now the agency loomed ahead, on a tributary called Rosebud Creek, set in an idyllic place untouched by the outside world, or so it seemed.

They reached the agency, a two-story log building built

in haste, and there a lean young Crow with an imperial gaze waited, his focus entirely on the old woman in the wagon.

He was a stranger, and yet she seemed to know who he was, and when he offered her his hand as she alighted, she seemed almost shy.

The Stars and Stripes cracked and snapped on the stockade's staff as Many Quill Woman reached the hard clay, and stared at this rough settlement of log buildings, adobe structures, and lodges, many with smoke streaming horizontally from them.

"I am Aleek-chea-ahoosh," he said. "Plenty Coups."

Victoria was being welcomed by the chief.

thirty-nine

It was so good to hear Absaroka words. Victoria huddled on the wagon seat, shivering in her thin blanket, hearing the words she had thirsted for all those years on the Wind River Reservation. Now the words rose up around her, words out of her childhood, the drawn-out words, the abrupt words, the words that only an Absaroka could understand perfectly. She shivered in the flood of words.

Now she was meeting the young chief of the Mountain Crows, as white men called them. Plenty Coups was his name, and she had heard of him, and perhaps had seen him as a boy long before, when she and Skye had lived among the People. Yes, she had seen this tall boy, who had become a great warrior, had counted so many coups people had lost track, and who had received so many visions that the Absaroka people revered him for being a seer as well as a warrior and now a leader.

This place on the Sweetwater, it was a strange place for the Absaroka people to be as winter came. This was foothill country, and it would soon be engulfed in snow, just when the People should be farther down onto the prairies, wintering in river bottoms where there would be plenty of cottonwood to fuel the lodge fires.

But here they were, in a rude place where the white men were erecting an earthen stockade and throwing up log houses, including the two-story one that housed the Crow Agency. There weren't many of the People in sight, she thought, but her eyesight was bad, and so was her hearing, and she was shivering in her blankets as the Absaroka words flooded over her like summer sunshine.

"Many Quill Woman, we rejoice. We have wondered how you and the beloved friend I cannot name were doing, so far away," the young chief was saying. "We heard he had left us, but we had no word of you, and now we rejoice to see you."

"The one we cannot name lies in a graveyard beside his younger wife," Victoria said, adhering to the forms. The dead could not be named, for it would violate their spirits.

"And what of my brother Arrow and his family?" she asked. "I should like to see them while I can."

"Ah, Many Quill Woman, the one of whom you speak . . ."

She knew then that Arrow, too, was gone from this world.

"That one is walking the star path, and so is his woman, but his children live and will be pleased to see you."

Eight winters had passed since she had been among the People, and now she was acutely aware that life and death had continued their cycle, and that she had missed much of the affairs of her people.

"But Grandmother, I see you are shivering in this cold. It would please me if you and your son, the son of our friend who lived among us for so long, would come to my lodge, which is that one." He pointed to a square log cabin with smoke curling up from a stovepipe.

"Come. Bring the wagon. The horse will be taken care of. I will give the word."

"We would be pleased to," said Dirk.

The young chief helped Many Quill Woman off the wagon and onto the frozen ground, where cold seemed to come up through her moccasins and made her feet numb. At the door stood a young Absaroka woman in cloth skirts, and a doeskin tunic covering her upper body.

"Grandmother, this is my woman, Strikes the Iron," the chief said. "And this is Many Quill Woman, wife of the man who fought beside the People and protected the People and gave to the People, who lies among the Shoshones now."

Strikes the Iron smiled brightly and ushered Victoria inside, where her shivering slowed a little, but was not conquered by the heat from the cast-iron stove. This was a dark and damp place, not like a good buffalo-hide lodge, with its winter lining up and dozens of thick robes on the ground to stay the cold rising out of the earth.

The world had changed, she thought. A huddle of log buildings, an earthen stockade for the soldiers, and when the snows came, a sorrow of cold. She remembered happier times, when the People collected in great lodges warmed plentifully by tiny fires, to tell stories, to hear the seers and keepers tell of where the People came from, and to hear of all the things that happened in the winters of the past. And to play games, and flirt, and sing, and tell funny stories, and gossip.

Still, here were the chief and his woman, making her comfortable. And Dirk, too, who had not a drop of Absaroka blood in him, but was made as welcome as a son of the People. They did not have robes on the ground here, and they sat on benches around the sides of the wooden lodge, which doubled as beds at night. The earth was covered with the split logs known to white men as puncheons, and these things were not as good, and they slowed the conversation because people were too far apart, and it was hard to hear. But of all this she kept quiet, for the flow of words over her was Absaroka, and the honey of her tongue caught in her head and lifted her spirits, so that her heart was full of joy.

She huddled on a bench with her blanket tightly about her, her dim gaze upon the young chief, who was dressed in white men's clothing, his hair in braids, his eyes watching her with affection. Soon Strikes the Iron placed tea before her, and she sipped, hoping to warm her body, but her body was too light, lighter than a feather, and tea brought no heat to it.

The chief remembered her husband, whose name could not be said here, as the Englishman who helped the People fend off the Siksika and the Lakota and the Cheyenne; who came to live among the People, and shared their fate, and employed his big Sharps rifle on the buffalo hunts so all might have meat.

And then, as word of her arrival swept the Absaroka people, Victoria's clan and kin began to knock on the door, but these were mostly children and grandchildren of people she remembered, boys and girls she barely knew, except for the names of their elders. Here was a grandchild of Walks Backward, and a boy born of Ridge Walker, and a baby, scarcely a few weeks old, born of a son of the brother whose name she could not utter. And these were presented to her as gifts, the young people of her tribe, the clan sisters and clan brothers, where her blood ran in other veins.

They came, tapped on the door, and Strikes the Iron opened it to still more, until the log house was jammed with Absaroka people, who had come from miles around to catch a glimpse of Mr. Skye's wife, the old medicine woman of the Absaroka people who had traveled and fought where no other Absaroka had ever gone.

She stared at them dimly, for her eyes were poor, but she could still hear the tongue given her at birth, and she listened carefully to these people, and to the young chief, who introduced each young Absaroka to the great grandmother they had known only in story and legend.

The light faded, and Plenty Coups took each visitor to the door and then they disappeared into the twilight, and soon the chief's cabin was as quiet as it had been when she first stepped in. She had seen her People. She had not expected ever to see them again. But here she was, among them, and she had seen them with her own eyes, and heard them speak her own tongue, and she was glad. She belonged to them, and all the time with Skye had not dimmed her belonging to the Absaroka, the people of the large-beaked bird that white men had mistranslated into crow.

It was cold in the room, but the others didn't seem to notice it.

"You will stay with me," the chief said. "We will make good robe beds and you will be warm."

She didn't think she would ever be warm, but she nodded.

This cabin was something like a lodge, with shelf seating and bedding around the periphery, and a stove in the middle. She wanted a lodge. She wanted a Crow village outside this door, with the lodges raised in an orderly half-circle, their doors facing east, with just the right amount of space between each lodge, enough to give each lodge its own privacy, but in the midst of neighbors and all the People. But now there were scattered cabins, and no villages at all.

Still, this was home; she had returned, like a lost child finding her family. She was among the speakers of her tongue, and that made her giddy and light-headed and her body was weightless.

She learned many things about the first Crow Agency on Mission Creek, and how it was windy and white men didn't like the wind, and how gold had been the excuse to drive the Absaroka people east, which they didn't mind because they were closer to the sacred buffalo out on the plains. So they were here, learning to farm and raise stock in a place where farming was no good and the white men didn't plant anything.

Still, she had returned, and felt light, and that was what mattered most. In the morning at first light she would go outside to welcome Father Sun and raise her old arms to the great blessing of the day.

"Grandmother, you're nodding. We will prepare the robes for you," Plenty Coups said, and instantly Strikes the Iron piled smooth, rich buffalo robes on the shelf to the right of the door, the place of honor in this wooden lodge, and Many Quill Woman was soon tucked in, a small sweet smile pursing her lips.

She drifted into a light sleep, and found herself in the midst of flower-strewn dreams.

She was a beautiful girl, one her mother had pridefully dressed in softest and whitest doeskin, and she was sitting on a sunny ridge watching a tiny rattlesnake as it watched her. A bold magpie lit on her lap and began chattering, and that stirred the tiny snake to coil itself. The magpie enjoyed the event, chattering happily, and when the snake struck, the magpie pecked it, and the snake slid away. She laughed, and the magpie pecked her hand delicately, and whirred away. That was delightful.

She grew in beauty, and her family knew it, and she was often dressed in quilled doeskin, and her hair was combed until it glowed, and sometimes braided and tied with red ribbons. She lived in a time of flowers, and wherever the People went, they were surrounded by flowers. In the summer, there were alpine flowers; in the fall, out on the plains, there were fall flowers and bushes burning with berries waiting to be plucked and mixed with meat to make pemmican.

The boys noticed and shyly watched her as she bloomed, and she knew they were thinking of taking her into their own lodges when the time came, and some of them contrived to talk to her when she was fetching water, and some played a flute or left small gifts at the lodge door, and her parents knew that soon most of the boys among the Kicked-in-the-Bellies would come to the lodge, bearing gifts, their eyes burning.

But then one day she felt a strange calling in her breast, and she told her mother she would go away to the place of visions, where boys often went, to await with prayer and fasting whatever had been ordained. She went only with a small robe, and lay quietly watching the night skies, which were alive with falling stars, and she felt confused. Why was she there, all alone, in the vastness of the night? But dawn came, salmon in the east, and with it a flock of magpies, silent on wing, hushed instead of noisy, serene instead of agitated. They were herky-jerky birds with a waddle that made them awkward, yet she knew at once that she, the beautiful Absaroka daughter, would be given both a spirit helper all her days, and a mission.

She had lain quietly in the dawn light, feeling the sun's rays paint her, and all the magpies—more than she could count—settled close to her, and she was given to know things; she would lead a most unusual life and would not be given in marriage to any boy, but to someone who would be a great mystery. The magpies would give her medicine powers. She would be a medicine woman, with an inner knowledge of other mortals, and the power to heal and prophesy. And the magpies would be her protectors, for so long as she never lifted a hand against them, or her People, or the innocent.

She took that great vision back to her village, and told it to the elders, and they purified her with sweetgrass smoke, and became a woman set apart.

She waited for the next dream to come, because there were many flowers in it, strange flowers she had never seen, flowers from far-away places, with names she didn't know. She knew this dream would be about the man she had wed, the strange one both fierce and tender, who had strange notions, and who loved her in some way so beautiful it was unfathomable to her, and she loved him back in the same manner, even as she continued to heal and prophesy, and to fight, for she had become a warrior woman, fearless, skilled with bow and rifle, beside this strange man. Now the petals were falling, drifting like a spring shower out of the heavens, and she saw no magpies at all. She wanted to dream about this man, and remember his face, and remember how it was when he held her in his arms, but her dream would not take her there, to the sacred places, and she began only to feel cold, first a little chill, and then very cold, and the petals stopped falling out of the blue sky, and then the dream stopped, and she could dream no more.

forty

She was gone. The dream keepers came for her, and now she was a weightless husk. Her spirit had been the heaviest thing within that ancient frame. She lay serenely in her robe, very still. Dirk stood beside the shelf bed, suddenly brimming with loss.

Strikes the Iron had found her thus, and summoned Plenty Coups, even while Dirk slept, and then they had awakened him in the rose dawn of a clear December day. He absorbed her absence. She was on her way. The star trail would take her some imaginable distance away.

He thought of her request to come here, to be among her People at the last. She had received her wish and now her life was fulfilled. She had come back to the people of her girlhood, to the relatives and friends and tongue and wisdom and ways she had known. She had returned to that which had stamped her, made her an Absaroka, given her a name, given her those medicine powers, given her those skills with a bow and arrows. He thought she was somewhere in her upper seventies, but those details, the family history, were confusing, and he simply wasn't sure. There would be no white men's records: birth, parents, marriage, death, place. The Crows had no parish records.

He sat next to her, feeling a tug for this Crow mother, the older wife of Mister Skye, this woman who had no child of her own, and loved him as much as his Shoshone mother, who brought him into the world.

"Her wish was to come here, and I brought her, and now all that she asked has happened," he said to the chief.

"I count it a blessing to have met her, talked with her, and offered her my hospitality," he replied. "It was like opening the door to a magical person."

"I should have expected it," Dirk said. "But I didn't."

"It is good that you didn't," Plenty Coups said. "Have you any thoughts about what to do next?"

"Grandfather, she is one of yours. I don't know what to do."

"You are her son," the chief said, firmly returning the decisions to Dirk.

"She would want to be given to the sun," Dirk said.

"Yes! That is good!" said Strikes the Iron.

"I will do that," Dirk said. "But I would like for you, Grandfather and Grandmother, to choose a place and direct me in the ways of the People."

"It will be done."

"Should I go find the Indian agent?"

"Major Armstrong? He does keep a book of births and deaths, and all who are enrolled at this agency. But Many Quill Woman was not enrolled. And he did start a cemetery, and wants us to bury our own as white men do, but the People don't like it, and the earth is not a good place."

Dirk knelt next to his Crow mother, who lay so still. He wanted to memorize her face, but there was nothing to memorize, and no photographs or tintypes or drawings that he knew of, so he would remember her only in small fragments: laughter, wit, a tender hand upon his father's face, a rowdy story.

He stood, slowly.

"Grandfather, is there a ritual, a way of mourning? I am not of your blood."

Plenty Coups gazed through the real-glass window upon an autumnal scene, and shook his head. "We have no crier now. There once was one who would go through the village, from lodge to lodge, with the news. And then the women would gather and mourn, and prepare the body to be given to the sun. Now . . . those ways are gone."

There were no lodges visible; no village or winter camp, the lodges pitched in half-circles and facing east. There was only a scatter of rude cabins, most leaking smoke, scattered willy-nilly without heeding the old ways, or the old disciplines.

Dirk peered out into the emptiness of the settlement, and realized that Absaroka life had been shattered in many ways with the advent of the reservation.

"Grandfather, I will bury her as she would have wanted. To do that, I will need your wisdom."

"We will do this as she would want," the chief said. "Go harness your horse; bring the wagon. We will cover Many Quill Woman in the old way."

Dirk clambered into his coat and stuffed his hat down, and plunged into a bitter morning. No one stirred. The scatter of cabins and the earthen walls of the post gave him the sense of being in a white men's frontier settlement rather than at the center of Crow Indian life. He threw an icy harness over the dray, and slipped an icy bit into the dray's mouth, which it tried to spit out, and eventually hooked the wagon to the tugs and steered the dray to the chief's small cabin. In all that while, he saw no other person braving the wind.

He parked there, and went indoors, and found that Strikes the Iron had wrapped Victoria in a blanket, and then a beautiful robe, and had tied the entire bundle with thong, so that no part of his Crow mother peeked out at him, and there was only the tightly bound bundle. The chief's wife slipped into a capote, the chief chose only a blanket, and then he collected two axes and a ball of thong.

He nodded to Dirk, who knew what to do. He lifted his Crow mother, who weighed nothing, and carried her into the bitter air, and settled her carefully in the wagon bed. And then the three of them climbed to the seat, and Dirk looked expectantly at the chief.

Plenty Coups pointed, and his finger directed Dirk to a lengthy trail stretching south and west, away from the mountains and toward long, naked ridges stretching into the Yellowstone valley.

They rode quietly, the horse settling into the task, and the wagon creaked through icy-skimmed puddles and over frosted grass. At a point where one majestic ridge declined toward the distant valley, he pointed again, and Dirk steered the wagon off the trail, toward a promontory with a grove of naked cottonwoods nearby.

It would be a good and fitting place for Many Quill Woman, first wife of Barnaby Skye.

A signal from the chief, and Dirk halted. It was quiet and cold and lonely, perhaps two miles from the agency. Far to the north lay the Yellowstone valley, the living heart of the country the Absarokas claimed as their own.

Dirk walked slowly to the promontory, and then to the nearby stand of cottonwoods, and finally to a great willow standing among the cottonwoods. A limb split into a narrow vee, facing north. It would do.

The chief handed Dirk an axe and took the other, and between them they cut crosspieces that would span the vee, and as swiftly as they completed a crosspiece, Strikes the Iron anchored it to the willow tree with thong, carefully tying each piece. They worked patiently, ignoring the cold, and in a while they had completed the platform that would become Victoria's final home.

Now, at last, giving Victoria to the sun, the wind, the night skies, the rain, the snow, the spring zephyrs, the heat of summer, proved to be hard and hurtful. He didn't want to let go of her. And yet it was necessary to do what had to be done. The chief and his wife waited, for this was a task for Dirk alone. He peered at that bundle lying in the wagon bed, and then gently lifted it, feeling the softness of the richly tanned buffalo robe, feeling the tight cords that bound it together. He carried his Crow mother to the scaffold and lifted as high as he could, higher than his head, and then rolled her onto the platform. And then he straightened her until she lay exactly in its center, facing upward toward the skies.

Plenty Coups sang a song, long and mournful, the tongue strange to Dirk's ear, even if its message was not. He saw tears forming under the eyes of the chief's woman.

A magpie alighted in a willow branch, dark and saucy white, up there in the latticework of naked limbs. Then another, and another, and then still more, whirring down into the willow, settling silently on the limbs. And then there were a dozen, and twenty, and fifty, and a hundred alighting silently at this place in the heart of Absaroka country.

And then, when it seemed that every magpie for miles

around had settled in the willow tree, the entire flock lifted off, flapping upward, and then around, in a giant circle, a great spiral that grew larger and larger in the bright blue, with the willow tree at the vortex. At last the great congregation of black-and-white birds vanished quietly into the morning sky, and there was not so much as a crow or a hawk or a sparrow in the endless heavens.

For some reason, Dirk found himself smiling.

They rode quietly back to the agency, their backs to the wind, and Dirk welcomed the warmth of Plenty Coups' log house.

It was not a time for speaking. He settled himself on the bed shelf where his Crow mother had slept, dreamed, and died. Something of her lingered there. He felt alone, even though this good leader of a good people welcomed him and his wife slipped to his side, sometimes with tea, and other times just to offer company.

He didn't belong among the people of the large-beaked bird. All gone: his father Barnaby Skye, his mother Mary of the Shoshones, his Crow mother Victoria. All that remained were the stories, things he learned through childhood and manhood about this man and his women and his amazing horse Jawbone, who carved a joyous life for themselves in a wild world. All his life he had heard stories about his parents, all his life he had heard not just of their prowess and courage, but also their goodness. Barnaby Skye was a memorable man; Victoria and Mary were just as memorable.

Chief Many Coups left Dirk to his silences and busied themselves with other things. They sent word out to the People that Many Quill Woman had begun the journey among the stars, and others could find her on the promontory if they wished. A few came to the house, and quietly laid their hands upon Dirk, who accepted their blessings with a smile and a nod and thanksgiving.

Then, later that chill day, the chief approached Dirk.

"Do not leave us," he said.

"Thank you, but I must."

"You could teach us. You know the tongue. You taught the Shoshones."

"The Indian Bureau would not permit it, Grandfather. They discharged me."

"The Methodist missionaries are going to start a school here in a while."

"I am not one of them and I have too many things inside of me."

In truth, Dirk felt close to all things. He was more than Crow and Shoshone. He was more than Indian and white. He didn't want to build a cabin here or on the Wind River Reservation, where he would wait for his monthly allotments and loaf through the days, being only half of himself. He was more than a believer and more than a disbeliever. The Jesuits had educated him, but his own religion was larger than theirs. He had learned the Shoshone mysteries, the very mysteries that brought the boy, Owl, to his doom, but his vision of life was larger than that. He was more than a white man, able to move easily among white people, like his father, and more than a Shoshone, too. He had no family and yet he belonged to a larger family. He did not know his grandparents. He had no history like his father or his mothers. No English relatives, no Crow ones, and only some distant Shoshone cousins. But he was rich in family and friends because he had two bloods.

"Thank you, Grandfather and Grandmother. Tomorrow,

if you will permit it, I will take leave of you. I brought her here, and her wish was fulfilled, and now it is time for me to go."

They did not object.

In the morning he would hitch up the dray and go away, to somewhere as high as the heavens.